'You made me believe you were something you were not.'

He raised his eyebrows at that. *Just as she had made him believe she was someone she was not.*

It fuelled her anger and sense of injustice.

'All those nights, Ned... And in between them you were here, living in your mansion, dancing at some ball with the latest diamond of the *ton* hanging on your arm. Seeking to ally yourself with some earl's daughter while you played your games in Whitechapel.'

He said nothing.

'You would have bedded me and cast me aside.'

'Would I?'

His voice was cold, hard, emotionless. There was something in his eyes when he said it that unnerved her. It made her feel as though she was the one who had got this all wrong. She reminded herself of the shabby leather jacket and boots he had worn—a disguise. She reminded herself of what had passed between them in the darkness of a Whitechapel alleyway while he'd been living a double life here.

'Now that matters are clear between us there is no need to speak again. Stay away from me, Ned.'

AUTHOR NOTE

You first met this heroine, Miss Emma Northcote, in my earlier book, A DARK AND BROODING GENTLEMAN. With Emma and her family suffering such difficult times, I felt she deserved a story of her own. And a worthy hero of her own, too!

I found him in Ned Stratham, a man of the dark streets in London's East End, seemingly ordinary, but who turns out not to be so ordinary after all. He's a wolf amongst pampered pedigree dogs—in more ways than one!

So here is Emma and Ned's story of destiny and love and happiness. I sincerely hope you enjoy reading it.

With warmest wishes.

THE GENTLEMAN ROGUE

Margaret McPhee

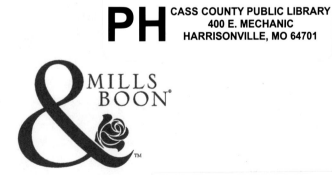

MILLS
BOON®

First published in Great Britain 2014
by Mills & Boon, an imprint of Harlequin (UK) Limited,
Large Print edition 2015
Harlequin (UK) Limited, Eton House, 18-24 Paradise Road,
Richmond, Surrey TW9 1SR

© 2014 Margaret McPhee

ISBN: 978-0-263-25523-2

Harlequin (UK) Limited's policy is to use papers that are natural,
renewable and recyclable products and made from wood grown in
sustainable forests. The logging and manufacturing processes conform
to the legal environmental regulations of the country of origin.

Printed and bound in Great Britain
by CPI Antony Rowe, Chippenham, Wiltshire

Margaret McPhee loves to use her imagination—an essential requirement for a trained scientist. However, when she realised that her imagination was inspired more by the historical romances she loves to read rather than by her experiments, she decided to put the ideas down on paper. She has since left her scientific life behind, retaining only the romance—her husband, whom she met in a laboratory. In summer, Margaret enjoys cycling along the coastline overlooking the Firth of Clyde in Scotland, where she lives. In winter, tea, cakes and a good book suffice.

Previous novels by the same author:

THE CAPTAIN'S LADY
MISTAKEN MISTRESS
THE WICKED EARL
UNTOUCHED MISTRESS
A SMUGGLER'S TALE
  (part of *Regency Christmas Weddings*)
THE CAPTAIN'S FOBIDDEN MISS
UNLACING THE INNOCENT MISS
  (part of *Regency Silk & Scandal* mini-series)
UNMASKING THE DUKE'S MISTRESS*
A DARK AND BROODING GENTLEMAN*
HIS MASK OF RETRIBUTION*
DICING WITH THE DANGEROUS LORD*
MISTRESS TO THE MARQUIS*

The Gentleman Rogue features characters
you will have met in *A Dark and Brooding Gentleman*.

And in Mills & Boon® Historical *Undone!*

HOW TO TEMPT A VISCOUNT*

**Did you know that some of these novels
are also available as eBooks?
Visit www.millsandboon.co.uk**

For Gran & Grandad
and
for Agnes & John
with love

Chapter One

London—August 1811

Emma de Lisle watched the man covertly from the corner of her eye. He was sitting at his usual table, over at the other side of the room, his back to the wall, a clear view of the door. On the table before him sat his pint of porter, his almost-finished plate of lamb chops and, beside it, his faded leather hat.

He moved the small ivory disc over the back of his hand, just as he always did, the trick making the disc look like it was magically tumbling one way over his fingers and then all the way back, forward and back, forward and back in that slow easy rhythm. He sipped from the tankard and seemed comfortable just sitting there on his own, eating, drinking, watching—a part of the bustle of the taproom of the Red Lion Chop-House, and yet not a part.

'All right?' A short brown-toothed man muttered as he passed, giving a sullen nod of his head in the man's direction.

The man gave a nod in return and the little disc disappeared from his fingers into his jacket. Emma had noticed him before. Just as she noticed him now. Because of the way he ran the small ivory circle over his fingers. Because a slice of one dark-blond eyebrow was missing, a tiny scar cutting in a straight line clear through it, and because the eyes beneath those brows were the olour of a clear summer sky. But most of all, she noticed him because he intrigued her.

The faded brown-leather jacket he wore was cracked with age. Beneath the table she knew he wore scuffed boots that matched the jacket. His hat was leather, too, worn smooth, smoky-brown, dark beside his hair. Clothes that had lasted a lifetime, ageing with the man that wore them. Yet beneath his jacket was a shirt that, in contrast to most others she saw in here, was good quality, white and freshly laundered, and his fingernails were clean and trimmed. He kept to himself and was always on his own. And there was something about him, something of self-containment and strength, of intelligence and power. But all of it understated, quiet, kept beneath the surface. He did not seem to care what others thought of him. Unlike the other men in Whitechapel he did not make any effort to either intimidate or impress. Never tried to make conversation, just kept his thoughts to himself. He was clean-shaven, handsome too in a rugged sort of way, although handsome men should have been the last thing on Emma's mind.

'Three mixed-grill platters!' Tom, the cook, yelled, jolting her from her speculation.

'Coming, Tom.' Emma dragged her eyes away from the man, her moment of respite gone. She hurried up to the kitchen hatch, and, using the cloth dangling from the belt around her waist, quickly shifted the scalding plates on to her large wooden tray. In a much-practised move, she hefted the whole tray up to balance it on her shoulder, before bustling across the room to make her delivery.

'Here we are, gentlemen. Three of our very best mixed-grills.' She presented each of the three men round the table with an enormous platter.

On the way back to the bar she cleared two tables, took two orders for more beers, and noticed a new party of men arriving to be fed.

'I'll see to the new boys, Em,' Paulette, the Red Lion's other serving wench, said as she passed Emma.

'Four pints of ale ready over here, Emma!' Nancy, the landlady, called, setting the last of the pints down on the bar with a thud that sent the froth of their heads cascading in a creamy waterfall down the outsides of the pewter tankards.

Emma bustled over. Collected all four on to her tray and went to deliver them to the table nearest to the front door.

'Thanks, darlin'.' The big black-haired man leered down the cleavage that her low-cut chemise and tight-laced bodice of her scarlet work dress exposed. She disliked this dress and how much it revealed. And she disliked men like him. He grinned, revealing teeth that matched his hair as his hand slid against her hip.

She slapped his fingers away, kept her tone frosty. 'Keep your hands to yourself.' Wondered if she would ever get used to this aspect of the job.

He laughed. 'You're a feisty one and no mistake. But I like a challenge.' His hand returned, more insistent this time, grabbing her buttock and squeezing as he hauled her close. 'Just as much as I like that fancy rich accent of yours. Makes you sound like a real lady it does. And I've never had a lady. Come on, darlin', I'll make it worth your while.' The stench of ale and rotten teeth was overpowering. His friends around the table cheered and sniggered.

Emma fixed him with a cynical and steely stare. 'Hard though it is to believe, I must decline. Now unhand me and let me get on with my work or you will have a bar full of thirsty, hungry men waiting to be served to contend with.'

Black-Hair's grin broadened. He pulled her to him, wrenching the tray from her hand, and dropping it to clatter on the floor. 'The other wench can see to them. You can see to me, darlin'.'

Oh, Lord! She realised with a sinking heart and impending dread that he was not going to release her with nothing worse than a slap to the bottom. He was one of those that would pull her down on his lap and start fondling her. Or worse.

'I will see to nothing. Release me before Nancy sees your game and bars you.'

She was only dimly aware of the shadow of the figure passing at close quarters. She was too busy trying to deal with the black-haired man and extricate herself from his grip. So when the deluge of beer tipped like an almighty cascade of brown rain over the lout's head she was as shocked as he.

Black-Hair's grin was wiped. Emma was forgotten in an instant. He released her, giving an almighty roar of a curse.

Emma didn't need an invitation. Making the most of her opportunity, she grabbed her tray and backed clear of the danger.

Black-Hair was spluttering and wiping beer from screwed-up eyes with great rough tattooed hands. His hair was sodden and glistening with beer. It ran in rivulets down his cheeks and over his chin to drip its tea-coloured stain on to the grubby white of the shirt that covered his barrel chest. The shoulders of his shabby brown-woollen jacket were dark as rain-soaked earth. Even the front of his grey trousers was dark with it. He stank like a brewery.

His small bloodshot eyes swivelled to the perpetrator.

The hubbub of chatter and laughter and clank of glasses had ceased. There was curiosity and a whispered hush as everyone watched.

Emma shifted her gaze to follow that of the black-haired lout and saw the subject of her earlier covert study standing there. Tall, still, calm.

'Sorry about that. Slip of the hand.' The words might have offered apology, but the way the man said them suggested otherwise. His voice was the same East End accent as theirs, but low in tone, clear in volume, quietly menacing in its delivery.

'Oh, you'll be damn sorry all right!' Black-Hair's chair legs scraped loud against the wooden floorboards as he got to his feet. 'You'll be pissing yourself, mate, by the time I've finished with you.'

The man let his gaze drop pointedly to the dark sodden front of Black-Hair's trousers, then rose again to meet his eyes. There was a glimmer of hard amusement in them. He raised the eyebrow with the scar running through it, the one that Emma thought made him look like a handsome rogue. 'Looks like you got there first.'

The crowd sniggered at that.

Black-Hair's face flushed puce. His little piggy eyes narrowed on the man like an enraged bull. He cracked his knuckles as he made a fist.

By some unspoken command Black-Hair's four friends got to their feet, making their involvement clear. Any trace of curiosity and amusement fled the room's atmosphere. It was suddenly sharp-edged with threat.

The hush spread. Every man in the chop-house was riveted on what was unfolding before Emma.

The nape of her neck prickled.

'Settle down, boys,' said Nancy. 'There's no

harm done. Sit down and drink your pints before they get warm.'

But not one of the men moved. They all stayed put, stood where they were, eyeing each other like dogs with their hackles raised.

'We don't want no trouble in here. You got a disagreement, you take it outside.' Nancy tried to come closer, but two men stepped into her path to stop her progress, murmuring advice—two regulars intent on keeping her safe.

No one heeded her anyway. Not the black-haired villain and his cronies. And not the man.

In the background Paulette's face, like every other, was lit with excited and wary anticipation.

The man's expression was implacable. He looked almost amused.

'I'm going to kill you,' said Black-Hair.

'And there was me thinking you were offering to buy me a replacement porter,' said the man.

'You ain't gonna be able to hold a pint of porter, let alone drink one, I swear.'

Emma's blood ran cold. She knew what men like this in Whitechapel did to one another. This was not the first fight she had seen and the prospect of what was coming made her feel queasy.

The man smiled again, a smile that went nowhere near those cool blue eyes. 'You really want to do this?' he asked with a hint of disbelief and perplexity.

'Too late to start grovelling now,' said Black-Hair.

'That's a shame.'

There was not one sound in the whole of the chop-house. The silence hissed. No one moved. All eyes were on the man, Emma's included. Staring with fascinated horror. Five ruffians against one man. The outcome was certain.

The black-haired man stepped closer to the man, squaring up to him, violent intent spilling from every pore.

She swallowed. Felt a shiver chase over her skin.

The man did not seem to feel the same. He smiled. It was a cold, hard smile. His eyes showed nothing of softness, not one hint of fear. Indeed, he looked as if he welcomed what would come. The blood. The violence. Five men against one. Maybe he really did have a death wish after all.

'Someone stop them. Please,' she said, but it was a plea that had no hope of being answered.

An old man pulled her back. 'Ain't no one going to stop them now, girl.'

He was right. She knew it and so did every single person in that taproom.

The black-haired brute cracked his knuckles and

stretched his massive bull neck, ready to dispense punishment.

Emma held her breath. Her fingers were balled, her nails cutting into her palms.

The man's movement was so fast and unexpected. One minute he was standing there. The next, he had landed a head butt against the lout's nose. There was a sickening crunch. And blood. A lot of blood. Black-Hair doubled over as if bending in to meet the man's knee that hit his face. The speed and suddenness of it shocked her. It shocked the men in there, too. She could tell by the look on their faces as they watched the black-haired giant go down. The ruffian was blinking and gasping with the shock of it as he lay there.

Emma watched in disbelief. Every muscle in her body tensed with shock. She held her breath for what would happen next.

'Too late to start grovelling,' the man said.

Leaning one hand on the floor, Black-Hair spat a bloody globule to land on the toe of the man's boot and reached for a nearby chair.

'But if you insist...' The man stepped closer to Black-Hair, his bloodied boot treading on the giant's splayed fingers, his hand catching hold of the villain's outstretched hand as if he meant to help him to his feet. But it was not help he offered. He gave the wrist a short sharp twist, the resulting crack of which made Emma and the rest of the audience wince.

Black-Hair's face went ashen. He made not one sound, just fainted into a crumpled heap and did not move.

In the stunned amazement that followed no one else moved either. There was not a sound.

'He might need a little help in holding his porter,' said the man to Black-Hair's friends.

'You bastard!' One of them spat the curse.

The man smiled again. And this time Emma was prepared.

The tough charged with fists at the ready.

The man's forehead shattered the villain's cheekbone while his foot hooked around his ankle and felled him. When the rat tried to get up the man kicked his feet from under him. This time Black-Hair's friend stayed where he was.

The other three men exchanged shifty glances amongst themselves, then began to advance. One slipped a long wicked blade that winked in the candlelight.

'Really?' asked the man.

The sly-faced man came in, feigned attack, drew back. Came in close again, circling the man.

'Too scared?' asked the man.

A curl of lip and a slash of the blade was his opponent's only response.

But the man kicked him between the legs and there was an ear-piercing scream. Emma had never heard a man scream before. It made the blood in her veins turn to ice. She watched the knife clatter to the floor forgotten while the sly-faced villain dropped like a stone, clutching himself and gasping.

The man looked at the two remaining thugs.

For a tiny moment they gaped at him. Then they turned tail and ran, pelting out of the chop-house like hares before a hound.

The man stood there and watched them go.

But Emma was not looking at the fleeing villains. Rather, she was looking at the man. She could not take her eyes off him. There was what looked like the beginning of a bruise on his forehead. The snow-white of his shirt was speckled scarlet with blood from Black-Hair's nose. His dark neckcloth was askew. He was not even out of breath. He just stood there calm and cool and unperturbed.

The slamming of the front door echoed in the silence.

No one spoke. No one moved. No one save the man.

He smoothed the dishevelment from his hair, straightened his neckcloth and walked through the pathway that cleared through the crowd before him.

They watched him with respect. They watched him with awe. Soft murmured voices.

Fists and feet were what gained a man respect round here. Standing up for himself and what he believed in. Physicality ruled. The strongest, the toughest, the most dangerous. And the man had just proved himself all three.

Some regulars from the crowd half dragged, half carried the injured away.

The man returned to his table, but he did not sit down. He finished the porter in one gulp and left more coins beside the empty tankard than were needed for payment. He lifted his hat and then his eyes finally met Emma's across the taproom.

Within her chest her heart was still banging hard against her ribs. Through her veins her blood was still rushing with a shocked fury.

He gave her a nod of acknowledgement and then turned away and walked out of the place, oblivious to the entire crowd of customers standing there slack-jawed and staring at him.

Emma stared just as much as all the others, watching him leave. And even when the door had closed behind him she still stood there looking, as if she could see right through it to follow him. Six months in Whitechapel and she had never seen a man as strong, as ruthless or as invincible.

'Don't think he'll be having any trouble for a while,' said Nancy, who was standing, hands on hips, bar cloth in hand, watching.

'Who is he?' Emma asked in soft-voiced amazement.

'Goes by the name of Ned Stratham. Or so he says.'

Emma opened her mouth to ask more, but Nancy had already turned her attention away, raising her voice loud and harsh as she called out to the taproom audience, 'Show's over, folks. Get back to your tables before your chops grow cold and your ale grows warm.'

Emma's gaze returned to linger on the front door and her thoughts to the man who had just exited through it.

Ned Stratham.

A fight seemingly over a pint of spilled porter. And yet Emma was not fooled, even if all the others were.

Ned Stratham did not know anything about her other than she served him his dinner and porter. He was a man who had barely seemed to notice her in the months he had been coming here. A man who kept to himself and quietly watched what unfolded around him without getting involved. Until tonight.

It had not been fighting in any sense that a gentleman would recognise, it had been raw and shocking and, if she were honest, much more effective. It followed no rules. It had not been polite or genteel, nor, on the surface of it, honourable or chivalric.

'Backlog of chops in the kitchen, Emma,' Nancy's voice interrupted.

Emma nodded. 'I am just coming.'

Seemingly a taproom brawl over a clumsy accident and yet… In her mind she saw again that blue gaze on hers, so piercing and perceptive.

'Emma!' Nancy yelled again. 'You want it in writing?'

Lifting her tray, Emma headed for the kitchen. Ned Stratham's table had been nowhere near Black-Hair's and any man who could tumble a disc over his knuckles had no problems with balance.

And she knew that, despite his method, what Ned Stratham had just done was chivalric in every sense of the word. She knew that what he had just done was save her from Black-Hair.

* * *

Ned Stratham saw the woman again a week later on his visit to the Red Lion. His meal had been delivered by the other serving wench, but it was Emma who came to collect his cleared plate and empty tankard.

Her dark hair was clean and pinned up, her pale olive skin clear and smooth, unmarked by pox scars. Her teeth were white and straight. She was too beautiful for Whitechapel. Too well-spoken, too. It made her stand out. It made her a target for men like the dark-haired chancer last week. He already knew that she wore no wedding band upon her finger. No husband. Unprotected in an area of London where it was dangerous for any woman, let alone one like her, to be so.

'Do you wish another pint of porter, sir?' Her voice was clear, her accent refined and out of place on this side of town.

'Thank you.' He watched in silence as she shifted his plate, cutlery and tankard to sit on her empty wooden tray. But once the table was cleared she did not hurry off as usual. Instead she hesitated, lingering there with the tray in her hands.

'I did not get a chance to thank you, last week.'

Her eyes were a dark-brown velvet. Warm eyes, he thought as he looked into them. Beautiful eyes.

'For what?' he asked.

'Spilling your drink.'

'A clumsy accident.'

'Of course it was.' She smiled in a way that told him that she understood exactly what he had done. The hint of a dimple showed in the corner of her mouth.

It made him smile, too.

She was always polite and professional, and friendly with it, as if she genuinely liked people. But unlike most other serving wenches he had never seen her flirt with any man, even though that would have earned her more tips. She did her job with a capable efficiency and sense of purpose that he liked.

He turned his gaze to focus on the tumble of the small pale-ivory token across his knuckles. No matter how beautiful she was, there was a part of him that wanted her to just walk away as she had done all the other times, to attend to other punters on other tables. There were things on his mind more important than beautiful women. Things he had spent a lifetime chasing. Things upon which he had to stay focused to bring to fruition. He did not want distractions, not of any kind.

And the truth was he had not wanted to inter-
vene last week, but he could not have just sat there
and turned a blind eye while a woman was forced
against her will, whatever the level of it. He had
known men like the black-haired tough all his
life. What started out as 'fun' soon escalated to
something else.

He watched the rhythmic smooth tumble of the
token over the fingers of his right hand. It was a
movement so long practised as to no longer be a
trick but a reflex, a part of himself.

'I will fetch your porter.' He didn't look up at
her but he knew she was still smiling. He could
hear it in her voice.

Ned said nothing more. Just kept his focus on
the token, effectively dismissing her.

He heard her turn and walk away. Shifted his
eyes momentarily to her retreating figure, to the
soft sway of her hips. The smallest of glances; no
risk to the ripple of his fingers that was as instinc-
tive and easy to him as breathing. And yet, in that
moment, for the first time in years, he fluffed the
move like a novice. The token tipped from his
hand, straight off the table, landing edge up on
the floorboards to roll away with speed.

His heart skipped a beat. He was already on
his feet and following, but the token was way in

front and heading for the crowded bar. But Emma, as he'd heard her called, reached a foot forward and, with the toe of her boot, gently stopped it, balanced the tray on her hip and retrieved it from the floor.

Ned watched as she rubbed the token against the bodice of her dress, dusting off the dirt that marred its smooth pale surface. Her gaze moved over the worn ivory, studying it.

She turned to him as he reached her.

Their eyes held for a tiny second before she passed the token to him.

'Thank you,' he said.

'For what? I trust the inadvertent and clumsy tread of my boot did your property no harm.' Her eyes held his.

He couldn't help himself. He smiled.

And so did she.

Her eyes watched the token as he slipped it safely inside his jacket. 'What is it?'

'My lucky charm.'

'Does it work?'

'Without fail.'

Her eyebrows rose ever so slightly, but she softened the cynicism with a smile that did things to him that no other woman's smile ever had. It kept him standing here, talking, when he should have walked away.

'You don't believe me.'

'A lucky charm that works without fail...?' She raised her eyebrows again, teasingly this time. 'Perhaps I should ask to borrow it.'

'Are you in need of good luck?'

'Is not everyone?'

'Emma!' Nancy shouted from the bar. 'Six pints of porter here!'

'Ned Stratham.' He did not smile, but offered his hand for a handshake.

'Emma de Lisle.'

Her fingers were feminine and slender within his own. Her skin cool and smooth, even within the warmth of the taproom. The touch of their bare hands sparked physical awareness between them. He knew she felt it, too, from the slight blush on her cheeks and the way she released his hand.

'Emma!' Nancy, the landlady, screeched like a banshee. 'Get over here, girl!'

Emma glanced over her shoulder at the bar. 'Coming, Nancy!

'No rest for the wicked,' she said, and with a smile she was gone.

Ned resumed his seat, but his eyes watched her

cross the room. The deep red of the tavern dress complimented the darkness of her hair and was laced tight to her body so that he could see the narrowness of her waist and the flare of her hips and the way the material sat against her buttocks. There was a vitality about her, an intelligence, a level of confidence in herself not normally seen round here.

He watched her collect the tankards from the bar and distribute them to various tables, taking her time en route to him. His was the last tankard on the tray.

'What's a woman like you doing in a place like this?' he asked as she set the porter down before him.

Her eyes met his again. And in them was that same smile. 'Working,' she said.

This time she didn't linger. Just moved on, to clear tables and take new orders and fetch more platters of chops.

He leaned back against the wooden panelling on the wall and slowly drank his porter. The drift of pipe smoke was in the air. He breathed it in along with the smell of char-grilled chops and hoppy ale. Soaking up the atmosphere of the place, the familiarity and the ease, he watched Emma de Lisle.

He had the feeling she wouldn't be working here

in the Red Lion for too long. She was a woman who was going places, or had been to them. Anyone who met her knew it. He wondered again, as he had wondered many times before, what her story was.

He watched how efficiently she worked, with that air of purpose and energy; the way she could share a smile or a joke with the punters without it delaying her work—only for him had she done that. The punters liked her and he could see why.

She didn't look at him again, not in all the time it took him to sup his drink.

The bells of St Olave's in the distance chimed eleven. Nancy called last orders.

Ned's time here for tonight was over. He drained the tankard. Left enough coins on the table to pay for his meal and a generous tip for Emma de Lisle, before lifting his hat and making his way across the room to the front door.

His focus flicked one last time to where Emma was delivering meat-laden platters to a table of four.

She glanced over at him, her eyes meeting his for a tiny shared moment, and flashed her wonderful smile at him, before getting on with the job in hand.

He placed his hat on his head and walked out

of the Red Lion Chop-House into the darkness of the alleyway.

I trust the inadvertent and clumsy tread of my boot did your property no harm. He smiled. Emma de Lisle was certainly one hell of a woman. A man might almost be tempted to stay here for a woman like her. Almost.

He smiled one last time, then set off through the maze of streets he knew so well. As he crossed the town, moving from one parish to the next, he shifted his mind to what lay ahead for tomorrow, focusing, running through the details.

The night air was cool and his face grim as he struck a steady pace all the way home to Mayfair.

Chapter Two

'Is that you, Emma?' her father called at the sound of her key scraping in the lock. She could hear the wariness in his voice.

She unlocked the door and let herself into the two small rooms that they rented.

'I brought you a special supper—pork chops.'

'Pork?' He raised his eyebrows in surprise. 'Not usual for there to be any pork left.'

There had not been. Pork was expensive and the choicest chop they offered. It was also her father's favourite, which was why Emma had paid for them out of her own pocket, largely with the generous tip Ned Stratham had left, the rest covered by Nancy's discount. 'Happy Birthday, Papa.' She dropped a kiss to his cheek as he drew her close and gave her a hug.

'It is my birthday? I lose track of time these

days.' He sat down in one of the spindly chairs at the bare table in the corner of the room.

'That is what happens with age,' Emma teased him. But she knew it was not age that made him forget, but the fact that all the days merged together when one just worked all the time.

She hung her cloak on the back of the door, then set a place at the little table, unwrapped the l idded plate from its cloth and finally produced an earthenware bottle. 'And as a treat, one of the finest of the Red Lion's porters.'

'You spoil me, Emma,' he chided, but he smiled. 'You are not having anything?'

'I ate earlier, in the Red Lion. And you know I cannot abide the taste of beer.'

'For which I am profoundly thankful. Bad enough my daughter chooses to work in a common tavern, but that she would start drinking the wares…' He gave an exaggerated shudder.

'It is a chop-house, not a tavern as I have told you a hundred times.' She smiled. Although the distinction made little difference in reality, it made her father feel better. But he would not feel better were he to see the Red Lion's clientele and her best customers. She wondered what he would make of a man like Ned Stratham. Or what he would say had he witnessed the manner in which Ned had bested five men to defend her.

Her father smiled, too. 'And I suppose I should be heartily grateful for that.'

'You know the tips from the chop-house pay very well indeed, much better than for any milliner or shop girl. And it will not be for ever.'

'Perhaps not,' he said thoughtfully.

'No perhaps about it, Papa,' she said sternly. 'Our savings begin to grow. And I have made an application for a position in Clerkenwell. It is not Mayfair, but it is heading in the right direction.'

'Managing a chop-house.'

Managing a tavern, but she did not tell him that. 'One step at a time, on a journey that will eventually lead us back to our own world.'

He smiled. 'My dear girl, have I told you that you are stubborn as a mastiff?'

'Once or twice. I wonder where I might have acquired such a trait? I do not recall my dear mama having such a defect.'

He chuckled. 'Indeed, I own the blame. The apple does not fall so very far from the tree.' He gently patted her hand. 'Come, take a seat. You must be tired after working all evening.'

Emma dropped into the seat opposite. 'Not so tired at all.' And although her feet were aching it was the truth. She thought of Ned Stratham and the interaction that had passed between them earlier that evening and smiled. He was a man without an inch of softness in him. Probably more dangerous than any of the other men that came to the chop-house, and the men that came to the Red Lion were not those anyone would wish to meet alone on a dark night. Definitely more dangerous, she corrected, remembering precisely what he had done to Black-Hair and his cronies. And yet there was something about him, something that marked him as different. Pushing the thought away, she focused her attention on her father.

'How were the docks today?'

'The same as they ever are. The good news is that I managed to get an extra shift for tomorrow.'

'Again?' The fatigue in his face worried her. 'Working a double shift is too much for you.' Working a single shift in a manual job in the London Docks' warehouses was too much for a man who had been raised and lived as a gentleman all his life.

'What is sauce for the goose is sauce for the gander,' he said. 'Do not start with your scolding, please, Emma.'

She sighed and gave a small smile. It was his birthday and she wanted what was left of it to be nice for him. There would be other days to raise the issue of his working double shifts. 'Very well.'

'Fetch your cup. I shall propose a toast.'

She did as he bid.

He poured a dribble of porter into her cup. Raised his own tankard in the air. 'God has granted me another year and I am happy and thankful for it.' But there was a shadow of sadness in his eyes and she knew what he was thinking of. 'To absent loved ones,' he said. 'Wherever Kit is. Whatever he is doing. God keep him safe and bring him home to us.'

'To absent loved ones,' she echoed and tried to suppress the complicated swirl of emotions she felt whenever Kit's name was mentioned.

They clunked the cups together and drank down the porter. Its bitterness made her shudder. Once it had been champagne in the finest of cut-crystal glasses with which he made his birthday toast and the sweetest of lemonades, extravagantly chilled with ice. Once their lives had been very different from the ones they lived here.

As if sensing her thought, he reached his hand to hers and gave it a squeeze. Her eyes met his, sombre for a moment with shared dark memories, before she locked the memories away in the place they belonged. Neither spoke of them. It was not their way. She forced a smile to her face. 'You should eat those pork chops before they grow cold.'

'With pleasure, my dear girl.' Her father smiled in return and tucked into the meal with relish.

Across town the next day, within the dining room of a mansion house in Cavendish Square, a very distinguished luncheon was taking place.

The fireplace was black marble, carved and elaborate. The walls were red, lined with ornate paintings of places in Scotland and overseas Ned had never been. Above the table hung an enormous chandelier from which a thousand crystal drops danced and shimmered in the slight breeze from the opened window. There were two windows in the room, both large, bowed in style, both framed with long heavy red damask curtains with fringed swags and tails. Both had blinds that were cream in colour and pulled high.

Out in the street beyond, the sky was bright with the golden light of a summer's afternoon. It glinted on the silver service and crystal of the glasses on the polished mahogany table stretched out like a long banqueting table from kings of old. Enough spaces to seat eighteen. But there were only five men dining from the sumptuous feast. Seated in the position of the principal guest was the government minister for trade. On his left was the minister's secretary. Directly opposite the minister was the biggest mill owner in the north and one away was a shipping magnate whose line was chief to service the West Indies and the Americas. A powerful collection of men, and seated at their heart, in the position of host, was Ned Stratham.

He fed them the best of fine foods and rich sauces prepared by a chef who had once been employed by the Prince Regent. He ensured that his butler and footmen were well trained enough to keep the men's glasses flowing with expensive French wines. A different one suited for each dish.

Ned knew how to play the game. He knew what was necessary for success in business and influence over policy.

'I can make no promises,' said the minister.

'I'm not asking you to,' replied Ned.

'And the source of the figures you quoted?'

'Sound.'

'You really think it would work?'

Ned gave a nod.

'You would be taking as much a risk as us, maybe even more so as it is your money on the line.'

'Maximum gain comes from maximum venture.'

'If the vote were to go against us and the bill fail…'

'You would survive it.'

'But would you?' the minister asked.

'That's not your problem.' Ned held his gaze while the seconds stretched, until eventually the minister for trade nodded.

'I will set the necessary mechanisms in motion tomorrow.'

'Then, we're agreed.' Ned held out his hand for a handshake.

The minister swallowed. A shadow of unease shifted through his shrewd eyes. It was one thing to say the words, but another to shake on it. A handshake for men like him placed their honour on the line.

There was a silence that was awkward for them all save Ned. He took a sort of wry pleasure in such moments; using gentlemen's discomfort of him and his dubious breeding to his own ends.

The other three looked nervous, waited to see what the minister would do.

Ned kept his gaze on the other man's. Kept his hand extended. Both were steady.

The minister smiled and finally shook Ned's hand. 'You have convinced me, sir.'

'I'm glad to hear it.'

* * *

It was after six by the time the luncheon finally ended and four of the most influential men in the country left Cavendish Square.

The butler and two footmen returned to the dining room, standing with their backs against the wall. Faces straight ahead, eyes focused on some distant point. Ned marvelled that gentlemen discussed the details of confidential business before servants, as if they were not men, as if they could not see or hear what was going on. Ned knew better. He never made the same mistake.

He sat alone at the table, the wine glass still halffull in his hand. The sunlight which streamed in through the windows lit the port within a deep ruby-red and made the monogram engraved on the glass's surface sparkle—S for Stratham.

The minister had squirmed, but in the end the deal had been done. It would be good for much more than Ned. He felt a sense of grim satisfaction.

The butler cleared his throat and came to hover by his elbow. 'More port, sir?'

'No, thank you, Clarkson.' Ned wondered what Clarkson would do if he were to ask for a porter. But gentlemen in Mayfair did not drink porter. Not in any of their fancy rich establishments. Not even in their own homes. And Ned must keep up the guise of a gentleman.

But porter made him think of Whitechapel, and the Red Lion…and Emma de Lisle. With those perceptive dark eyes, and that vitality and warm, joyful confidence that emanated from her.

He glanced out of the window, at the sunlight and the carriage that trundled past, and felt the waft of cool air break through the cigar smoke that lingered like a mist within the dining room.

He had other business to attend to. But it didn't have to happen tonight.

Ned set the fine crystal goblet down upon the table. Got to his feet.

The butler appeared by his side again.

'I'm going out, Clarkson.'

'Very good, sir. Shall I arrange for the carriage?'

'No carriage.' Not for where Ned was going. 'It's a fine evening. I'll walk.'

Ned went to change into his old leather jacket and boots.

The heat from the kitchen mixed with that that had built up in the taproom through the summer's day to make the air of the Red Lion stifling. The chop-house's windows and doors were all open, but it made little difference.

Nancy had taken advantage of the heatwave and had her staff carry some tables out on to the street, so that the chop-house's customers could sit out there in the cool shade and drink their beer.

'Three pitchers of ale!' Nancy yelled and Emma hurried to answer.

Emma could feel the sweat dripping down her back and between her breasts. Never had a shift seemed so long. Her legs were aching and her feet felt like they were on fire. She lifted the tray, tried to blow a hair away from where it had escaped her pins to dangle in her eye and made her way across the taproom, hurrying out of the doorway, just as Ned Stratham was coming in.

She collided with him, almost dropping the tray. It was Ned who steadied it, stopping the slide of the pitchers and the ensuing disaster.

'Ned Stratham,' she said, and inside her stomach felt like a flock of starlings taking off from the fields as one to swoop across a sunset sky. 'Two nights on the trot? This is a first.' Sometimes weeks passed between his visits.

Those blue, blue eyes met hers and held for a second too long. 'You've been counting.'

'As if I would have time to be counting.'

She saw the hint of amusement in his eyes as he moved aside and let her pass through.

Emma did not look back. Just got on with serving the tableloads of customers that were outside in the alley. But all the while she was conscious that he was inside. Too conscious. She smiled wryly to herself and got on with clearing the outside tables before returning to the taproom.

There was not a seat to be had inside. Ned was leaning against the bar, comfortable, already sipping a porter. He looked unconcerned by the crowd, by the heat, by not having a chair or table.

'Six porters, two small beers and a stout, Emma!' Paulette shouted and thumped the last of the tankards down on the wooden counter beside Ned.

Emma continued her quick pace to the bar and, while unloading her tray, slid a glance in Ned Stratham's direction.

'Busy in here tonight,' he observed.

'There's a schooner in at the docks. We've had the full crew in since lunchtime.'

'Good business.'

'But bad timing. Tom did not come in today. Nancy is in the kitchen, cooking in his place.' She started loading up the fresh porters while she spoke.

'Bet that's made her all sweetness and light.'

'You know her so well.'

With impeccable timing, Nancy's face, beet-red with heat and running with sweat, appeared at the hatch as she thumped three plates down. 'Three mixed grills!' She flicked a crabbed gaze in Emma's direction.

'Where's me bleedin' platter?' someone shouted from the other side of the room.

'Any more of your lip and it'll be up your bleedin' backside,' Nancy snapped in reply and riveted the man with a look that would have blistered paint on a door.

Emma's and Ned's eyes met in shared silent amusement. 'Enjoy your porter,' she said and then she was off, collecting the platters on her way to deliver the porters.

'Come on, wench! My stomach thinks my throat's been cut! How long's a fellow got to wait in this place for a drink?' a punter shouted from the table in the middle of the floor.

'We're working as fast as we can!' screeched a flustered Paulette from behind the bar, her face scarlet and sweaty.

'Five porters, gentlemen.' Emma's voice, although quiet in comparison to the rowdy conversation, shouts and laughter in the place, stood out because she sounded like a lady. She worked quickly and efficiently, setting a tankard on the table before each man before moving on to deliver the rest of the drinks from her tray.

Ned watched her bustle across the room to the big table in the corner where the crew of the schooner looked three sheets past a sail. He felt himself stiffen as one of them copped a sly grope as she leaned across the table with a drink.

Her movement was subtle and slight, but very effective. The contents of the tankard ended up in the worm's lap.

The sailor gave a yelp, followed by a curse, staggering to his feet and staring down at the sodden stain rapidly spreading over his trousers. 'Look what the hell you've done!'

His crewmates were all laughing.

'I am so sorry,' she said without the slightest bit of sincerity. 'I will fetch you another porter. Let us just hope it does not go the same way as the first one.' And there was the steely hint of warning in her eye as she said it.

Grumbling, the man sat down.

'I wonder where you got that idea,' Ned Stratham said when she returned to the bar. He kept his focus on the token tumbling over his fingers.

'I wonder,' she said.

He moved his gaze to her. The strands of her hair had escaped its pins to coil like damp ebony ivy against the golden skin of her neck. The swell of her breasts looked in danger of escaping the red bodice. He could see the rise and fall of it with her every breath. Her cheeks were flushed with the heat and her eyes, sparkling black as cut jet, held his. They shared a smile before she hurried off across the room again. She was so vivid and vital and alive that the desire he normally held in check surged through him.

Ned wasn't the only one, judging by the way the sailors were looking at her. After months away at sea most men had two things on their mind—drink and women. They were tanked up on the first and were now seeking the second.

'What you doing later, darlin'? Me and you, we could step out for a little drink.'

'Hands off, Wrighty, she's coming home with me, ain't that right, Emma darling?' another said.

'Neither is possible, I'm afraid, gentlemen. I'm meeting my betrothed,' she said without missing a beat while clearing empties from their table.

'Shame.'

The other looked less than convinced. His gaze meandered with greed and lust over the length of her body as she returned to the bar. He wasn't alone. A man would have had to have water in his veins not to want her. And what was flowing in the veins of the sailors was far from water.

One drink, Ned had told himself. And yet he couldn't walk away now. Not even had he wanted to. He ordered another porter from Paulette.

It was an hour before the bustle waned and another two before Paulette rang the bell for last orders.

Half an hour later and what remained of the Red Lion's clientele had emptied into the alleyway outside.

Emma leaned against the edge of a table, taking the weight off her feet, while fastening her cloak in place. The taproom was empty. The tables had been wiped down, the stools upturned on the tabletops. The floor had been swept ready to be mopped the next day. Ned Stratham had gone some time while she had been in the kitchen helping Nancy scrape the grills clean. Gone without saying goodbye, she thought, and then realised how stupid that thought was. He was just a customer like all the rest. And if she had any sense in her head she should be glad of it.

'Ned Stratham's got his eye on you, Em,' Paulette teased with a sly face.

'Nonsense.' Emma concentrated on fastening

her cloak and hoped the dimness of the candle-light hid her blush.

'I saw the way he was watching you. Asking questions, too.'

'Too much time on his hands,' said Emma dismissively.

Paulette smirked. 'Don't think so.'

'What a night!' Nancy swept in from the kitchen. 'Tom better show tomorrow or there'll be trouble.'

Nancy unlocked the front door to let Emma and Paulette leave. 'Watch yourself, girls, we got a few stragglers.'

Emma gave a nod as she and Paulette stepped out into the alleyway.

The last of the evening light had long since faded to an inky dark blue. The day's heat had cooled. Behind them the kitchen door closed with a slam. A lone sailor stood waiting before them.

Emma met Paulette's eyes.

'It's all right, Em. George said he'd wait for me. He's the boatswain off the ship that's in,' explained Paulette.

Emma lowered her voice. 'Paulette—'

'I know what I'm doing, honest, Em. I'll be all right,' Paulette whispered and walked off down the alleyway with the boatswain.

Behind her Emma heard Nancy slide the big

bolts into place across the door, locking her out into the night. The only light in the darkness was that from the high-up kitchen window.

Emma turned to head home, in the opposite direction to the one that Paulette and her beau had taken, just as two men stepped into the mouth of the alley ahead.

Chapter Three

'Emma, darlin', you've been telling us porkies.' Through the flicker of the kitchen lamps she recognised the sailor who had asked her to step out with him for a drink. He was unshaven and the stench of beer from him reached across the distance between them. His gaze was not on her face, but lower, leering at the pale skin of her exposed *décolletage*. Her heart began to thud. Fear snaked through her blood, but she showed nothing of it. Instead, she eyed the men with disdain and pulled her cloak tighter around herself.

'Good job we came back for you, since there's no sign of your "betrothed." Maybe now we can get to know each other a bit better.'

'I do not think so, gentlemen.'

'Oh, she don't think so, Wrighty. Let us convince you, darlin'.' They gave a laugh and started to walk towards her.

Emma's hand slid into the pocket of her cloak, just as Ned Stratham stepped out of the shadows by her side.

She smothered the gasp.

His face was expressionless, but his eyes were cold and dangerous as sharp steel. He looked at the men. Just a look. But it was enough to stop them in their tracks.

The sailor who had done the talking stared, and swallowed, then held up his hands in submission. 'Sorry, mate. Didn't realise…'

'You do now,' said Ned in a voice that for all its quiet volume was filled with threat, and never shifting his hard gaze for an instant.

'All right, no offence intended.' The sailors backed away. 'Thought she was spinning a line about the betrothed thing. She's yours. We're already gone.'

Ned watched them until they disappeared and their footsteps faded into the distance out on to St Catherine's Lane. Only then did he look at Emma.

In the faint flickering light from the kitchen window, his eyes looked almost as dark as hers, turned from sky-blue to midnight. He had a face that was daunted by nothing. It would have been tough on any other man. On him it was handsome. Firm determined lips. A strong masculine nose with a tiny bump upon its ridge. His rogue eyebrow enough to take a woman's breath away. Her heart rate kicked faster as her gaze lingered momentarily on it before returning to his eyes.

'What are you doing here, Ned?' she asked in wary softness.

'Taking the air.'

They looked at one another.

She's yours. The echo of the sailor's words seemed to whisper between them, making her cheeks warm.

'I didn't think you'd be fool enough to walk home alone in the dark through these streets.'

'Normally I do not. Tom lives in the next street up from mine. He usually sees me home safe.'

'Tom's not here.'

'Which is why I borrowed one of Nancy's knives.' She slid the knife from her pocket and held it between them so that the blade glinted in the moonlight.

'It wouldn't have stopped them.'

'Maybe not. But it would have done a very great deal of damage, I assure you.'

The silence hissed between them.

'You want to take your chances with the knife? Or you could accept my offer to see you home safe.'

She swallowed, knowing what he was offering and feeling her stomach turn tumbles within. 'As long as you understand that it is just seeing me safely home.' She met his gaze, held it with mock confidence.

'Are you suggesting that I'm not a gentleman?' His voice was all stony seriousness, but he raised the rogue eyebrow.

'On the contrary, I am sure you are the perfect gentleman.'

'Maybe not perfect.'

She smiled at that, relaxing a little now that the shock of seeing him there had subsided, and returned the knife blade to its dishcloth scabbard within the pocket of her cloak.

'We should get going,' he said. And together they began to walk down the alleyway.

Their footsteps were soft and harmonious, the slower, heavier thud of his boots in time with the lighter step of her own.

They walked on, out on to St Catherine's Lane. Walked along in silence.

'You knew those sailors would be waiting for me, didn't you?'

'Did I?'

'You do not fool me, Ned Stratham.'

'It's not my intention to fool anyone.'

She scrutinised him, before asking the question that she'd been longing to ask since the first night he had walked into the Red Lion. 'Who are you?'

'Just a man from Whitechapel.'

'And yet…the shirt beneath your jacket looks like it came from Mayfair. And is tailored to fit you perfectly. Most unusual on a man from Whitechapel.' He was probably a crook. A gang boss. A tough. How else did a man like him get the money for such a shirt? Asking him now, when they were alone, in the dark of the night, was probably not the wisest thing she had ever done, but the question was out before she could think better of it. Besides, if she did not ask him now, she doubted she would get another chance. She ignored the faster patter of her heart and held his eyes, daring him to tell her something of the truth.

'You've been eyeing up my shirt.'

She gave a laugh and shook her head. 'I could not miss it. Nor could half the chop-house. You have had your jacket off all evening.'

'But half the chop-house would not have recognised a Mayfair shirt.' Half in jest, half serious.

Her heart skipped a beat, but she held his gaze boldly, as if he were not treading so close to forbidden ground, brazening it out. 'So you admit it is from Mayfair?'

'From Greaves and Worcester.'

'How does a Whitechapel man come to be wearing a shirt from one of the most expensive shirtmakers in London?'

'How is a woman from a Whitechapel chophouse familiar with the said wares and prices?'

She smiled, but said nothing, on the back foot now that he was the one asking questions she did not want to answer.

'What's your story, Emma?'

'Long and uninteresting.'

'For a woman like you, in a place like this?' He arched the rogue eyebrow with scepticism.

She held her silence, wanting to know more of him, but not at the cost of revealing too much of herself.

'Playing your cards close to your chest?' he asked.

'It is the best way, I have found.'

He smiled at that. 'A woman after my own heart.'

They kept on walking, their footsteps loud in the silence.

He met her eyes. 'I heard tell you once worked in Mayfair.' It was the story she had put about.

'Cards and chest, even for unspoken questions,' she said.

Ned laughed.

And she smiled.

'I worked as a lady's maid.' She kept her eyes front facing. If he had not already heard it from the others in the Red Lion, he soon would. It was the only reasonable way to explain away her voice and manners; many ladies' maids aped their mistresses. And it was not, strictly speaking, a lie, she told herself for the hundredth time. She had learned and worked in the job of a lady's maid, just as she had shadow-studied the role of every female servant from scullery maid to housekeeper; one had to have an understanding of how a household worked from the bottom up to properly run it.

'That explains much. What happened?'

'You ask a lot of questions, Ned Stratham.'

'You keep a lot of secrets, Emma de Lisle.'

Their gazes held for a moment too long, in challenge, and something else, too. Until he smiled his submission and looked ahead once more.

She breathed her relief.

A group of men were staggering along the other side of the Minories Road, making their way home from the King's Head. Their voices were loud and boisterous, their gait uneven. They shouted insults and belched at one another. One of them stopped to relieve his bladder against a lamp post.

She averted her eyes from them, met Ned's gaze and knew he was thinking about the knife and how it would have fared against six men.

'It would still have given them pause for thought,' she said in her defence.

Ned said nothing.

But for all of her assertions and the weight of the kitchen knife within her cloak right at this moment in time she was very glad of Ned Stratham's company.

The men did not shout the bawdy comments they would have had it been Tom by her side. They said nothing, just quietly watched them pass and stayed on their own side of the road.

Neither of them spoke. Just walking together at the same steady pace up Minories. Until the drunkards were long in the distance. Until they turned right into the dismal narrow street in which she and her father lodged. There were no street lamps, only the low silvery light of the moon to guide their steps over the potholed surface.

Halfway along the street she slowed and came to a halt outside the doorway of a shabby boarding house.

'This is it. My home.'

He glanced at the building, then returned his eyes to her.

They looked at one another through the darkness.

'Thank you for walking me home, Ned.'

'It was the least I could do for my betrothed,' he said with his usual straight expression, but there was the hint of a smile in his eyes.

She smiled and shook her head, aware he was teasing her, but her cheeks blushing at what she had let the sailors in the alleyway think. 'I should have set them straight.'

'And end our betrothal so suddenly?'

'Would it break your heart?'

'Most certainly.'

The teasing faded away. And with it something of the safety barrier between them.

His eyes locked hers, so that she could not look away even if she had wanted to. A sensual tension whispered between them. Attraction. Desire. Forbidden liaisons. She could feel the flutter of butterflies in her stomach, feel a heat in her thighs. In the silence of the surrounding night the thud of her heart sounded too loud in her ears. Her skin tingled with nervous anticipation.

She glanced up to the window on the second floor where the light of a single candle showed faintly through the thin curtain. 'My father waits up for me. I should go.'

'You should.'

But she made no move to leave. And neither did he.

He looked at her in a way that made every sensible thought flee her head. He looked at her in a way that made her feel almost breathless.

Ned stepped towards her, closed the distance between them until they were standing toe to toe, until she could feel the brush of his thighs against hers.

'I thought you said you were the perfect gentleman?'

'You said that, not me.' His eyes traced her face, lingering over her lips, so that she knew he meant to kiss her. And God knew what living this life in Whitechapel had done to her because in that moment she wanted him to. Very much.

Desire vibrated between them. Where his thighs touched to hers the skin scalded. In the moonlight his eyes looked dark, smouldering, intense. She knew that he wanted her. Had been around Whitechapel long enough to know the games men and women played.

Emma's breath sounded too loud and ragged.

Their gazes held locked.

The tension stretched until she did not think she could bear it a second longer.

He slid his strong arms around her waist, moving slowly, giving her every chance to step away or tell him nay. But she did neither. Only placed her palms to rest tentatively against the leather breast of his jacket.

He lowered his face towards her.

She tilted her mouth to meet his.

And then his lips took hers and he kissed her.

He kissed her and his kiss was gentle and persuasive. His kiss was tender and passionate. He was the strongest, fiercest man she knew and yet he did not force or plunder. He was not rough or grabbing. It seemed to her he gave rather than took. Courting her lips, teasing them, making her feel things she had never felt before. Making her want him never to stop.

By its own volition one hand moved up over his broad shoulder to hold against the nape of his neck. Anchoring herself to his solidity, to his strength and warmth.

He pulled her closer, their bodies melding together as the kiss intensified. Tasting, touching, sharing. His tongue stroked against hers, inviting hers to a dance she did not know and Emma followed where he led.

He kissed her and she forgot about Whitechapel and poverty and hardship.

He kissed her and she forgot about the darkness of the past and all her worries over the future.

He kissed her and there was nothing else in the world but this man and this moment of magic and madness, and the force of passion that was exploding between them.

And when Ned stopped and drew back to look into her face, her heart was thudding as hard as a blacksmith hitting his anvil and her blood was rushing so fast that she felt dizzy from it.

'You should go up now, before I change my mind about being the perfect gentleman.' He brushed the back of his fingers gently against her cheek.

With trembling legs she walked to the front door of the boarding house and let herself in. She did not look round, but she knew Ned Stratham still stood there watching her. Her heart was skipping in a fast, frenzied thud. Her blood was rushing. Every nerve in her body seemed alive. She closed the door quietly so as not to wake the neighbours. Rested her spine against its peeling paint while she drew a deep breath, calming the tremor in her body and the wild rush of her blood, before climbing the stairwell that led to her father and their rented rooms.

'It is only me, Papa,' she called softly.

But her father was sound asleep in the old arm-chair.

She moved to the window and twitched the curtain aside to look down on to the street.

Ned Stratham tipped his hat to her. And only then, when he knew she was home safe, did he walk away.

Emma blew out the candle to save what was left. Stood there and watched him until the tall broad-shouldered figure disappeared into the darkness, before turning to her father.

Even in sleep his face was etched with exhaustion.

'Papa,' she whispered and brushed a butterfly kiss against the deep lines of his forehead.

'Jane?' Her mother's name.

'It is Emma.'

'Emma. You are home safe, my girl?'

'I am home safe,' she confirmed and thought again of the man who had ensured it. 'Let me help you to bed.'

'I can manage, my dearest.' He got to his feet with a great deal of stiffness and shuffled through to the smaller of the two rooms.

The door closed with a quiet click, leaving Emma standing there alone.

She touched her fingers to her kiss-swollen lips and knew she should not have kissed Ned Stratham.

He was a Whitechapel man, a man from a different world than her own, a customer who drank in the Red Lion's taproom. And he was fierce and dangerous, and darkly mysterious. And she had no future here. And much more besides. She knew all of that. And knew, too, her mother would be turning in her grave.

But as she moved behind the partitioning screen and changed into her nightdress, in her nose was not the usual sweet mildew, but the lingering scent of soap and leather and something that was just the man himself. And as she pulled back the threadbare covers and climbed into the narrow makeshift bed, in her blood was a warmth.

Emma lay there, staring into the darkness. They said when the devil tempted he offered a heart's desire. Someone tall and dangerous and handsome. She closed her eyes, but she could still see those piercing blue eyes and her lips still tingled and throbbed from the passion of his kiss.

When exhaustion finally claimed her and she sank into the blissful comfort of sleep she dreamed of a tall, dangerous, handsome man tempting her to forbidden lusts, tempting her to give up her struggle to leave Whitechapel and stay here with him. And in the dream she yielded to her heart's desire and was lost beyond all redemption.

Tom did not come to the Red Lion the next night, but Ned Stratham did.

Their gazes held across the taproom, the echoes of last night rippling like an incoming tide, before she turned away to serve a table. Butterflies were dancing in her stomach, but she knew that after what had happened between them, she had to rectify the matter. She emptied her tray, then made her way to where he sat alone.

Those blue eyes met hers.

She felt her heart trip faster and quelled the reaction with an iron hand. Faced him calmly and spoke quietly, but firmly enough that only he would hear.

'Last night, we should not have, *I* should not have… It was a mistake, Ned.'

He said nothing.

'I'm not that sort of a woman.'

'You're assuming I'm that kind of a man.'

'Lest you had forgotten, this is a chop-house not so far from the docks. All the men in here are that kind of a man.'

He smiled at that. A hard smile. 'Not gentlemen, but scoundrels.'

'I did not say that.'

'It's what you meant.'

He glanced across the room to where Paulette was working behind the bar before returning his gaze to hers.

Nancy's curses sounded from the kitchen.

And she knew he knew that Tom had not come in again, that there was no one to see her home.

Ned looked at her with eyes that made no pretence as to the man he was, with eyes that made her resolutions weaken.

'Emma!' Nancy's voice bellowed.

'It is not your duty to see me home.'

'It is not,' he agreed.

As their gazes held in a strange contest of wills, they both knew it was already decided. Ned Stratham was not going to let her take her chances with a kitchen knife through the Whitechapel streets tonight.

'Get yourself over here, Emma!' Nancy sounded as if she were losing what little patience she possessed.

Ned did walk her home. And he did kiss her. And she gave up pretending to herself that she did not want it or him.

* * *

He came to the Red Lion every night after that, even when Tom had returned. And every night he walked her home. And every night he kissed her.

Ned tumbled the token over his fingers and leaned his spine back against the old lichen-stained stone seat. St Olave's church clock chimed ten. Down the hill at the London Docks the early shift had started five hours ago.

The sky was a cloudless blue. The worn stone was warm beneath his thighs. His hat sat on the bench by his side and he could feel a breeze stir through his hair. His usual perch. His usual view.

His thoughts drifted to the previous night and Emma de Lisle. Two weeks of walking with her and he could not get her out of his head. Not those dark eyes or that sharp mind. She could hold her own with him. She had her secrets as much as he. A lady's maid who had no wish to discuss her dismissal or her background. She was proud and determined and resourceful. There weren't many women in Whitechapel like her. There weren't *any* women like her. Not that he had known across a lifetime and he had seen about as much of Whitechapel as it was possible to see.

Life had not worn her down or sapped her energy. She had a confidence and a bearing about her comparable with those who came from a lifetime of wealth. She had learnt well from her mistress. A woman like Emma de Lisle would be an asset to any man in any walk of life; it was a thought that grew stronger with the passing days.

And he wanted her. Ned, who did not give in to wants and desires. He wanted her with a passion. And he was spending his nights and too many of his days imagining what it would be like to unlace that tight red dress from her body, to bare her and lay her down on his bed. Ned suppressed the thoughts. He was focused. He was disciplined. He kept to the plan. It was what had brought him this far.

The plan had never involved a woman like her. The plan had been for someone quite different. But she was as refreshing as a cool breeze on a clammy day. She was Whitechapel, the same as him, but with vision that encompassed a bigger view. She had tasted the world on the other side of London. He had a feeling she would understand what it was he was doing, an instinct that she would feel the same about it as he did. And part of being successful was knowing when to be stubborn and stick to the letter of the plan and when to be flexible.

His gaze shifted.

The old vinegar manufactory across the road lay derelict. Pigeons and seagulls vied for supremacy on the hole-ridden roof. Weeds grew from the crumbling walls.

Tower Hill lay at his back. And above his head the canopy of green splayed beech leaves provided a dapple shelter. He could hear the breeze brush through the leaves, a whisper beside the noises that carried up the hill from the London Docks; the rhythmic strike of hammers, the creak and thud of crates being moved and dropped, the squeak of hoists and clatter of chains, the clopping of work horses and rumbling of carts.

A man might live a lifetime and never meet a woman like Emma de Lisle.

Ned's fingers toyed with the ivory token as he watched the men moving about in the dockyard below, men he had known all of his life, men who were friends, or at least had been not so very long ago, unloading the docked ship.

Footsteps drew his attention. He glanced up the street and recognised the woman immediately, despite the fact she was not wearing the figure-hugging red dress, but a respectable sprig muslin and green shawl, and a faded straw bonnet with a green ribbon hid her hair and most of her face.

Emma de Lisle; as if summoned by the vision in his head. She faltered when she saw him as if contemplating turning back and walking away.

He slipped the token into his waistcoat pocket and got to his feet.

She resumed her progress. Paused just before she reached him, keeping a respectable distance between them.

'Ned.'

Last night's passion whispered and wound between them.

He gave a nod of acknowledgement.

Once, many years ago, he had seen a honeycomb dripping rich and sweet with golden honey. In this clear, pure daylight her eyes were the same colour, not dark and mysterious as in the Red Lion.

Their gazes held for a moment, the echoes of last night rippling like a returning tide.

'It seems that destiny has set you in my path again, Ned Stratham. Or I, in yours.'

'And who are we to argue with destiny?'

They looked at one another for the first time in daylight.

The road she was walking led from only one place. 'You have come from the dockyard.'

'My father works there. I was delivering him some bread and cheese.'

'He has a considerate daughter.'

'Not really. He worked late last night and started early this morning.'

But she had worked late last night, too, and no doubt started early this morning. A shadow that moved across her eyes and a little line of worry etched between them. 'Delivering his breakfast is the least I can do. He has a quarter-hour break at—'

'Half past nine,' he finished.

She lifted her eyebrows in unspoken question.

'I used to work on the docks.'

'And now?'

'And now, I do not. Cards and chest,' he said.

She laughed and the relaxed fascination he felt for her grew stronger.

'Five o'clock start. Your father will be done by four.'

'If only.' She frowned again at the mention of her father. Twice in five minutes; Ned had never seen her look worried, even on the night when she had thought herself alone facing the two sailors in the alleyway. 'He is on a double shift in the warehouse.'

'Good money, but tiring.'

'Very tiring.' She glanced down the hill at the dockyard with sombre eyes. 'It is hard work for a man of his age who is not used to manual labour.'

'What did he do before manual labour?'

She gave no obvious sign or reaction, only stood still as a statue, but her stillness betrayed that she had not meant to let the fact slip.

Her gaze remained on the dockyard. 'Not manual labour,' she said in a parody of his answer to her earlier question. She glanced round at him then, still and calm, but in her eyes were both defence and challenge. Her smile was sudden and warm, deflecting almost. 'I worry over my father, that is all. The work is hard and he is not a young man.'

'I still know a few folk in the dockyard. I could have a word. See if there are any easier jobs going.'

The silence was like the quiet rustle of silk in the air.

'You would do that?'

'There might be nothing, but I'll ask.' But there would be something. He would make sure of it. 'If you wish.'

He could see what she was thinking.

'No strings attached,' he clarified.

Emma's eyes studied his. Looking at him, really looking at him, like no woman had ever looked before. As if she could see through his skin to his heart, to his very soul, to everything that he was. 'I wish it very much,' she said.

He gave a nod.

There was a pause before she said, 'My father is an educated man. He can read and write and is proficient with arithmetic and mathematics, indeed, anything to do with numbers.'

'A man with book learning.'

She nodded. 'Although I'm not sure if that would be of any use in a dockyard.'

'You would be surprised.'

They stood in silence, both watching the dockworkers unloading the ship, yet her attention was as much on him as his was on her.

'Whatever you do for a living, Ned, whatever illicit activity you might be involved in…if you can help my father…'

'You think I'm a rogue…' He raised his brow. 'Do I look a rogue?'

Her gaze dropped pointedly to the front of his shirt before coming back up to his face. It lingered on his scarred eyebrow before finally moving to his eyes.

'Yes,' she said simply.

'My Mayfair shirt.'

'And the eyebrow,' she added.

'What's wrong with the eyebrow?'

'It does give you a certain roguish appearance.'

He smiled at that.

And she did, too.

'And if I am a rogue?'

She glanced away, gave a tiny shrug of her shoulders. 'It would not affect how I judge you.'

'How do you judge me, Emma?'

She slid a sideways glance at him. 'Cards and chest, Ned.'

He laughed.

'I should go and leave you to your contemplation.'

They looked at one another, the smile still in her sunlit eyes.

'Join me,' he said, yielding for once in his life to impulse. His eyes dared hers to accept.

He saw her gaze move to his scarred eyebrow again, almost caressingly.

He crooked it in a deliberate wicked gesture.

She smiled. 'Very well, but for a few moments only.' She smoothed her skirt to take a seat on the bench.

He sat down by her side.

A bee droned. From the branches overhead a blackbird sang.

Emma's eyes moved from the dockyards to the

derelict factory, then over the worn and pitted surface of the road mosaicked with flattened manure, and all the way along to the midden heap at its far end.

'Why here?' she asked.

'I grew up here. It reminds me of my childhood.'

'A tough neighbourhood.'

'Not for the faint of heart,' he said. 'Children are not children for long round here.'

'Indeed, they are not.'

There was a small silence while they both mused on that. And then let it go, eased by the peace of the morning and the place.

'It is a beautiful view,' she said.

Ned glanced round at her, wondering whether she was being ironic. 'Men in gainful employment are always a beautiful sight,' he said gravely.

'I was not thinking in those terms.' She smiled. 'It reminds me of a Canaletto painting.' Her eyes moved to the old manufactory. 'It has the same ruined glory as some of his buildings. The same shade of stone.'

'I wouldn't know. I've never seen a Canaletto painting.'

'I think you would like them.'

'I think maybe I would.'

Her gaze still lingered on the derelict building

as she spoke. 'A ruined glory. There are pigeons nesting in what is left of the roof. Rats with wings, my father used to call them,' she said.

'Plenty good eating in a rat.'

She laughed as if he were joking. He did not. He thought of all the times in his life when rat meat had meant the difference between starvation and survival.

'One day it will be something else,' he said. 'Not a ruined glory, but rebuilt.'

'But then there will be no more violets growing from the walls.'

'Weeds.'

'Not weeds, but the sweetest of all flowers. They used to grow in an old garden wall I knew very well.' The expression on her face was as if she were remembering and the memory both pained and pleased her.

Emma looked round at Ned then and there was something in her eyes, as if he were glimpsing through the layers she presented to the world to see the woman beneath.

'I will remember that, Emma de Lisle,' he said, studying her and everything that she was. A man might live a lifetime and never meet a woman like Emma de Lisle, the thought whispered again in his ear.

Their eyes held, sharing a raw exposed honesty.

Everything seemed to still and fade around them.

He lowered his face to hers and kissed her in the bright glory of the sunshine.

She tasted of all that was sweet and good. She smelled of sunshine and summer, and beneath it the scent of soap and woman.

He kissed her gently, this beautiful woman, felt her meet his kiss, felt her passion and her heart. Felt the desire that was between them surge and flare hot. He intensified the kiss, slid his arms around her and instinctively their bodies moulded together, as their mouths explored. He was hard for her, felt her thigh brush against his arousal, felt the soft press of her breasts against his chest, the slide of her hand beneath his jacket to stroke against his shirt, against his heart.

And then her palm flattened, pressed against his chest to stay him.

Their lips parted.

'It is broad daylight, Ned Stratham!' Her cheeks were flushed. Her eyes were dark with passion and shock. 'Anyone might see us.'

He twitched his scarred eyebrow.

She shook her head as if she were chiding him, but she smiled as she got to her feet.

He stood, too.

A whistling sounded and a man's figure appeared from the corner, trundling his barrow of fish along the road—Ernie Briggins, one of the Red Lion's best customers. 'Morning, Ned.'

Ned gave a nod.

Ernie's eyes moved to Emma with speculation and a barely suppressed smile. 'Morning, Emma.'

'Morning, Ernie.' Emma's cheeks glowed pink.

Ernie didn't stop, just carried on his way, leaving behind him the lingering scent of cod and oysters and the faint trill of his reedy whistle.

Emma said nothing, just raised her brows and looked at Ned with a 'told you so' expression.

'I better get you safely home, before any more rogues accost you.'

'I think I will manage more safely alone, thank you. Stay and enjoy your view.' Her eyes held to his. 'I insist.' She backed away. Smiled. Turned to leave.

'Emma.'

She stopped. Glanced round.

'I'm going out of town for the next week or so. I have some business to attend to. But I'll be back.'

'Developed a compulsion for the porter, have you?'

'A compulsion for something else, it would

seem,' he said quietly. 'We need to talk when I return, Emma.'

'That sounds serious.'

'It is.' He paused, then asked, 'Will you wait for me?'

There was a silence as her eyes studied his. 'I am not going anywhere, Ned Stratham.'

Their eyes held, serious and intent, for a second longer. 'I will wait,' she said softly.

They shared a smile before she turned and went on her way.

He watched her walk off into the sunlight until she disappeared out of sight.

A man might live a lifetime and never meet a woman like Emma de Lisle. But not Ned.

A fancy new dress and Emma wouldn't be out of place in Mayfair. Ned smiled to himself and, lifting his hat, began the long walk back across town.

The letter came the very next morning.

Emma stood in the rented room in the bright golden sunshine with the folded and sealed paper between her fingers, and the smile that had been on her face since the previous day vanished.

It had taken a shilling of their precious savings to pay the post boy, but it was a willing sacrifice.

She would have sold the shoes from her feet, sold the dress from her back to accept the letter and all that it might contain.

Her heart began to canter. She felt hope battle dread.

The paper was quality and white, her father's name written on the front in a fine hand with deep-black ink. There was no sender name, no clue impressed within the red-wax seal.

She swallowed, took a deep breath, stilled the churn in her stomach. It might not be the letter for which her father and she had both prayed and dreaded all of these two years past.

The one o'clock bell tolled in the distance.

She placed the letter down on the scrubbed wooden table. Stared at it, knowing that her father would not finish his shift before she left for the Red Lion, knowing, too, that he would probably be asleep by the time she returned. She was very aware that the answer to what had sent her mother to an early grave and turned her father grey with worry might lie within its folds.

Kit. She closed her eyes at the thought of her younger brother and knew that she could not get through the rest of this day without knowing if the letter contained news of him. Nor would her father. He would want to know, just the same as

Emma. Whether the news was good…or even if it was bad.

She pulled her shawl around her shoulders, fastened her bonnet on her head and, with the letter clutched tight within her hand, headed for the London Docks.

Chapter Four

Emma knew little of the warehouse in which her father worked. He had spoken nothing of it, so this was her first insight into the place that had become his world as much as the Red Lion had become hers.

All around the walls were great racks of enormous shelving stacked with boxes and bales. The windows in the roof were open, but with the heat of the day and the heavy work many of the men were working without shirts. She blushed with the shock of seeing their naked chests and rapidly averted her gaze, as she followed the foreman through the warehouse. Eventually through the maze of shelving corridors they came to another group of shirtless men who were carrying boxes up ladders to stack on high shelves.

'Bill de Lisle,' the foreman called. 'Someone here to see you.'

One of the men stepped forward and she was horrified to see it was her father.

'Papa?' She forgot herself in the shock of seeing his gaunt old body, all stringy from hard labour.

'Emma?' She heard her shock echoed in his voice. In a matter of seconds he had reclaimed his shirt and pulled it over his head. 'What has happened? What is wrong to bring you here?'

'A letter. Addressed to you. I thought it might contain news of...' She bit her lip, did not finish the sentence.

'If you will excuse me for a few moments, gentlemen,' her father said to the men behind him. 'And Mr Sears,' to the foreman who had brought her to him.

Her father guided her a little away from the group.

'Bill?'

'It is what they call me here.'

She gave a small smile. The smile faded as she passed the letter to him. 'Maybe I should not have brought it here, but I thought...' She stopped as her father scrutinised the address penned upon it. 'The writing is not of Kit's hand, but even so... Someone might have seen him. Someone might know his whereabouts.'

Her father said nothing, but she saw the slight

tremble in his fingers as he broke the red-wax seal and opened the letter. He held it at arm's length to read it since his spectacles were long gone.

She swallowed, her throat suddenly dry with anticipation. Rubbed her clammy palms together and waited. Waited until she could wait no more.

'Is it good news?'

Her father finished reading and looked up at her. 'It is the best of news, Emma…'

The breath she had been holding escaped in a gasp. Her heart leapt. The terrible tight tension that held her rigid relaxed.

'…but it does not concern your brother.'

The warm happiness flowing through her turned cold. She glanced up at her father. 'I do not understand.'

'The letter is from Mrs Tadcaster, who was second cousin to your mama. She writes to say that the Dowager Lady Lamerton's companion has run off with one of the footmen.'

'Why is that good news?'

'Because, my dear—' he smiled '—the dowager is in need of a new companion, a woman of gentle breeding who would understand what was required of her and might start in the position with immediate effect.'

The penny dropped. Emma suddenly realised

why her mother's cousin had written to impart such trivial gossip. She knew where this was leading. And she should have been glad. Indeed, had it been only a few weeks ago she would have been. But much had happened in those weeks and the feeling in the pit of her stomach was not one of gladness.

'Mrs Tadcaster had spoken to her ladyship of you and Lady Lamerton has agreed to take you on as her companion.'

Emma could not say a word.

'Such sudden and surprising news after all this time. Little wonder you are shocked.'

She was shocked, but not for the reasons her father thought.

We need to talk when I return.

That sounds serious.

It is. Will you wait for me?

Ned's words and all they might mean had not left her mind since yesterday. Her stomach felt hollow.

'I cannot go.'

'Why ever not?' He stared at her

How could she tell him about Ned? Not a gentleman, but a Whitechapel man. A man who was tougher and more dangerous than all he had warned her against. A man who could best five men in a tavern fight and who had worked on these same docks. A man who made magic somersault in her stomach and passion beat through her blood. Whose kiss she wanted to last for ever… and who had implied he wanted a future with her.

'I could not possibly contemplate leaving you here alone.'

'Nonsense. It would be a weight off my mind to know that you were living a safe, respectable life with the Dowager Lady Lamerton. Do you not think I have enough to worry over with Kit?'

'I understand that, but you need not worry over me.'

'You are a serving wench in a tavern.'

'It is a chop-house, Papa,' she corrected him out of force of habit.

'Emma, chop-house or tavern, it makes no difference. Do you think I do not know the manner of men with whom you must deal? Do you think there is a night goes by I am not sick with worry until Tom sees you safely home and I hear you coming through that front door?'

She felt guilt turn in her stomach at the thought of him worrying so much while she enjoyed being with Ned.

'Were you with Lady Lamerton, I could find lodgings closer to the docks. There are always fellows looking for someone to share the rent on a single room. It would be easier for me. Cheaper. More convenient. And they are a good enough bunch in here. Tease me a bit, but that is the extent of it.'

'Lady Lamerton will see this as an opportunity to glean every last detail of our scandal from me. You know she is chief amongst the gossipmongers and has a nose like a bloodhound.'

'Clarissa Lamerton likes to be queen of the *ton*'s gossip, not its subject. She will grill you herself, but protect you from all others. What is this sudden change of heart, Emma? This argument is usually the other way around. You have always been so strong and committed to returning to society and tracing Kit.'

Emma glanced away.

'Lady Lamerton's ability to discover information is all the more reason to accept the position. You would be well placed, in one of the best households in London, to hear news of Kit. Lady Lamerton's son has an association with Whitehall. Rest assured young Lamerton will hear if there is anything to be heard and thus, too, his mother. You have to take this opportunity, Emma, for Kit's sake and mine, as well as for your own. You know that without me telling you.'

She did. That was the problem. She understood too well what he was saying and the truth in it.

'If you stay here, you are lost. It is only a matter of time before one of these men makes you his own. Indeed, it is a miracle that it has not already happened.'

She glanced down at the floor beneath their feet so that he would not see the truth in her eyes.

But he reached over and tilted her face up to his. 'You are a beautiful young woman, the very image of your mother when I met and married her. I want a better life for you than that which a husband from round here could offer you.'

She wanted to tell him so much, of Ned and all that was between them, but she could not. Not now, not when her duty was so pressing.

'As if I would have a husband from round here.' Her forced smile felt like a grimace.

Will you wait for me? In her mind she could see that soul-searching look in Ned's eyes.

And hear her own reply. *I am not going anywhere, Ned Stratham...I will wait.*

'I am glad you have not forgotten your vow to your mother, Emma.'

'How could I ever forget?' She never would, never could. Family was family. A vow was just that, even if it was at the expense of her own happiness. She felt like her heart was torn between her family and the man she loved.

She told herself that Ned might not love her, that she might have misunderstood what it was he wanted to talk to her of. After all, he had made no promises or declarations, and despite all those late-night conversations and all their passion, they knew so little of each other. But in her heart, she knew.

She knew, but it did not change what she had to do.

'You know you have to take this chance, Emma.' Her father's eyes scanned hers.

'Yes.' One small word to deny the enormity of what was in her heart.

'I will go past the mail-receiving office on the way home, pay for paper and some ink and write to Mrs Tadcaster.'

She gave a nod.

'Let me escort you from this place.'

Emma placed her hand on his arm and walked with him, without noticing the shirtless men who stopped working to watch her pass with silent appreciation.

She was thinking of all the days and nights she had worked so hard to escape Whitechapel, of all the times she had prayed for just such an opportunity. And now that her prayer had finally been answered she did not want to leave.

She was thinking of a man whose hair the sun had lightened to the colour of corn-ripened fields and whose eyes matched the cloudless summer sky outside; a man who had captured her heart, and to whom there would be no chance to explain.

On the afternoon of Ned's return from Portsmouth, he went straight to a meeting in White's Club. But now the meeting was concluded, the necessary introductions made and ideas discussed. He shook hands with the Earl of Misbourne, Viscount Linwood, the Marquis of Razeby and Mr Knight.

'If you will excuse me, gentlemen?' A nod of the head and he and his friend and steward, Rob Finchley, were out of the room and walking down the corridor.

Further down the corridor, he saw the small group of men who knew his secret. Men who were bursting with longing to take him down, to expose his real identity, but could not. They knew what would happen if they did. He met each of their gazes in turn across the distance, held them so that they would remember why they could not tell what itched upon their tongues to be out. And in return they glowered with all their haughty disdain.

Rob cursed beneath his breath. 'They look at you as if you're a gutter rat in their midst.'

Ned smiled at the group of arrogant young noblemen. It had the desired effect, twisting the knife a little deeper. 'But remember what it costs them to stand there and suffer my presence.'

Rob grinned. 'I feel better already.'

They were still smiling as they crossed St James's Street and climbed into the waiting gig. It was a top-of-the-range model, sleek, glossy black exterior, cream leather seats; a small white circle enclosing a red diamond shape adorned the front plate. Ned did not look back. Just took up the reins and drove off.

'I think you hooked Misbourne.'

'Let's hope.' The wheels sped along. Ned kept his eyes forward concentrating on the traffic. 'I can't make Dawson's ball tonight.'

'Not like you to miss a big event like Dawson's.'

'I have a commitment elsewhere.' His face was closed and impassive, his usual expression when it came to dealing with friend and foe alike.

'All the bigwigs are going to be there.'

'I know.'

There was a small silence before Rob said, 'Must be important, this other commitment.'

'It is.' Ned slid a glance at his friend, let his eyes linger for a moment, in that quiet confrontational way, and smiled.

Rob smiled, too. 'All right, mate. I get the hint. I'll stop fishing about your mystery woman.'

A few hours later, Ned walked alone into the Red Lion Chop-House. Some heads nodded at him, recognising him from the weeks before. Ned felt the usual comfort and ease that sat about the place, felt it as soon as he crossed the parish boundary that divided the East End from the rest of London. The taproom was busy as usual, the tables and rowdy noise of the place spilling out into the alleyway in front. His eyes scanned for Emma, but did not find her.

The first suspicion stroked when he saw that it was Paulette who came to serve him.

'Your usual, is it?'

He gave a nod. 'Emma not in tonight?'

'Thought you might ask that.' She smiled a saucy knowing look. 'Emma's gone. Landed herself some fancy job as a lady's maid again. An offer she couldn't refuse apparently, lucky mare. She left a message for you, though. Said to tell you goodbye. That she was real sorry she couldn't tell you in person. Said she hoped you would understand.'

He dropped a coin into her hand for passing on the message. 'Forget the lamb and the porter.' He didn't wait.

There were other chop-houses in Whitechapel. Other serving wenches. But Ned didn't go to them. Instead he made his way up along Rosemary Lane to Tower Hill and the ancient stone bench beneath the beech trees. And he sat there alone and watched the day shift finish in the docks and the night shift begin. Watched the ships that docked and the ships that sailed. Watched until the sun set in a glorious blaze of fire over the Thames and the daylight faded to dusk and dusk to darkness.

Had she waited just one week…a single week and how different both their lives would have been.

Loss and betrayal nagged in his gut. He breathed in the scent of night with the underlying essence of vinegar that always lingered in this place. And he thought of the scent of soap and grilled chops and warm woman.

He thought of the teasing intelligence in her eyes and the warmth of her smile.

He thought of the passion between them and the sense that she made his world seem a better place.

He thought of what might have been, then he let the thoughts go and he crushed the feelings. Emma de Lisle had not waited. And that was that.

Ned was not a man who allowed himself to be influenced by emotion. He had his destiny. And maybe it was better this way. No distractions, after all.

He heard the cry of the watch in the distance. Only then did he make his way back across town to the mansion house in Cavendish Square.

Along the Westminster Bridge Road in Lambeth, the evening was fine and warm as Emma and the Dowager Lady Lamerton approached Astley's Amphitheatre.

'I say, this is really rather exciting,' her new employer said as they abandoned the carriage to the traffic jam in which it was caught and walked the remaining small distance to the amphitheatre's entrance.

'It is, indeed.' It was only Emma's third day returned to life in London's high society, albeit at a somewhat lesser level to that she had known, and already she was aware that there was a part of her that had settled so smoothly it was as if she had never been away—and a part that remained in Whitechapel, with her father...and another man.

She wondered again how her father was managing in his new lodging. Wondered if he was eating. Wondered if Ned Stratham had returned to the Red Lion yet and if Paulette had passed on her message.

'In all of my seventy-five years I have yet to see a woman balancing on one leg upon the back of a speeding horse,' said Lady Lamerton. Her walking stick tapped regular and imperious against the pavement as they walked.

Emma hid her private thoughts away and concentrated on the dowager and the evening ahead. 'I hope you shall not find it too shocking.' She tucked her arm into the dowager's, helping to stabilise her through the crowd.

'But, my dear, I shall be thoroughly disappointed if it is not. This latest show is quite the talk of the *ton*. Everyone who is anyone is here to see it.'

Emma laughed. 'Well, in that case we had best go in and find our box.'

As being seen there was more important than actually watching the show, Lady Lamerton and Emma had a splendid vantage point. There was the buzz of voices and bustle of bodies as the rest of the audience found their seats.

'Do look at that dreadful monstrosity that Eliza Frenshaw has upon her head. That, my dear, is what lack of breeding does for you, but then her father was little better than a grocer, you know,' Lady Lamerton said with the same tone as if she had just revealed that Mrs Frenshaw's father had been a mass murderer. Then had the audacity to nod an acknowledgement to the woman in question and bestow a beatific smile.

Emma drew Lady Lamerton a look.

'What?' Lady Lamerton's expression was the hurt innocence that Emma had already learned was her forte. 'Am I not telling the truth?'

'You are never anything other than truthful,' said Emma with a knowing expression.

The two women chuckled together before Lady Lamerton returned to scrutinising the rest of the audience with equally acerbic observations.

Emma let her eyes sweep over the scene in the auditorium before them.

There was not an empty seat to be seen. The place was packed with the best of the *ton* that had either remained in London for the summer or returned early. Ladies in silk evening dresses, a myriad of colours from the rich opulence of the matrons to the blinding white of the debutantes, and every shade in between. All wearing long white-silk evening gloves that fastened at the top of their arms. Their hair dressed in glossy ringlets and fixed with sprays of fresh flowers or enormous feathers that obscured the view of those in the seats behind. Some matrons had forgone the feathers in favour of dark-coloured silk turbans. There was the sparkle of jewels that gleamed around their pale necks or on their gloved fingers that held opera glasses. Like birds of paradise preening and parading. Only two years ago and Emma had been a part of it as much as the rest of them. Now, beautiful as it was, she could not help but be uncomfortably aware that the cost of a single one of those dresses was more than families in Whitechapel had to survive on for a year.

There were many nodded acknowledgments to Lady Lamerton and even some to Emma. Emma nodded in return, glad that, for the most part, people accepted her return without much censure.

Her eyes moved from the stalls, up to the encircling boxes and their inhabitants. To the Duke of Hawick and a party of actresses. To Lord Linwood and his wife, the celebrated Miss Venetia Fox. To the Earl of Hollingsworth, and his family and guest.

Lady Hollingsworth did not nod. The woman's eyes were cool, her nose held high in disdain. Emma met her gaze boldly. Refused to be embarrassed. Smiled with amusement, then moved her gaze along to Hollingsworth's daughter, Lady Persephone, with her pale golden-blonde hair and her perfect pout, and the way she was flirting with the gentleman by her side, no doubt the suitor Hollingsworth was hoping to land for her. The gas lighting dimmed just as Emma's gaze shifted to the man, but for one glimmer of a second she saw him. Or thought she saw him. And what she saw made her heart miss a beat and her stomach turn a somersault.

The music started. The ringmaster, red-coated and waxen-moustached, the ultimate showman, appeared, his booming voice carrying promises of what lay ahead that drew gasps of astonishment from the audience. The performance was starting, but Emma did not look at the ring. Her focus was still on Lady Persephone's suitor. On the fine dark tailored tailcoat, on the gleam of white evening wear that showed beneath. On the fair hair and face that was so like another, a world away in Whitechapel, that they might have been twins. And yet it could not be him. It was not possible.

Her eyes strained all the harder, her heart thudding faster. But in the dimmed light and across the distance she could not be sure.

As if sensing her stare his eyes shifted to hers and held for a second. She moved her gaze to the stage, embarrassed to have been caught staring.

Six white horses galloped with speed around the ring while the scantily clad women on their backs rose in unison to balance on one leg.

There were gasps and applause.

'Heaven's above,' muttered the dowager, but she applauded.

Emma clapped, too, but she was barely seeing the horses or the women on their backs.

It could not be him, she told herself again and again. But every time she stole another glance in his direction the man was watching her and her heart missed a beat at the uncanny familiarity. She stopped looking, aware that she was giving a strange man altogether the wrong impression. The lights would come up at the interval and she would see she was imagining things.

Ned was too much on her mind. The touch of his kiss. The feel of his strong arms around her. The promise in those last words between them. *But I'll be back... We need to talk when I return, Emma.*

I am not going anywhere, Ned Stratham. I will wait.

Guilt squeezed at her heart. She wondered what he had said when he discovered her gone, wondered if his heart ached like hers. Had she stayed he would have bedded her. Had she stayed he might have married her. She closed her eyes at that. Reined her emotions under control. Was careful not to look at Lady Persephone's beau again.

The interval arrived at long last.

The lights came up.

'Tolerably interesting, I suppose,' pronounced Lady Lamerton with a sniff. 'Would you not say?'

Emma smiled. 'I would agree wholeheartedly.'

Then, as Lady Lamerton's footman arrived to take her drinks order, Emma's eyes moved to the Hollingsworths' box.

Both the earl and the suitor were gone, leaving only Lady Hollingsworth and Lady Persephone surveying with smug arrogance. Emma's heart dipped in disappointment.

What if he did not return before the lights dimmed once more?

It was not him. It could not be him. It was ridiculous to even think such a thing.

The moments stretched with an unbearable slowness. She focused all her attention on the dowager. Only when the bell sounded for the end of the interval, only when she knew the dowager's gaze engaged once more on the melee of bodies returning to their seats, did she look again at the Hollingsworths' box.

The man was there, looking directly at her. But this time she did not avert her gaze.

She could not move, just sat there and blatantly stared.

Her heart was hammering fit to burst, her breath was caught in her throat. Something constricted around her chest and squeezed tight at her heart. She felt as though all the world had rolled away to leave nothing in its wake, save Emma and the man at whom she stared.

Only Emma and Ned Stratham.

Chapter Five

In those tiny seconds that stretched between them to an eternity Ned knew that fate was playing tricks with him. He saw a reflection of his own shock in Emma's face. And with it was hurt exposed raw and vulnerable, there for a heartbeat, and then replaced with accusation and angry disbelief. Her eyes flicked momentarily to Lady Persephone by his side before coming back to his.

Ned's gaze lingered on Emma even after she had turned her face away.

'Is everything all right, Mr Stratham? You seem a little preoccupied.'

'Forgive me, Lady Persephone.' He forced his attention to her rather than Emma.

He could feel his blood pumping harder than in any fight, feel the shock snaking through his blood.

'Such a pleasure that you agreed to accompany us tonight, sir.' Lady Persephone smiled and struck a pose to show her face off to its best. She was pampered, self-obsessed and with the same disdainful arrogance that ran through most women of her class. Her figure was plump and curvaceous from a lifetime of good living. Pale golden-blonde ringlets had been arranged artfully to cascade from her where her hair was pinned high. Her dress was some kind of expensive white silk edged with pale-pink ribbon. Her shawl was white, threaded through with gold threads that complemented her hair. A fortune's worth. Little wonder that Hollingsworth needed an alliance.

'The pleasure is all mine.' He made the glib reply with a smile that did not touch his eyes.

She fluttered her eyelashes, but as the lights went down, his eyes were not on the earl's daughter or the sleek black stallion that had galloped into the amphitheatre ring, but on the woman who sat by the Dowager Lady Lamerton's side. A woman he had last seen walking down a deserted sunlit road in Whitechapel on a morning not so long ago.

He watched her too often during the remaining performance, but she did not look at him again, not once, her attention as fixed with determination upon the ring below as the smile on her face.

The performance was long. Very long. He bided his time.

The end came eventually. He escorted Lady Persephone and her family out.

Across the crowd in the foyer he could see Emma and Lady Lamerton making their way towards the staircase.

Emma glanced up, met his gaze with icy accusation before she turned and was carried away with Lady Lamerton and the crowd.

'If you will excuse me,' he said smoothly to the Hollingsworths.

'But, Mr Stratham!' He heard the shock and petulance in Lady Persephone's voice.

'Well, I never—' Hollingsworth was beginning to say, but Ned did not stay to hear the rest. He was already weaving his way through the crowd towards the staircase down which Emma had disappeared.

He caught up with her in the crowd on the ground floor, came up close behind.

'Emma,' he said her name quietly enough that only she would hear as he caught a hold of her arm, unnoticed in the crush that surrounded them, and steered her into a nearby alcove.

She tried to snatch her hand free of his grip, but he held her firm. 'Do not "Emma" me!'

Her spine was flush against the wall. He stood in close to protect her from the sight of passing eyes. So close he could smell the familiar enticing scent of her, so close that his thighs brushed against hers.

Anger was a tangible thing between them, flushing her cheeks, making her dark eyes glitter.

'Not a Whitechapel man after all, Ned Stratham.'

'Always a Whitechapel man,' he said with unshakeable steadfastness. 'Not a lady's maid after all, Emma de Lisle.'

She ignored the jibe, held his gaze with a quiet fury. 'Tell me, upon your return to Whitechapel, was it of your courtship with an earl's daughter that we were to have "talked"?'

'Had you waited, as you said you would, you would know.'

They were standing so close he could see the indignation that flashed in her eyes and feel the tremor that vibrated through her body.

'Know that all those nights you were not walking out with me in Whitechapel you were here, in Mayfair, paying court to Lady Persephone? Know that there was more than one woman on the re-ceiving end of your charms? Know that you were lying through your teeth to me when you implied you had a care for me, for your care was all for another?' Her breath was ragged. 'I am glad I did not wait to hear you spin more of your lies.'

'I am not the one who lied.'

'And yet here you are in high society.'

'With good reason.'

'Oh, spare me, please!' Her breasts brushed against his chest with every breath she took.

'No,' he said in a low voice. 'You will have your explanation, Emma, and I will have mine.'

Where his hand still held hers he felt the sud-den leap of her pulse.

'I do not think so, Ned. You should return to Lady Persephone. I am sure she will be wondering where her suitor has got to. Just as Lady Lamer-ton will be seeking me.'

The accusation rippled between them.

He pinned her with his gaze, but she did not fal-ter, just held it with hot hard defiance.

'We will talk, Emma.' He released her and stepped aside.

She held his gaze for a moment longer. 'Hell will freeze over first, Ned Stratham.' She stepped out into the flow of the crowd just as Lady Lamerton, who had almost reached the front door, peered behind.

He stood where he was and watched until Emma had negotiated her way through the bodies to reach the older woman. Only once they had disappeared through the front door did he step out into the crowd.

'I look forward to hearing more of your news. Yours with affection...' Within the drawing room of her Grosvenor Place home the Dowager Lady Lamerton finished dictating the letter. 'Compose another one in the same vein to Georgiana Hale. Not a straight copy, you understand, in case the unthinkable happens and they see each other's correspondence.' Lady Lamerton gave a shudder at the thought.

'Of course.' Emma passed the letter to Lady Lamerton for her signature. 'And the part about Dorothy Wetherby... I believe that Mrs Hale and Mrs Wetherby are cousins.'

'Good lord, I had forgotten. You are quite right, my dear. No mention of Dorothy Wetherby's latest exploits.' She smiled what Emma had come to call her mischievous smile. 'That would certainly put the cat amongst the pigeons.' She chuckled as she signed her name and passed the paper back to Emma.

'We had quite the time of it last night, did we not?' demanded Lady Lamerton.

'Indeed.' Emma busied herself in blotting the letter dry and finding the sealing wax. She did not want to speak of last night. She did not want to think of it. Not when she had already lain awake half the night thinking of nothing else.

'I do not see what all the fuss was about. It was not as shocking as was implied.'

'Some aspects of it were very shocking,' said Emma, although those aspects had not occurred within the ring.

'Perhaps to you with your innocence and na-ïvety...'

She smiled at that, but it was an ironic smile. Oh, she had been naïve, all right. Naïve to trust Ned Stratham. Even after all she had learned in these past two years. Pretending he was a White-chapel man. Pretending he was considering a fu-ture with a serving wench when he was serious only about landing himself a title. Liar! Damna-ble liar! She was so angry, at him, and at herself for believing him. When she thought what she had felt for him...what she had done with him... When she thought how close she had come to turning down the opportunity to return to society and all it might allow her to do for Kit…and all for a man who had deceived her. She wondered if anything of what he had said had been true. But then when she had thought about it during those long hours of the night, how much had he actually told her of himself? Answering questions with questions. And in her efforts to protect her own secrets she had not pressed him.

'But not to a woman of my position and experience of life and the world.'

Emma gave another smile, but said nothing.

'How was it seeing so many familiar faces again, my dear?'

'Most interesting.'

She thought of Lord Hollingsworth and his family in the box at the amphitheatre, Ned sitting beside Hollingsworth's daughter, and felt something twist in her stomach.

'I could not help notice the appearance of some new faces amidst the old. Faces I do not know.'

'We have had a few new arrivals since you were last in society, Emma.'

'And some betrothals and weddings, no doubt.'

'Oh, indeed. And some most scandalous. The Earl of Misbourne's son, Viscount Linwood, married the actress Miss Fox and was caught up in the most appalling murder scandal. And Misbourne's daughter, Lady Marianne, a meek and mild little thing who wouldn't say boo to a goose, was married with rather suggestive haste to a gentleman who, let us just say, was the antithesis of what one would have anticipated Misbourne to have chosen. But then there always has been something rather shady about that family.' She leaned closer, her eyes sparkling as she relived the gossip.

'Lady Persephone must have made her come out by now.' Emma hoped she was not being too obvious in what she wanted to ask.

'Indeed,' said the dowager. 'She came out this Season and took very well—very well indeed.'

Emma felt nauseous. 'She is betrothed?'

'Heavens, no! Hollingsworth has pockets to let and needs her to make an alliance to rectify the problem. All the interest in Lady Persephone was from other titles or gentlemen with insufficient funds for Hollingsworth's liking. He is angling to catch her Mr Stratham.'

Just the mention of his name made her stomach squeeze a little tighter. She swallowed.

'Mr Stratham,' she said lightly as if the name meant nothing to her. 'I do not believe I have heard of that gentleman.'

'One of the *ton*'s new faces. Made his money

from trade overseas amongst other things.' The dowager could not quite keep the censure from her tone. 'A self-made man, but enormously wealthy.' She paused for effect and met Emma's eyes to deliver the golden piece of information. 'Lives in a mansion in Cavendish Square.' One of the most elite addresses in London.

'He must be wealthy indeed.' Yet he had pretended to live in the Whitechapel streets the same as her. Had walked her home to the shabby boarding house in which she and her father had lodged. She closed her eyes at the memory of those nights and all they had entailed.

'But Hollingsworth is not the only one seeking Mr Stratham's money. Devonport, Longley and a number of others are, too. Stratham is in a strong position to negotiate the best deal.'

'A host of earl's daughters to pick from,' she said and hoped the dowager did not hear the bitter edge to her voice.

'Quite.' Lady Lamerton nodded. 'Although in the past month it has to be said he seems to have been rather distracted from the marriage mart. No doubt making the most of his bachelorhood before he makes his decision and commits himself.'

'No doubt,' Emma said grimly. 'And his pedigree?' She wanted to know more of this man who had duped her so badly, this man who had lied to and betrayed her.

'No one knows quite where Edward Stratham came from, although his accent betrays something of common roots.'

Whitechapel. The word whispered through Emma's mind, but she dismissed it.

'He is a member of White's Club, but according to m'son does not attend much. And other than his steward, Mr Rob Finchley, Stratham has no close friends or confidantes.'

'Even you have been able to discover nothing else of him?'

Lady Lamerton puffed herself at Emma's subtle acknowledgement of her prowess in the gleaning of information from persons of interest, as she liked to say.

'Stratham keeps his own counsel and when it comes to discussing matters he has no wish to discuss...how can I put it?' She thought for a moment and then said, 'He is not a man whom one can press.'

Emma understood very well that Ned Stratham was not the sort of man to be intimidated.

'But for all he is trade, he is a handsome devil and such eyes as to have half the ladies in London in a swoon.'

Emma felt the tiny clench of the muscle in her jaw. 'And what news of Miss Darrington? How does she fare?'

'Now there is a story and a half.' Having exhausted the available gossip on Ned Stratham, Lady Lamerton was more than happy to move on to another subject. 'There was the most dreadful scandal concerning Miss Darrington and the Marquis of Razeby.'

Emma finished sealing the letter and settled comfortably in her chair to listen.

It was later that same day, at half past two, when Emma and Lady Lamerton arrived outside the circulating library for the dowager's weekly visit. Emma waited as Lady Lamerton was helped down the carriage step by a footman. A rather saucy romantic novel hidden between two books on art, as per the dowager's instruction, was tucked under Emma's arm. Lady Lamerton deemed it perfectly acceptable to be reading erotic art books, but heaven forbid that she be seen with a racy romance.

'How did you enjoy the novel?' Emma asked.

'Absolute poppycock,' the dowager pronounced as she leaned upon her walking stick. And then added with a smile, 'But immensely enjoyable poppycock. A rather wicked story all about a devilishly handsome, if rather dangerous, gentleman.' She gave a little amused chuckle and Emma smiled.

She was still smiling as she glanced along the pavement they were about to cross to reach the library door and then the smile vanished from her face. For there, strolling towards them, was Ned Stratham.

Those blue eyes met hers.

Her heart missed a beat before racing fit to burst. She deliberately shifted her gaze, ignoring him, as if he were not there.

Please God... But her prayer went unanswered. Lady Lamerton saw him at once. 'Why, Mr Stratham. We were just talking of you.'

Emma felt her face scald.

'Only good things, I hope.'

'Is there anything bad?' enquired the dowager sweetly.

Ned smiled. 'Now, that would be telling.'

Lady Lamerton gave a laugh. 'La, sir, you are quite the rogue.'

'Indeed, I am, ma'am.' His smile painted the words of truth as those of jest.

Then his eyes moved to Emma and lingered.

She held her head high. Feigned a calmness she

did not feel. Inside her heart was beating nineteen to the dozen, but she met his gaze coolly.

'I do not believe you have met m'companion, sir.'

'I have not had that pleasure,' he said. 'I would have been sure to remember.'

No insinuations that they had met before. No hints over Whitechapel.

Their eyes held.

She swallowed.

'May I introduce Miss Emma Northcote,' Lady Lamerton said.

Ned seemed to still and for the flicker of a second Emma saw something that looked like shock in his eyes. Then it was gone and he was once more his quiet assured self.

Only then did she remember that he knew her as de Lisle.

Her eyes held his, waiting for him to make some comment on her change of name. Her breath held, waiting as that tiny moment seemed to stretch. The atmosphere between them was obvious.

'I am pleased to meet you, Miss Northcote.' His voice was as cool as his gaze. He gave a curt bow.

'Likewise, Mr Stratham.' She dropped the smallest curtsy.

There was a deafening silence, which Ned made no effort to fill.

'We are for the circulating library, sir,' said Lady Lamerton. 'Are you?'

'No.' He did not elaborate.

The dowager inclined her head, dismissing him. 'Your servant, ma'am.'

His eyes moved to Emma's again.

This time there was no perfunctory smile on his lips and the look in his eyes made her shiver. 'Miss *Northcote*.' The slightest emphasis on her name.

She gave a nod and turned away to escort the dowager into the library.

There was no sound of his footsteps upon the pavement and she had the feeling that he was standing there, watching her. It made her feel nervous. It made each step feel like an eternity. But she did not yield to the urge to glance behind. Not until Lady Lamerton was through the door and Emma, too, was safe inside the library.

He was still standing there, just as she had thought. And there was something in the way he was looking at her, something focused and hard, as if he were seeing her for the first time, as if he were scrutinising her. Something of accusation that made her uncomfortably aware that she had not been entirely honest with him.

Only then did he dip his head in a final acknowledgement and turn and walk away.

Rob was waiting for him in his study when Ned got back to the mansion in Cavendish Square.

His friend and steward glanced round from where he was examining the arrangement of swords and sabres mounted upon the wall. 'I came early. Wanted to check over a few things before we left for Misbourne's.'

Ned gave a nod, and passed his cane and hat to Clarkson. Then peeled off his gloves and did the same.

The door closed with a quiet click behind the departing butler.

Ned walked straight to his desk and, ignoring the crystal decanter of brandy that sat there on the silver salver, opened the bottom drawer and took out a bottle of gin. He poured two generous measures into the matching crystal glasses. Passed one to Rob and took a deep swig from the other.

He could feel his friend's eyes on him and knew it didn't look good, but right at this minute he didn't give a damn.

'You all right, Ned?'

'I've been better.'

'You look like you've just seen a ghost.'

That was certainly one way of putting it.

'Business deal gone bad?' Rob asked.

Nothing so simple. 'Something like that.'

'Not Misbourne. Not the—'

'No.' He cut Rob off. Took another swig of the gin, relishing the raw kick of it. 'Not Misbourne.'

'That's a relief, at least.'

'Yes.'

There was a silence. Ned's mind was whirring. His blood still pumping hard as if he'd just floored ten men. He could feel a cold sweat on his upper lip, a clamminess on the palms of his hands. He took another gulp of gin to numb the tremor of shock that still ran through him.

'If you need to call off with Misbourne...'

'I don't.' Ned met his friend's gaze. 'I need Misbourne on board. And missing a lunch he's arranged will set him against me.'

'It's just a lunch.'

'Nothing with these men of the *ton* is just a lunch.'

'If he asks about any of the details...'

'Leave the details to me.'

Rob gave a nod.

Ned finished the rest of the gin and set the glass down on the desk.

'Let's walk. I could do with some fresh air.' To calm the pound of his blood and shutter the disbelief that was coursing through his body.

Rob nodded.

Ned rang the bell for his butler. There would be time to think later and there was much riding on Misbourne.

Ned was well practised at putting emotion aside. He did it now, coldly, deliberately, and got on with the task in hand.

'More tea?' Emma asked, teapot poised in hand to refill the dowager's delicate blue Sèvres teacup.

The afternoon sunlight filled Lady Lamerton's little parlour, making it bright and warm. Dust motes floated in the sunbeams to land on the circulating library's latest romance novel on the embroidered tablecloth of the tea table before them.

On the sideboard at the other end of the parlour, a book on antiquity and a heavyweight tedious literary novel had been discarded until they were required for next week's return visit to the library.

'Thank you, my dear.' Lady Lamerton gave a small nod.

Emma poured the tea.

'So what did you make of our Mr Stratham?'

'Tolerable enough, I suppose.' Emma managed to keep her hand steady and concentrated on adding a splash of cream and three lumps of sugar to the dowager's cup, just the way she liked it.

'Tolerable?' The dowager looked at her aghast as she accepted the cup and saucer from Emma. 'With those eyes?'

'A pair of fine eyes do not make the man.'

'So you did notice,' said the dowager slyly. 'And I must say he seemed rather struck by you.'

'Hardly.' Emma took satisfaction in her calm tone as she topped up her own teacup.

'Indeed, I do not think I have seen any woman make such an impression upon him.'

Emma remembered again that expression on his face outside the library. The intense scrutiny in his eyes. The force of something that seemed to emanate from him. Something angry and accusatory that he had no right to feel. She took a sip of tea and said nothing.

'I wonder if he will be at Hawick's ball tonight,' the dowager mused.

Emma felt a shiver ripple down her spine. 'Is it likely?'

'Most likely, indeed.'

We will talk, Emma. She thought of the cool

promise that had been in his eyes and the utter certainty in those quiet words. She swallowed and resolved not to leave the dowager's side for the entirety of the evening.

The Duke of Hawick's ballroom was heaving. It seemed that the entirety of the *ton* had returned early to London, and were here, turned out for the event since the rumour had got out that the Prince Regent himself might be present.

It was as warm as an evening in the Red Lion, even though there were no adjacent kitchens here that fanned the heat. No low ceiling or small deep-sunk windows, and bricks that held the heat in summer and the cold in winter. It was a huge room of wealth and opulence that would have been beyond the imagination of most of those who frequented the Red Lion Chop-House. The massive chandelier held a hundred candles whose flames made the crystals glitter and sparkle like diamonds. The windows were numerous and large, the sashes pulled up to allow a circulation of fresh air. At the back of the room were glass doors that opened out on to a long strip of town garden similar to that at the back of the mansion house in Cavendish Square. All of that open glass and air and yet still the place was too warm because of the throng of guests.

'Another fine evening,' Lord Longley said and lifted a glass of champagne from the silver salver that the footman held before him.

'Indeed.' Ned accepted a glass of champagne, too. Took a sip without betraying the slightest hint that he hated the stuff. He was all too aware of the way Longley ignored Rob's presence. 'You have met my steward, Mr Finchley.'

Longley could barely keep the curl from his upper lip as he gave the smallest of acknowledgements to Rob before returning his attention to Ned. He thought Rob beneath him. And Ned, too, but swallowed his principles for the sake of money.

'Harrow tells me you were at Tattersall's saleroom the other day looking at the cattle.' Tattersall's was the auction house where the *ton* went to buy their horses. Ned could hear the slight sneer that Longley always had in his voice when he spoke to him. Felt the edge of anger that he always felt amongst these men born to titles and wealth and privilege and who lived in a world far removed from reality.

'Browsing the wares.' Ned's eyes were cool. 'Were we not, Mr Finchley?'

'And fine wares they were, too,' said Rob.

'Matters equine take a knowledgeable eye.' *Which you do not have.* That patronising air that Longley could not quite hide no matter how hard he tried. 'And experience. I would be happy to teach you a thing or two.'

'How kind.' Ned smiled.

The sentiment behind the smile was lost on Longley.

'Where do you ride?'

'I don't.'

'I did not know that,' said Longley and tucked the tidbit away to share with his friends in White's should matters not work out between him and Ned as he was hoping. 'I suppose I should have realised, what with your not having come from—' He stopped himself just in time.

Ned held Longley's gaze.

The earl glanced away, cleared his throat and changed the subject to why he was standing here in Ned's company tonight. 'Lady Juliette is in good spirits tonight.' Lady Juliette, Longley's daughter for whom he was seeking a match with new money.

'You must be pleased for her.' From the corner of his eye he saw Rob struggle to stifle a grin.

'Do not need to tell you that she was quite the

diamond of this year's Season. I am sure you are already aware of her.'

'Very aware.'

Longley smiled.

'Quite the horsewoman as I recall,' said Ned.

Longley's smile faltered as he realised the mistake he'd just made. He squirmed. 'Not so much these days.' He cleared his throat again. 'Excuse me, sir. I see Willaston and have a matter to discuss with him.'

A small bow and Longley took himself off, leaving Ned and Rob standing alone.

There was a silence before Ned spoke. 'There's something you need to know, Rob. The Dowager Lady Lamerton has a new companion.'

'You think I'm in with a shout?' Rob grinned.

Ned did not smile. His eyes held Rob's. 'Her name is Miss Emma Northcote.'

Rob's grin vanished. 'Northcote? I thought the Northcotes were long gone. Moved away to the country.'

'So did I.' Ned thought of the truth of Emma Northcote and her father's circumstance—the nights in the Red Lion Chop-House; the narrow street with its shabby lodging house; and the London Dock warehouse—and something tightened in his throat. He swallowed it down. Gave a hard smile. 'It seems we were wrong.'

'Hell.' A whispered curse so incongruous in the expensive elegance of their surroundings as the shock made Rob forget himself. 'That's going to make things awkward.'

'Why?' Ned's expression was closed.

'You know why.'

'I did nothing wrong. I've got nothing to feel awkward over.'

'Even so.'

'It isn't going to be a problem. *She* isn't going to be a problem.' Not now he knew who she was.

Both men's gazes moved across the room as one to where Lady Lamerton sat with her cronies…and her companion.

Northcote, not de Lisle, the worst lie of them all.

He looked at the long gleaming hair coiled and caught up in a cascade of dark roped curls at the back of her head, at the sky-blue silk evening dress she was garbed in, plain and unadorned unlike the fancy dresses of the other ladies and obviously paid for by Lady Lamerton. She wore no jewellery. He knew that she would have none. The *décolletage* of her dress showed nothing other than her smooth olive skin. Long white silk evening gloves covered her arms and matching white slippers peeped from beneath the dress.

She had seen him the minute she entered the ballroom. He knew it. Just as he knew she was ignoring him.

'No,' said Rob quietly. 'Knowing you, I don't suppose she will.'

Ned's eyes shifted from Emma to Rob. 'Would you hold this for me?' He passed his glass to Rob. 'There's something I have to do.'

'You can't be serious…'

Ned smiled a hard smile.

'Tell me you're not going over there to get yourself introduced?' Rob was staring at him as if he were mad.

'I'm not going over there for an introduction. Miss Northcote and I have already had that pleasure.'

Rob looked shocked.

'But the lady and I didn't get a chance to talk.'

The music came to a halt. The dance came to an end. The figures crowded upon the floor bowed and curtsied and began to disperse.

Ned glanced across the floor to Emma once more.

'This won't take long.'

'Ned…' Rob lowered his voice and spoke with quiet insistence.

But Ned was already moving smoothly through the crowd, crossing the ballroom, his focus fixed on Emma Northcote.

Chapter Six

'Oh, my!' Emma heard Miss Chichester exclaim as she stared in the direction where Ned Stratham stood talking with Mr Finchley and Lord Longley. 'You are not going to believe this, Miss Northcote, but Mr Stratham—'

Emma resisted the urge to look round. 'I do not understand why Mr Stratham is of such fascination to the ladies of the *ton*,' she interrupted. 'He is just trade, for all his money.' It was a cruel and elitist remark, but after what he had done he deserved it.

Miss Chichester's eyes widened. Her pale cheeks flushed ruddy. She gave a soft, breathless gasp and pressed a hand to her *décolletage*.

'Indeed I am, Miss Northcote,' Ned Stratham's voice said. That same soft East End accent, that same slight edge underlying the quiet words.

Emma's heart stuttered. Her stomach turned end

over end. She froze for a second before turning to look up into those too-familiar cool blue eyes.

'Mr Stratham,' she said with a controlled calm that belied the trembling inside. 'You surprise me.'

He smiled. 'Evidently.'

She held his gaze as if she were not embarrassed at being caught out and ashamed of her words, but the seep of heat into her cheeks betrayed her. However, she offered no apology.

The silence stretched between them.

His eyes never faltered for a moment. He stood there, all quiet strength and stillness, with those eyes that knew her secrets and those lips that had seduced her own. 'I am here to ask you to dance, Miss Northcote.'

Her stomach gave a somersault.

Beside her she heard Miss Chichester give a quiet gasp.

'I thank you kindly for your magnanimous offer, sir.' Emma held his gaze with a determined strength, knowing that, in this battle of wills, to look away would be to admit defeat. 'But I am obliged to refuse. I am here as Lady Lamerton's companion, not to dance.'

His mouth made a small dangerous curve, making fear trickle into her blood at what he meant to do. Too late she remembered that one word from his mouth could destroy her. One word and her return to the *ton* and all that meant for her brother would be over. Her mouth turned dry as a desert.

He turned his attention to Lady Lamerton. Only then did Emma notice that all of the ladies around them had fallen silent and that Lady Lamerton and her friends were watching with avid interest.

'I am sure that Lady Lamerton would be able to spare you for some small time.' He looked at Lady Lamerton with that quiet confidence in his eyes. Cocked the rogue eyebrow.

All eyes turned to the dowager, like a queen with the presiding vote over a court.

'Mr Stratham has the right of it, Emma.' Lady Lamerton turned her focus to Ned. 'I trust you will return m'companion to me safely, sir.'

'Safe and sound, ma'am.' Ned smiled at Lady Lamerton.

Safe and sound. The very air around him vibrated with danger.

All of the tabbies watched in rapt amazement.

His eyes switched back to Emma, the bluest blue eyes in all the world, so cool and dangerous, and filled with the echoes of shared intimacies between them. 'Miss Northcote.' He held out his hand in invitation. 'Shall we?'

Her eyes held his for a tiny moment longer,

knowing that he had manoeuvred her into a corner from which there was no escape. Then she inclined her head in acknowledgement.

He might have won the battle but it did not mean he would win the war.

She placed her hand in his, rose to her feet and let him lead her out on to the dance floor.

They joined the nearest set for a country dance that was neither progressive nor too fast for conversation.

'What game are you playing, Ned Stratham?'

'No game. We need to speak with a degree of privacy. This provides the perfect opportunity.'

She glanced around to all the pairs of eyes fixed upon them, to all the murmurs being whispered behind fans and into ears. 'You call this privacy? Our every move is under scrutiny.'

'Indeed. Apparently I am a source of fascination for the ladies of the *ton*.'

She blushed and eyed him with anger. She was very aware of the warmth of his hand around hers, of the proximity of his body. 'I have already told you I will not listen to more of your lies.'

'But I was not the one who was telling the lies, was I, Emma?'

'Given what you did, I do not think I owe you

any explanation as to why I did not wait. And as for a lady's maid, I have undertaken such duties in the past. For a month.'

'A month.' He paused. 'As the daughter of the maid's master.' He looked at her.

'Strictly speaking it was not a lie.'

'Strictly speaking.'

She pressed her lips firm. Glanced away.

He leaned closer, so that she felt the brush of his breath against her cheek, felt the shiver tingle down her spine and tighten her breasts.

'And as we are speaking strictly, the little fact of your name, Miss *de Lisle…*' His blue eyes seemed to bore into hers.

'It was not a lie. De Lisle is my mother's name.'

'Your mother's name. But not yours.'

She swallowed again. Her mouth was dry with nerves. He was making it sound as if she were the one in the wrong. 'My father and I could hardly admit the truth of our background. That we were fallen from society. That we were of that privileged class so despised in Whitechapel. Do you think we would have been accepted? Do you think Nancy would have given me a job in the Red Lion?'

'No.' His eyes held hers, unmoved by the

argument. 'But it does not change the fact that you lied to me, Emma Northcote.'

'Small white lies that made no difference.'

Something flashed in his eyes, something angry and passionate and hard. Something in such contrast to the cool deliberate control normally there that it sent a shiver tingling down her spine and made her heart skip a beat. 'They would have made all the difference in the world.'

The dance took them apart, leading them each to change places with the couple on their right. She took those few moments to try to compose herself before they were reunited once more and his hand closed over hers, binding her to him. And to this confrontation she had no wish to conduct upon a crowded dance floor.

'Do not seek to turn this around,' Emma said. 'You made me believe you were something you were not.'

He raised his eyebrows at that. *Just as she had made him believe she was someone she was not.*

It fuelled her anger and sense of injustice.

'All those nights, Ned… And in between them you were here, living in your mansion, dancing at some ball with the latest diamond of the *ton* hanging on your arm. Seeking to ally yourself with some earl's daughter while you played your games in Whitechapel.'

He said nothing.

'You would have bedded me and cast me aside.'

'Would I?' His voice was cold, hard, emotionless. There was something in his eyes when he said it that unnerved her.

Had she waited, she would know for sure.

Had she waited it would have been too late.

The dance played on, their feet following where it led. There was only the music and the scrape and tread of slipper soles against the smooth wood of the floorboards. Only the sound of her breath and his. Given all that was at stake, she had to know. She had to ask him.

'Are you going to tell them the truth of me? That I was a serving wench in a chop-house in Whitechapel? That my father is a dockworker? That we lodged in one of the roughest boarding houses in all London?'

'Are you going to tell them that I was a customer in the same chop-house?'

They looked at one another.

'You they would forgive. Me, you know they would not.'

'They would be a deal less forgiving of me than

you anticipate.' He smiled a hard smile. 'But do not fear, Emma. Your secret is safe with me.'

She waited for the qualifier. For what he would demand for his silence.

He just smiled a cynical smile as if he knew her thoughts. Gave a tiny shake of his head.

It made her feel as though she was the one who had got this all wrong. She reminded herself of the shabby leather jacket and boots he had worn—a disguise. She reminded herself of what had passed between them in the darkness of a Whitechapel alleyway while he was living a double life here. For all his denials he was a liar who had used and made a fool of her.

'Now that matters are clear between us, there is no need to speak again. Stay away from me, Ned.'

He smiled again. A hard, bitter smile. 'You need not worry, Emma Northcote,' he taunted her over her name. 'I will stay far away from you.'

'I will be glad of it.'

He studied her eyes, as if he could see everything she was, all her secrets and lies, all her hopes and fears. Then he leaned closer, so close that she could smell the clean familiar scent of him and feel his breath warm against her cheek, so close that she shivered as he whispered the words into her ear, 'Much more than you realise.'

Her heart was thudding. Her blood was rushing. All that had been between them in the Red Lion and the alleyway, and at the old stone bench, was suddenly there in that ballroom.

They stared at one another for a moment. Then he stepped back, once more his cool controlled self.

'Smile,' he said. 'Every eye is upon us and you wouldn't want our audience to think we were discussing anything other than the usual petty fripperies that are discussed upon a ballroom floor.'

He smiled a smile that did not touch his eyes.

And she reciprocated, smiling as she said the words, 'You are a bastard, Ned Stratham.'

'Yes, I am. Quite literally. But I deem that better than a liar.'

His words, and their truth, cut deep.

The music finally came to a halt.

The ladies on either side of her were curtsying. Emma smothered her emotions and did the same.

Ned bowed. 'Allow me to return you to Lady Lamerton.'

She held his gaze for a heartbeat and then another. And then, uncomfortably aware that every eye in the ballroom was upon them, she touched the tips of her fingers to his arm and let him lead her from the floor.

* * *

Ned and Rob were in Gentleman John Jackson's pugilistic rooms in Bond Street the next morning. At nine o'clock the hour was still too early for any other gentleman to be present. After a night of gentlemen's clubs, drinking, gaming and womanising—which were, as far as Ned could make out, the chief pursuits of most men of the gentry and nobility—gentlemen did not, in general, rise before midday. After a bout of light sparring together, Ned and Rob were working on the heavy sand-filled canvas punchbags that hung from a bar fixed along the length of one wall.

Rob sat on the floor, back against the wall, elbows on knees, catching his breath. Ned landed regular punches to the sandbag.

'What the hell was that about with Emma Northcote last night?' Rob asked.

'I wanted to speak to her.'

'About what?'

'To verify her identity.'

'And you needed to dance with her for that?'

'I had to put all those lessons with that dancing master to use at some time. I paid him good money.'

Rob raised his eyebrows. His expression was cynical. 'I take it she is who we think.'

'What gives you that impression?'

'Maybe the fact that you're knocking two tons of stuffing out of that punchbag.'

Ned raised an eyebrow, then returned to jabbing at the sandbag, right hook, then left hook. Right hook, then left. 'She doesn't change anything. We go on just as before.' He landed a left-handed blow so hard that it almost took the punchbag clear off its hook. He ducked as it swung back towards him, punched it again, and again. Kept up the training until his knuckles were sore and his arms ached and the keenness of what he felt was blunted by fatigue.

Rob threw a drying cloth up to him and got to his feet, gesturing with his eyes to the doorway with warning. 'That it, is it, Stratham?' he said, reverting to a form of formality now that they had company.

Ned caught the cloth and mopped the sweat from his face as he glanced round to see who it was that had entered.

There was only the slightest of hesitations in the Duke of Monteith and Viscount Devlin's steps as they saw who was in the training room using the equipment.

Ned met Devlin's eyes. The viscount returned the look—cold, insolent, contemptuous—before walking with Monteith to the other end of the room.

Ned and Rob exchanged a look.

'Your favourite person,' said Rob beneath his breath.

'It just gets better and better.' Ned smiled a grim smile, as he and Rob made their way to the changing rooms.

Within the dining room of Lady Lamerton's town house a few streets away, Emma and the dowager were at breakfast.

'It is just as I suspected, Mr Stratham dancing with you at Hawick's ball is all the gossip, Emma,' Lady Lamerton said as she read the letter within her hand.

The clock on the mantel ticked a slow and sonorous rhythm.

'I cannot think why. It was only one dance.' Emma did not speak while the footman moved from Lady Lamerton's side, where he filled her cup with coffee, to Emma's and stood waiting, coffee pot in hand.

She gave a nod, watching while the steaming hot liquid poured from the pot into the pretty orange-and-gold-rimmed cup. The aroma of coffee wafted through the air. She added a spot of cream from the jug and took a sip of the coffee.

Sunlight spilled in through the dining-room window. sparkling through the crystal drops of the chandelier above their heads to cast rainbows on the walls.

Lady Lamerton set the letter down on the growing pile of opened papers and reached for the next one. She glanced up as she broke the seal. 'Because, my dear, Mr Stratham has not previously been seen upon a dance floor. He does not dance.'

Emma took another sip of coffee and tried to smile, as if what had happened upon the dance floor last night was nothing. 'That must be somewhat of a disadvantage when he is at an Almack's ball.'

'Hardly,' said the dowager. 'If anything it is the opposite. It has created rather a stir of interest. The women see it as a challenge. The Lewis sisters have a sweepstake running as to who will be the first to tempt him upon a floor. It is considered to be an indicator of when he has made his choice of bride.'

Emma smiled again to hide the anger she felt at that thought. 'Well, last night certainly disproved that theory.'

'Indeed, it did. And will have made the Lewis

sisters a deal richer.' The dowager paused and looked at the letter in her hand. 'They are all positively agog to know of what he spoke.'

If they only knew. 'Nothing of drama or excitement. I already told you the details.' Last night in the ballroom when there had been a subtle questioning which Lady Lamerton had parried with the air of a hawk, with its wings shielding its food for its own later consumption. And in the carriage on the way home the hawk had eaten...although not of the truth.

'The weather and other trivialities are hardly going to satisfy them, Emma. Especially as the pair of you appeared to be having quite the conversation.'

Emma took another sip of coffee and said nothing.

Lady Lamerton held her spectacles to her eyes and peered at the letter again. 'Apparently they are taking bets on whether he will dance again. And if it will be with you.'

Emma suppressed a sigh at the *ton*'s preoccupations. An hour's walk away and the preoccupations and world were very different.

'Fetch my diary, Emma, and check when the next dance is to be held.'

'It is next week, on Thursday evening—the

charity dance at the Foundling Hospital.' Emma knew the line of thought the dowager's mind was taking. 'And even if Mr Stratham is there, I made it quite clear to him that my duty is as your companion and not to dance.'

'Much as I admire your loyalty, my dear, you are quite at liberty to dance with him. Indeed—' she glanced with unmistakable satisfaction at the unusually large pile of letters the morning post had brought '—it would be quite churlish not to.'

'He will not ask me.' *Stay away from me, Ned. You need not worry, Emma Northcote. I will stay far away from you.* The echo of their words rang in her head. And she remembered again, as she had remembered in the night, the look in his eyes—cool anger and other things…

Emma smiled as if it were nothing and led the conversation away from Ned Stratham. 'What are you wearing tonight for dinner at Mrs Lewis's?'

Her tactic worked. 'My purple silk and matching turban. I thought you could wear your dove-grey silk to complement me.'

'It would match well,' Emma agreed and listened as Lady Lamerton discussed a visit to the haberdashery to buy a feather for the turban.

Ned would stay away from her. And she would be glad of it.

More glad than you realise.

And a tingle ran over the skin at the nape of her neck at what those strange words might mean.

'I see Mr Stratham is here,' Lady Lamerton said *sotto voce* not five minutes after they had entered the drawing room of Mrs Lewis's Hill Street house that night.

'Is he? I had not noticed,' Emma lied. He and his steward, Rob Finchley, were over by the windows talking with Lord Linwood and another gentleman, one whom Emma vaguely recognised but could not quite place. Ned was smartly dressed in the best of tailoring, his fair hair glinting gold in the candlelight. He looked as at ease here as he had in Whitechapel. Beneath that polished surface emanated that same awareness, that same feeling of strength and danger held in control. His eyes met hers, hard, watchful and bluer than she remembered, making her heart stumble and her body shiver. She returned the look, cool and hard as his own, and curved her lips in a smile as if he bothered her not in the slightest, before returning her attention to Lady Lamerton.

Their hostess appeared, welcoming them, telling Lady Lamerton how wonderful she looked and asking which mantua maker was she using these days.

Emma saw some of the women who had been friends of hers in what now seemed a different life. Women who had attended the same ladies' educational seminary, who had made their come-outs at the same time, and against whom her competition in the marriage mart had necessitated spending a fortune on new wardrobes. They were dressed in the latest fashions, immaculately *coiffured*, safe in their little group. Emma knew how penniless ladies' companions were viewed in their circle, the whispered pity; she, after all, had once been one of the whisperers. Not out of malice, but naïvety and ignorance. But who her father had been, and who she had been amongst them, still held influence for, despite her reduced status, most smiled and gave small acknowledgements. Only a few turned their heads away.

'Lady Lamerton, how very delightful to find you here.' Mrs Faversham arrived, all smiles and politeness, but with the barely concealed expression of a gossip hound on the scent of a story. 'And Miss Northcote, too.' Her eyes sharpened and lit as she looked at Emma.

'Mrs Faversham,' cooed Lady Lamerton and smiled that smile that, contrary to its softness, indicated when it came to gossip she was top dog and would be guarding her object of interest with ferocity. Emma's father had been right.

'Such a shame I missed Hawick's ball. It seems it was quite the place to be. I heard that Mr Stratham finally took to the dance floor. But one can never be sure with such rumours.'

'I can confirm the truth of it, my dear Agatha.'

'Indeed?' Curiosity was almost bursting out of her. 'You must come to tea, dear Lady Lamerton. It has been an age since we visited together. Would tomorrow suit?'

'I am taking tea with Mrs Hilton tomorrow. My tea diary is quite booked these days. But I might be able to squeeze you in at the end of the week… if that would be agreeable to you.'

'Most agreeable.' Mrs Faversham smiled and could not help her eyes straying to Emma once more. 'And will Miss Northcote be there?'

But Emma was saved by the sound of the dinner gong.

The table was beautifully arranged with a central line of squat candelabras interspersed by pineapples. In the middle was a vast arrangement that involved the head and tail feathers of a peacock. Emma tensed, worrying that she would find herself seated beside Ned, but, for all his wealth, in the hierarchy of seating at a *ton* dinner table trade was still looked down upon and Ned and his steward were seated further down the table. A lady's companion, effectively a servant, was deemed higher because her family had once been one of them.

Lord Soames, one of her father's oldest and dearest friends, took his place by her side.

'And how is your papa fairing out in rural Hounslow, young Miss Northcote?' he bellowed on account of his deafness.

'He is well, thank you, Lord Soames.' She nodded and smiled, aware that the volume of Lord Soames's voice was loud enough to be heard all around. Loud enough for Ned to hear those few seats away.

'Glad to hear it, m'dear. You must tell him when you see him next that his presence is sorely missed.'

'I will.' She smiled again and smoothly changed the subject. 'Such uncommonly good weather we have been having.'

'What's that you are saying? Speak up, girl.'

'I was merely commenting upon the pleasant weather of late.'

Lord Soames held his ear trumpet to his ear. 'Did not catch a word of it, Miss Northcote.'

'Miss Northcote was speaking of the good weather,' a man's voice said from close behind. It was a voice that Emma recognised: aristocratic, educated, with a slight drawl of both careless sensuality and arrogance. She stiffened.

'Splendid weather indeed,' agreed Lord Soames with a nod and sat back in his chair to await his dinner.

'Good evening, Miss Northcote,' the voice drawled and its owner sat down in the vacant chair to her right.

The blood was pounding in her temple. She felt a little sick. Took a deep breath to steady herself before she looked round into the classically sculpted face of Viscount Devlin.

'I think you are mistaken in your seat, sir.' Her eyes looked pointedly at the small white place card with the name of Mr Frew written upon it.

Devlin lifted the place card and slipped it into a pocket of his dark evening tailcoat. 'I do not think so, Miss Northcote.'

Emma blinked at his audacity, met his gaze with a fierceness and flicked her focus a few seats along to where Mr Frew was sitting meekly. The gentleman had the grace to look embarrassed before rapidly averting his eyes.

She returned her gaze to Devlin, her face as much a mask as his, even if her heart was still pumping hard with anger and loathing beneath. She knew that she could not start causing a fuss, or refuse to sit beside him. Guests were already sliding sly glances their way. Everybody would be watching to see her reaction to him. Everybody remembered her mother's very public castigation of him and his friends. Everybody knew the history of him and her brother.

So she smiled, even if her eyes held all the warmth of an arctic night, and kept her voice low. 'What are you doing, Devlin?'

'Enjoying an evening out at dinner.' He smiled, too. That lazy charming smile of his she had once thought so handsome.

Across the table Lord Fallingham had taken the seat beside Mrs Morley. His eyes met hers. He gave a nod of acknowledgement before he turned to Mrs Morley and engaged her in a conversation that had no room for anyone else.

She did not glance round at Lord Soames. She could hear Mrs Hilton on his left shouting a conversation with him.

Devlin smiled again as if he had known her thoughts.

She did not smile, just held his gaze and waited.

'So how have you been, Miss Northcote?'

'Never better...' Her mouth smiled. Her eyes did not. 'Until a moment ago. And you, sir?' A parody of politeness and sincerity.

His smile was broader this time, lazier, more charming. 'All the better for seeing you.' And yet there was something in his eyes that gave lie to his words.

'I cannot think why. Given your interchange with my family before we left London, I did not think that there was very much we had left to say to one another.'

He made no reply, just leaned back in his chair, and took a sip of his champagne as he watched her. 'How did you find Hawick's ball the other evening?'

By its own volition her gaze moved to Ned further down the table. His glance shifted to hers at the very same time. She looked away. Lifted her glass with a rock-steady hand.

'It was a pleasant enough affair.'

Devlin flicked a glance towards Ned before coming back to her. 'Pleasant enough to tempt

Mr Stratham on to the dance floor so I hear. A hitherto unheard-of feat.'

'I would not know, having been absent from society for so long.'

He smiled at the barb, a smile that did not touch his eyes. Took another sip of his champagne. 'It is quite the accomplishment, I assure you.'

'I will take your word for it.'

He smiled again.

'He's new money,' he said in that same disparaging tone with which all of the *ton* viewed self-made men.

'So I have heard.'

'Men like Stratham do not play by the rules of our world. Some of them do not play by any rules at all.' He paused, then added, 'Especially when it comes to women.'

'That is rather rich coming from you.' The whole of London knew that Devlin was an out-and-out rake.

'Maybe.' Devlin smiled. 'But *my* affairs are conducted with those who know the score.'

There was a silence and in it lay his unspoken insinuation over Ned. He held her gaze.

'Why are you telling me?'

'For the sake of my friendship with your brother.'

'Friendship? Is that what you called it?' She raised her brows.

'And even if it were not so, given Stratham has expressed such an…interest in you, I would not be a gentleman were I to keep quiet and say nothing.'

'One dance does not constitute an interest.'

'I think, in this case, it rather does.'

'I am sure you are well intentioned, sir.' She kept her voice quiet and light, as if they were in truth discussing nothing more than the weather or the latest summer theatre show. 'But what I do, and with whom, is not your concern.'

'Maybe not.' Devlin's gaze flicked down the table to Ned and when he looked at her again there was a strange, almost possessive expression in his eyes. 'And then again maybe it is more of my concern than you realise.'

The expression was gone so quickly that she doubted she had really seen it. She stared at him, wondering if he had just actually said those words.

He smiled again, that charming smile that had so many women fluttering their eyelashes and hoping to be the one that tamed him.

There was the clatter of dishes, the scrape of cutlery, the chink of glass and glug of wine being poured as the meal was served. Footmen were moving between them, offering dishes for their serving. All around was the hum of conversations and small laughter.

Emma felt the slink of unease in her stomach.

But when the footmen moved on, Devlin's attention was across the table. 'How was your chicken, Mrs Morley?'

'Superb as ever can be expected from...'

The conversation played on. The seconds ticked slow.

Emma's eyes moved down the table to where Ned was talking to Mr Jamison. He glanced up and met her eyes with cool speculation, before returning his focus to whatever it was Mr Jamison was saying.

Chapter Seven

The morning sky was a yawning blue. The air was fresh and perfect. Ned's gig, sprung for sport and speed, and dark and sleek as the panther rumoured to be kept by the Prince Regent in his Tower menagerie, skimmed smooth and light over the roads towards Hyde Park.

'Did you see that Devlin was seated beside Miss Northcote?' Rob spoke loud enough to be heard above the noise of both the gig's wheels and the horses' hooves.

'Devlin was not seated there. He intimidated Frew into swapping seats.' Ned kept his attention on the four matched-black horses trotting smartly before them.

'I wonder why.'

'I would guess that he wished to speak to Miss Northcote.'

'You think he's sweet on her?'

'Maybe. But she's sure as hell not sweet on him.' Whatever it was Emma felt for Devlin was more akin to dislike and anger judging by the look on her face when Devlin had first sat down. Certainly not a prearranged meeting and not one she wanted to be a part of. It shouldn't have made any difference. She was nothing to him. But it did make a difference.

'She does not like him. That's why he had to wait until she was at the dinner table before he approached. Because she would have walked away otherwise,' Ned said.

'Strange that she should dislike him so much.'

'Is it?'

He could feel the glance that Rob flicked his way. 'Maybe he didn't like you dancing with her.'

Ned smiled. 'I'm sure he didn't like me dancing with her.'

Rob chuckled.

There was the whir and rumble of the wheels, the clatter of the horses' hooves, the noise and hubbub of the traffic all around them. They stopped at the junction behind a queue of carriages and waited while a road sweeper darted out ahead, sweeping the fresh pile of steaming horse manure up into his shovel ahead of the two city gentlemen who followed and receiving a tip for his trouble.

The carriages in front moved off. Ned gave a flick of the rein and his team followed.

'You're getting too good at this carriage driving,' observed Rob with a grin. 'Lessons paid off well.'

Ned smiled.

They lapsed into silence as they sped past the buildings.

When Rob spoke again it was in a voice not to be heard by any others. 'Do you think Devlin said anything to her about...?'

'No.' Absolute. Categorical. 'Whatever Devlin feels about me, he will not drag Emma Northcote into it. It's more than his honour is worth.'

'You'll forgive me if I don't set so much store by gentlemen and their honour.'

Ned smiled a hard smile.

'Miss Northcote—she's not what I thought she'd be. Not spoiled and pampered like the rest of them.'

Ned made no comment, but he thought of her in the red tavern dress dealing with the men in the Red Lion. He thought of her in his arms in the darkened alleyway, her mouth meeting his with passion and sweetness. He thought of the warmth of her smile, of her irrepressible spirit and strength of character. And how he had wanted her in his bed, in his life…in his future. He pushed the thoughts away with a will of steel. 'Whatever she is makes no difference to us.'

Rob smiled and leaned back in his seat to enjoy the view of the fine town houses.

Ned drove the carriage onwards to Hyde Park.

Emma stood alone by the window in the dining room of the dowager's Grosvenor Place town house, watching London wake to another day.

The Fortnum and Mason cart was passing, the delivery boy perched high on the back ready to spring down and run in with the groceries ordered by housekeepers and wives. Two milkmaids were on the other side of the road, wooden yokes across their shoulders, balanced like a weighing scale with large wooden churns. There seemed a never-ending stream of coaches and carts and gentlemen on horseback taking their mounts for exercise in the park. A clamour of activity, which was the reason that Lady Lamerton had chosen the house.

The sky was blue, but mired with that slight haze that would burn off as the earliness of the morning advanced and the sun climbed high in the sky. It was going to be another hot day. Emma could feel the clammy warmth in the air already.

She massaged a hand against the tightness nipping the nape of her neck.

She was thinking about last night and Devlin… and Ned.

An uneasiness still sat upon her over Devlin's veiled suggestion that he had an interest in her and over his implication about Ned and gentleborn women.

How Devlin could even think that there could be anything between them… Devlin, after all, was one of the men responsible for Kit's downfall and the financial ruin of her family. And even were he not, he was a rake, a man who lived a life devoted to empty hedonism and lavish luxury. He had no thought for anything serious or meaningful. He spent his time bedding women of the *demimonde*, gaming and drinking. After her months in Whitechapel she could not like a man like him.

She thought of Ned seeking his pleasures on the other side of town as much as Devlin. She thought of Devlin's hints and wondered what it was Ned had done with another gentle-born woman. The thought made her chest tighten with a heavy rawness and sent a bitterness pumping again through her blood. Had he lied to her as he had lied to Emma? Had he deceived Emma as to what was between them? And over his offer to help her father? She closed her eyes at the thought of that small unnecessary cruelty.

And in her mind she saw again her father that day at the warehouse.

'Oh, Papa,' she whispered soft as a breath and that ever-present nagging sense of worry over him stole out from where it lurked in the shadows to fill her mind. And she thought, too, of what he would say if he ever discovered what she had done with Ned Stratham.

'Ah, here you are, Emma.' Lady Lamerton's voice made her start. She hid away those feelings. Took a breath and turned to face her employer.

'I did not mean to startle you, my dear.'

'The fault is all mine. I was wool-gathering and did not hear your approach.' She smiled and, moving from the window, directed the dowager's attention elsewhere. 'Cook has quite surpassed herself with the ham and eggs this morning.'

'She has a temperament that requires handling with kid gloves, but…' Lady Lamerton smiled and lowered her voice to share the confidence '…she is worth her weight in gold. Worked for the royal household for years. When she left, Amelia Hilton tried to snaffle her, but I got in first.' The dowager leaned on her walking stick and gave a very satisfied cat-that-got-the-cream smile that made Emma smile in earnest.

Emma lifted a plate from the heater and helped Lady Lamerton to a selection from the breakfast dishes before they both took their seats.

Lady Lamerton peered at the empty space before Emma. 'I trust you have eaten?'

'I have, thank you.' She knew how precious food was. How hungry a person could get. So she had eaten whether she had appetite or not.

'I see Mrs Lewis seated you beside Devlin. Hardly the most sensitive of seating arrangements given the history of your families.'

Emma made no comment.

'Did he upset you?'

'Not at all,' she lied and thought of Devlin's insinuation about Ned.

Lady Lamerton glanced across at Emma as she ate. 'And yet you have something weighing upon your mind.'

The butler appeared with a fresh pot of coffee and set it down on the table between them, sending wafts of steam and its rich roasted aroma through the air. By unspoken consent both Emma and Lady Lamerton waited until he had departed again before they resumed their conversation.

'I was thinking of my father,' Emma admitted,

aware that the older woman was no fool. It was the truth, just not all of it.

'Wondering how he is faring in Hounslow without you?'

In his small comfortable cottage living a quiet but respectable life in Hounslow. So many lies. Emma met Lady Lamerton's gaze. There was a formidable kindness in it. She wondered what Lady Lamerton would do if she knew the truth? Of Whitechapel and the hardship of life there, of the dockyard warehouse and the Red Lion Chop-House. Part of her wanted so much to tell. To unburden herself. To cease the dishonesty. But Emma knew she could not. She was under no mis-apprehensions. Lady Lamerton had a kind heart, but she would not understand. And she certainly would not have a woman who had been a serving wench living in her house, acting as her companion. So Emma just smiled in reply.

'I am taking tea with Mrs Hilton this afternoon. There is no need for you to come. Take the day off. Travel out to Hounslow and surprise your papa with a visit.'

And discover for herself the truth of how he was coping. 'If you are certain...'

'Quite certain. I would not say it were I not. As long as you are returned before evening. Remember we have agreed to a card evening at Lady Routledge's.'

'I will be back long before evening.' No woman wanted to be walking the Whitechapel streets at night. And that made her think of the night that Ned Stratham had stepped in to save her from the two sailors. Of his walking her home…and all it had led to. She stopped the thoughts. Closed her mind to them. Thought of her purpose in being here.

'I have been meaning to ask you whether Lord Lamerton has yet had word of Kit?' she asked.

'It is early days, Emma, and m'son continues with his enquires. We must leave the matter in his capable hands.'

'I am most grateful. My father will be, too.' It would be the first thing her father would ask.

'If there is word to be had, Lamerton will be the one to have it.'

'He will.' Emma smiled, but as she sipped her coffee the question on Emma's mind was what that word would be.

It was a couple of hours later when Emma made her way across town, walking at a brisk pace. The new olive-green walking dress, cream spencer, bonnet and gloves, all part of the wardrobe

Lady Lamerton had bought for her upon her arrival, allowed her to belong in Mayfair. But not so in the East End. It was only when she got into Spitalfields and then headed further east into Whitechapel that she was aware of the way people were looking at her.

Before, in her own old and shabby attire, or the serving dress lent to her by Nancy, she had fitted in, drawn no notice. Now her new and expensive clothing proclaimed her from another tribe, an intruder from another world. The further she trod into Whitechapel the more uncomfortable she became.

Streets that only a couple of weeks ago had been her home, her locale, seemed threatening. Men, lurking in doorways, eyed her with sly speculation. Women, sitting upon their steps, did not recognise her as Emma de Lisle, one of Nancy's girls from the Red Lion, but as someone who should not be here, someone who did not fit in. Only two weeks had passed, but already she had forgotten the depth of the darkness, the stench of the dirt and the cutting danger of this place.

Five miles separated Whitechapel and Mayfair. It might as well have been five thousand. They were worlds apart. Little wonder Ned changed his clothes to come here. She wished she had done the same.

But although her clothes were all wrong, she knew these people. She kept her head up, maintained her confidence and stayed true to herself.

It was with relief that she eventually reached the London Docks.

In the warehouse was the same foreman she had met before. He did not recognise her at first. Did a double take when she apologised for inconveniencing him and asked him if she might speak to her father.

'Of course, miss.' He gave a nod. 'Come right this way for Mr de Lisle.'

Not Bill this time, but Mr de Lisle. It struck her as odd, as did the fact he led her into an office at the front she had not noticed before.

Her father was not shirtless and glistening in sweat. The clothes he wore were new—a fine fitted tailcoat and matching breeches, pale shirt and stockings, dark neckcloth and waistcoat. His grey hair was cut short and tidy and combed neat. A new pair of spectacles was perched on the end of his nose. He was the very image of respectability, sitting there at a large desk in the middle of the room writing within a ledger. Like the gentleman he had once been. So many emotions welled up at the sight. Surprise and relief, pride and affection. She pressed her gloved fingers to her lips to control them.

'Emma!' He set the pen down in its wooden holder. Got to his feet, came to her and embraced her.

She heard the office door close behind the foreman.

'Oh, Papa! How on earth...?' She looked him up and down before gazing around them at the change in his environment.

'It is a miracle, is it not?' He laughed. 'The very day that you left the company deemed they had a need of someone who could manage the accounts in-house rather than farm it out to an office on the other side of town. A money-saving venture they said. They seemed to know that I had something of an education and offered me the job. Fate has dealt us both good fortune, Emma.'

'It seems that it has,' she said quietly.

'And the vast increase in wage means I can afford some very fine rooms not so far away in Burr Street, although I have not yet had a chance to write to Mrs Tadcaster so that she could inform you.'

'And you are eating?'

'Like a king. There are some splendid chop-houses in the vicinity.' There was a twinkle in his eye as he said it.

Her smile broadened. It was so good to see him like this.

'Now tell me all about how things are with you, my dear girl. I have been worrying over you.'

'I accepted the position with Lady Lamerton so that you would not worry.'

He smiled. 'Ah, it is true. But I confess that my worry is a great deal less than it used to be. And besides, it is a father's duty to worry over his daughter.'

'And a daughter's duty to worry over her father.'

They laughed and talked some more. She told him that young Lord Lamerton was making enquiries as to Kit's whereabouts. She told of her life with the Dowager Lady Lamerton, of what was the same in the *ton* and what had changed. But she made no mention of the newcomer Mr Stratham.

'You see,' said her father. 'Am I not proved right? Accepting the position was the best thing to do.'

'It was,' she said, but she did not smile.

Her last view of him as she left was of him sitting at the big wooden desk, a contented expression on his face, as he dipped his pen into the inkwell and wrote entries into the large ruled ledger open before him.

Emma left the London Docks and headed west towards Mayfair, walking with a hundred other people across roads and along pavements. All around was the hurried tread of boots and shoes, the buzz of voices, and, louder than all, the clatter of horses' shoes. But what she heard in her head as she walked were the words that Ned had spoken to her on a morning that seemed now to belong to another time and another world.

I used to work on the docks... I still know a few folk in the dockyard... I could have a word. See if there are any easier jobs going.

And she knew that it was neither fate that had rescued her father from hefting crates upon the warehouse floor, nor a miracle, but Ned Stratham.

Chapter Eight

Mrs Morley's picnic in Hyde Park took place three days after Ned and Rob's early morning drive in the same place. The weather had grown hotter and stickier. It was a select affair arranged by one of the *ton*'s *grande dames* to raise funds for her husband's regimental charity. The price of the tickets guaranteed only a select attendance; as did the limited number of places.

Ned was there, with Rob, not because he enjoyed such frivolous wastes of time, or displaying the style of his dress. Ned did not care about clothes or fashion or the style of his hair. He kept the knot in his cravat simple and had looked at his valet in disbelief when the man suggested tying rags in his hair overnight to curl it. To give the valet his due, he had not asked again. Ned was there because he knew the importance of maintaining a presence when it came to doing business with these men. And being on a level meant attending social functions like this on a regular basis. It meant dining with them and being a member of a gentlemen's club.

He nodded an acknowledgement at Lord Misbourne across the grass. Misbourne was of particular importance to him, more so than the others. But Ned had sown the seeds. Now he had to wait for Misbourne to come back to him.

'Quite the turnout,' he said, looking over to where Spencer Perceval, the prime minister, and the Prince Regent were speaking to Devlin and his cronies. Beyond them he could see Emma Northcote and Lady Lamerton.

'Old boys' club,' said Rob.

Ned gave a small smile of amusement and accepted a glass of champagne from the silver tray the footman offered.

'Such a fine day for our picnic, don't you think, Mr Stratham?' Amanda White, a pretty young widow of a certain reputation, announced her arrival. Her neckline was just a low enough cut to afford an unhindered view of her cleavage and transparent enough to more than suggest what lay beneath. She looked at him with bold, seductive eyes and a lazy, sensuous smile.

'A fine day, indeed, madam.'

'I'm positively famished and need some advice over which are the tastiest morsels on offer.' She glanced across at the feast of extravagant dishes set out on the line of tables, the tablecloths of which gleamed white in the sun. 'Whether to have the wafer-thin sliced chicken or ham. Or something bigger, more masculine and…substantial. Like steak. Such a choice as to quite confuse a lady.' She touched her teeth against her bottom lip, biting it gently. 'What do you think, sir?'

From the corner of his eye he could see Rob's gaze fixated on Amanda White's ample bosom.

'I think you need the guidance of a renowned epicure. What good fortune there is one so close at hand…' He glanced round at Rob. 'Mr Finchley…?'

'I would be delighted, ma'am,' said Rob and offered his arm.

Amanda White could not in all civility refuse. She eyed Ned for a moment, knowing full well what he had just done, but then she smiled and tucked her hand into the crook of Rob's arm.

Rob smiled, too, as he led her away towards the picnic tables.

Ned's eyes moved across the distance to where Emma Northcote and Lady Lamerton had stood, but both were gone. He located the dowager at the far edge of the party, talking intently with Mrs Hilton. His eyes were still scanning the crowd when he heard Emma's voice behind him.

'Mr Stratham.'

A tiny muscle tightened in his jaw. Other than that, not one other sign betrayed him.

'Miss Northcote.' He turned to face her. Did not smile. 'Shouldn't you be with Lady Lamerton?'

'She and Mrs Hilton are discussing something which they deem unsuitable for an unmarried lady to hear.' She gave a small ironic smile. And in that moment, standing there dressed in their finery with champagne glasses in their hands and the extravagance of pineapples upon a banqueting table, surrounded by the elite of London's *ton*, Whitechapel and all that had happened there whispered between them.

The hint of a breeze flicked lazily at the olive-green satin of her bonnet ribbons. The colour suited her dark complexion well, highlighting the velvet brown of her eyes and the glossy dark gleam of her hair.

Neither of them drank their champagne. Both stood there, glasses steady in hands, appraising the other with calm measure. She watched him with those same dark perceptive eyes as the woman he had met in the Red Lion.

'I came to thank you.' Her voice was quiet enough that only he would hear.

'I have done nothing for which you should thank me.'

A smile, there then gone. 'You helped my father.'

'Did I?'

They looked at one another across the small distance, aware of the layers of tension between them.

'You were not lying, after all.'

'No.' His eyes held hers, serious, focused, revealing nothing of the hard beat of his heart.

'But you *were* courting titles on the marriage mart.'

'Before you. And after.'

'And in between?'

'No.'

Her eyes scanned his. 'You really are from Whitechapel.'

'Born and bred.'

Their gazes still held locked. 'You needn't worry, Ned. Your secret is safe with me.' The very words he had spoken to her upon Hawick's dance floor.

He smiled a crooked smile.

And she smiled, too, that glorious warm smile of hers that revealed the small sensuous dimple.

Ned's gaze shifted to beyond Emma, to the four tall dark figures that were making a beeline for them.

'Miss Northcote,' Devlin said as he came to stand at her side. Monteith stood by Devlin. Fallingham and Bullford took her other flank. Aligning themselves around her. Aligning themselves against him. 'And…Mr Stratham.' There was a slight razor edge in the way Devlin said his name. The viscount held his gaze with disdain and contempt and a hint of threat.

Ned found the less-than-subtle attempt at intimidation amusing. He had grown up the hard way. He knew how to read people. He understood Devlin better than Devlin understood himself. And he knew exactly which buttons to press to play him.

'Lord Devlin.' He smiled. 'How nice of you all to come over.'

The remark hit the spot. Devlin stiffened, then forced a smile. 'Miss Northcote's company beckoned.' The viscount turned his attention to Emma. 'I trust you are enjoying the picnic, Miss Northcote.'

'Very much, thank you, Lord Devlin.' Her words were polite, but Ned could hear the cool tinge in them. Her smile was small, perfunctory. It did not touch her eyes. Her dimple remained hidden.

Her gaze skimmed over Devlin and his friends. Her poise was calm and controlled, yet beneath it Ned could sense her discomfort.

'And you? Are you enjoying being here?' Ned asked of Devlin.

'Not as much as you, it would seem. I do not suppose they have picnics where you come from. Where was it again? I am not sure you ever did say?' Devlin sipped at his champagne as he played a dangerous game.

Emma shifted with unease.

'Such an interest in me, Lord Devlin. How flattering. I could give you my life history—where I came from...how I came to be here... All the details, if you want. We never really have had a chance to chat.'

Devlin's eyes narrowed with contempt. 'I am a busy man. My time is precious. And I have no interest in trade.'

Emma's eyes widened at the implied insult.

Ned smiled. 'And yet here you are, sharing that precious time with me.'

Devlin bristled. A muscle twitched in his jaw as he clenched his teeth. He glared at Ned for a moment before addressing Emma. 'If you will excuse me, Miss Northcote.'

She gave a tiny nod of her head.

The four young noblemen made curt bows and walked away.

Emma and Ned looked at one another.

It could have been just the two of them standing there, as it had been that day at the old stone bench. But that day was long gone and was never coming back.

His eyes traced her face.

'Goodbye, Emma.' A small bow and he walked away.

That evening was one of Lady Lamerton's rest evenings, as she called them. One of two or three evenings a week when she stayed at home. To rest and nurture her strength and vigour and to make her presence all the more appreciated at the Foundling Hospital's ball the next evening. Every night and they grew tired of one, she said. Too few evenings and they thought one out of it. The trick was in getting the balance of nights in and nights out just right. And the dowager knew a thing or two about such subtleties of the *ton*, having spent a lifetime mastering its handling.

They sat together in the little parlour playing whist.

'Apparently the picnic raised more than three

thousand pounds for Colonel Morley's regimental charity.' Lady Lamerton eyed her cards.

'A very successful fundraiser. Mrs Morley must be happy.' Emma placed a card down on the pile.

The dowager gave a tut when she saw the card. Emma smiled at her.

And the dowager smiled, too. 'Positively crowing. You know she never got over Lamerton—God rest his soul—choosing me over her. Accepted Morley as a poor second best.'

'I did not know that.'

'It was so long ago that there are few enough of us left to remember.'

'Was it a love match between you and Lord Lamerton?'

'Good heavens, no!' She gave a chuckle as if it were an absurd suggestion. 'Lamerton needed my papa's fortune.'

As too many earls needed Ned's.

'I was in love with someone else.'

The revelation was so unexpected. It allowed Emma a glimpse into the past and the young and passionate woman that Lady Lamerton must have been.

The dowager placed her card down on top of Emma's with deliberation. When she looked up to meet Emma's gaze she smiled. 'Elizabeth Morley's contribution to the picnic was paltry. Considerably more is expected of the hostess than a few seed cakes. Little wonder her face was so sour when she saw the magnificence of my peach flans.' She gave a small cackle.

'You are incorrigible.'

'I am blessed with natural ability.'

They both smiled.

'I saw you talking to Devlin and Mr Stratham. Matters between you and Devlin seem amicable.'

They were hardly amicable, but in her role as the dowager's companion Emma could not be anything other than civil to him. She gave a smile that the dowager interpreted as agreement.

'You do know that Mr Stratham contributed the pineapples.'

'Rather too extravagant,' said Emma.

'I would describe it as a clever move. When it comes to cultivating the *ton*, he knows he must make his money work for him.'

Ned was a shrewd man. She thought of the way he had sat in the Red Lion all those months. Self-contained, serene, but with so much beneath. She thought, too, of Devlin's words about Ned and women. She hesitated just a moment, then spoke.

'And yet I heard a rumour concerning Mr Stratham.'

'A rumour, you say?' The dowager raised an eyebrow and looked interested.

'That Mr Stratham is less than discreet or honourable when it comes to women.'

'Rather a *risqué* rumour for the ears of an innocent.'

Emma smiled. 'I could not help overhearing a conversation as I was passing.'

Lady Lamerton smiled her appreciation of eavesdropping. 'It is a quite misinformed opinion, my dear. Stratham is not that manner of man at all.'

'And yet he did spend time with Mrs White at the picnic.' Emma thought of the vivacious young widow and the way her violet eyes had looked so seductively into Ned's, the way she had touched a gloved hand on more than one occasion to his arm.

'Amanda White is always angling after him, but without success.'

'That is surprising.'

'Not at all. He is focused upon his business interests and on securing himself the best marriage alliance for his money. Stratham undoubtedly attracts women, but however he conducts his affairs it is with discretion. There has been nothing untoward. And believe me, had there been, I would know.

Gentlemen of trade are not exactly welcomed with open arms into the *ton*. He is under constant scrutiny.'

There was a truth in that. Emma knew very well how the *ton* viewed self-made men.

'Who was speaking of him?' the dowager wanted to know.

'I could not see. I was trying to be discreet.'

'I must teach you better.'

They exchanged a smile, then went back to their cards.

With the last trick played the dowager had won again.

'You are too good at this,' said Emma.

The dowager chuckled.

As Emma shuffled the pack and dealt the cards again, her mind strayed to Ned and their conversation earlier that day.

But you were *courting titles on the marriage mart.*

Before you. And after.

And in between?

No.

He had not lied about her father. Maybe he was not lying about the rest of it.

She had the feeling that her initial reaction, natural though it was to finding Ned Stratham living the life of a gentleman in Mayfair, had been misjudged.

Ned had never hidden the fact that he kept secrets. He had not lied about his. He was right; she had been the one who had lied about hers, even if it was for the best of reasons.

But I'll be back.... We need to talk when I return... She remembered the look in his eyes, serious, intent, soul-searching. About their future, she had thought. A future together.

She wondered what would have happened had she waited for him as she said she would.

She wondered with all her heart what Ned Stratham would have said.

Within the main hall at the Foundling Hospital the next evening the ball was in full swing. The turnout was more than good. In one corner of the room a posse of musicians played Handel's music, on account of the many fundraising concerts the composer had played on behalf of the Hospital. The design inside the hall, like the rest of the building, was Palladian, yet simple and unadorned; the Hospital did not want to be open to accusations of extravagance.

Ned and Rob stood across the room from the musicians. It was a position that Ned had chosen from instinct drummed into him across the years. Always keep your back to the wall so that no one could surprise you from behind. Always have a clear view of the doorway—both to see who entered and for exiting purposes. Where they stood satisfied both criteria.

On their right was the wall lined with long rectangular windows that had no curtains or blinds, only shutters that were fixed open. On their left were the internal wall and doorway that led in from the hallway and chapel. The dying sunset outside lit the windows, casting the hall with a rosy glow. From the centre of the high ceiling hung a massive but unadorned chandelier lit with the flicker of candles. It was a glamorous event, select, fashionable, six months in the organising. Tickets had been priced at one hundred pounds and every single one had been sold. To the richest and most elite of the *ton*. Ned smiled at that thought.

Rob gave a faint gesture of his head towards the door. 'Thought that Devlin and his cronies would have been at the *demi-monde* masquerade ball in the Argyle Rooms. Wonder what they're doing here instead?'

'Supporting the Foundling Hospital.' Ned gave a wry smile.

Rob laughed. 'A nice thought that.'

'Very nice.'

'Would get right up their noses as much as you do, if they knew precisely where their money was going.'

'If things go well with Misbourne, it won't be too long before they discover it for themselves.'

Rob grinned.

But Ned suspected that there was more to Devlin's presence here than just a night out. As if on cue, Devlin glanced at Emma.

Ned didn't need to follow his gaze. He already knew that she and the Dowager Lady Lamerton were standing with a group of the *ton*'s tabbies at the other end of the room. He knew that beside her the other women seemed faded and bland and that, beneath her calm, capable, polite interchanges, Emma was as aware of him as he was of her.

Devlin scanned the rest of the crowd until his eyes finally met Ned's.

Ned curved his mouth in a smile, drew Devlin a tiny acknowledgement, at which the viscount couldn't quite hide his contempt.

'Caught looking and he doesn't seem too pleased about it if the expression on his face is anything to go by,' said Rob. 'He normally likes to pretend you're so beneath him that he doesn't even notice you.'

And yet they both knew that were there a thousand people in this room Devlin would still have noticed him.

Ned's gaze shifted to Emma Northcote one last time.

And at the very same time her eyes met his. Something rippled between them before she looked away, engaging her attention more fully on Lady Lamerton and the group of women around her.

Ned pushed the thought of her from his head. It did not matter whether she was here or not. He had business to attend to. 'Time to go and talk to Misbourne.'

Rob gave a nod.

The musicians finished their tuning and began to play the initial bars of the first dance.

Ned sat his empty glass on the tray of a passing footman before making his way with Rob across the dance floor.

Emma was standing with Lady Lamerton at the other end of the Foundling Hospital hall. Lady Lamerton's social life was such a whir of activity. It had been so long since Emma had lived amongst the *ton* that she had forgotten what it was like to have so many social engagements, to plan one's entire life around them. The Season and Little Season were possibly the most important events of the year. Wardrobes were built around them. Débutantes launched in them. Marriages forged. And money, huge amounts of money, spent on and because of them. Emma had grown up accepting it as normal, but since her return from Whitechapel she questioned it.

After six months in that other world she could see it with fresh eyes. The vast luxury of it. The wonder. The sophistication and elegance. It took her breath away at the same time as it made her feel uneasy. She wondered if this was how Ned must have felt when first he came to Mayfair; wondered if he still felt it or had grown used to it.

She glanced across the length of the hall at where he stood with his steward, Rob Finchley. The midnight-blue tailcoat served to show his strong square shoulders. Other men padded their shoulders, but Emma knew that Ned Stratham's required no padding. She remembered too well how lean and hard and strong his body was.

Her eyes moved over his white cravat and white-worked waistcoat. Dark breeches clung to those long muscular thighs that had pressed to hers.

White stockings and dark slippers. Hair that was cut short and cast golden by the candlelight.

And yet all his expensive tailoring did not disguise Ned's slight edge of danger and darkness. There was something untamed about him. Like a wolf amongst a pack of sleek, pampered, pedigree dogs. She thought of what it took to survive in a place like Whitechapel. She thought of what it must have taken him to rise up out of it.

Her ears pricked up at the mention of his name. It dragged her back to the presence of Lady Lamerton and the surrounding conversation.

'I would not have thought to find Mr Stratham here,' Mrs Quigley, a tabby with the sharpest claws, was saying. Her little eyes flicked a look of superiority in his direction.

'I would be more surprised over his absence,' Lady Lamerton said in a tone that put Mrs Quigley in her place. 'Given that Mr Stratham is a patron of the Foundling Hospital.'

That was news to Emma and apparently to Mrs Quigley, too.

'I have it from m'son that Edward Stratham is the hospital's most generous single donor.'

'Garnering favour with the prospective fathers through marriage,' said Mrs Quigley.

'Tush,' said Lady Routledge. 'Any prospective

fathers through marriage are likely to be up to their necks in River Tick and would be more impressed if Stratham kept the cash in his own coffers.'

'Indeed.' Lady Lamerton adjusted her walking stick. 'But who I am surprised to see here are Devlin and his friends.'

'Not their usual scene at all,' said Mrs Hilton.

'Would have thought it rather too tame for those dissolute young bucks,' said Lady Routledge. 'I hope they are not here to cause trouble.'

'They are here for something,' said Lady Lamerton. 'Take my word upon it.'

'Perhaps one of them has their eye on a respectable lady. Perhaps they have decided to give up their rakish ways and settle down. Perhaps Devlin's papa has finally had a word in his ear.' Mrs Quigley glanced across at Lady Lamerton.

'Stanborough has mentioned nothing to me.'

'That does not mean it is not true,' pointed out Mrs Morley.

The dowager drew her a look that would have felled a lesser woman.

The music started up, the rhythm of the notes thudding through Emma's head, through her blood. The first dance was announced.

Emma glanced across at Ned again and met

the full force of his gaze. It made the butterflies flock in her stomach and her heart strike a tattoo just the same as it had done in the Red Lion; maybe even more so given the mess of their entanglement.

In that look was that same strength of character, that same tight rein of self-control. Calm, watchful confidence with the hint of something so resonant that it sent a shiver through her whole body.

Emma glanced away. This was not the Red Lion. He was not the same man. And even if he were, it was too late. She was here with a purpose. She could not forget her brother or the vow she had sworn to her mother. She turned away to the dowager just as Mrs Quigley exclaimed in breathy shock, 'Oh, my! I do believe he is coming to ask Miss Northcote to dance. How…unexpected.'

For a tiny moment she thought Mrs Quigley meant Ned. Emma's heart banged hard enough to escape her ribcage but when she followed the woman's wide-eyed stare it was not Ned that stood there, but Devlin.

Her stomach dropped to meet her shoes. Her palms were suddenly clammy. As those arrogant eyes met hers she felt a flit of panic at the prospect of having to dance with him.

He turned his attention to Lady Lamerton.

'Ma'am, would you permit your companion to stand up with me for this dance?'

Asking the dowager rather than Emma. Playing by the rules of society. Yet it irked Emma, making her feel every inch the paid servant that she was, rather than a woman who had a right to answer for herself.

She looked around the small circle of ladies. Every one of them was staring at Lady Lamerton, eyes goggling, waiting with bated breath. Lady Lamerton was in her element, holding them all in the palm of her hand.

'I will, sir. But only if Miss Northcote is in agreement.'

All eyes swivelled to Emma, awaiting her reaction.

There was a calculated gleam in Devlin's eyes. He knew full well the stir it would create if she dealt him the direct insult of a refusal. He smiled his usual lazy, arrogant smile, that of a man who was used to getting what he wanted.

It was almost enough to tempt her to refuse him, just to see it wiped from his face. And had there not been Lady Lamerton to consider, and all that depended on Emma's position with her, she would have done it. But there *was* Lady Lamerton. And there was Kit.

So Emma met those arrogant dark eyes and gave a cool polite smile. 'Thank you, Lord Devlin, how could I refuse?'

He held out his hand to her.

She took a breath and, placing her hand in his, let him lead her out on to the dance floor.

Ned and Rob were with Misbourne, chief amongst the Hospital's governors. Rob stood back, watching the dance floor while Ned discussed financial matters with Misbourne. Even though Ned was listening to Misbourne he was aware of what it was his friend watched so intently.

His eyes cut a glance through the crowd upon the dance floor to one couple alone. Devlin's hand upon Emma's. A light touch here. A lingering touch there. They did not speak, only danced with smooth flowing steps. Polite, formal, nothing but respectable. Emma's expression was a mask that revealed nothing.

'You really think you can drum up the investment?' Misbourne asked.

'It's already done.'

'Then what do you need me for?'

'To represent the project amongst the great and good.' They would listen to Misbourne. He was an earl. He was part of the establishment.

Misbourne's sharp dark eyes narrowed as they fixed upon Ned. He stroked his beard and studied Ned as if trying to glean his measure. The earl was not devoid of prejudices and might have his own dark agendas, but Ned knew the man would do better for the Hospital than any other. And so it was to Misbourne that he made the proposition.

Misbourne gave a nod. 'Come round tomorrow at seven. We will discuss it over dinner.'

The matter was concluded.

Fallingham, Monteith and Bullford were chatting to Lady Lamerton and the rest of the tabbies. Buttering them up. Waiting. Ned had known for what as soon as they had ambled over there. Emma did not even have a chance to resume her seat after Devlin returned her from the dance floor before Fallingham had her back up. And after Fallingham, Bullford, and after Bullford, Monteith and then back to Devlin.

Misbourne's eyes missed nothing. 'Miss Northcote is quite the belle of the ball. Your dance with her the other night seems to have brought her into favour.' Nor had Emma's sudden popularity among the small group of society rakes gone unnoticed by others in the ballroom. Ned could hear the whispers. See the ripple of interest. And the speculation.

'Hasn't it just,' he said.

Emma had got through a full dance with Devlin. Danced with all the rest of his and her brother's friends with increasing discomfort. And betrayed nothing of how she felt about them. But then Devlin came again for a second dance. Pushing his luck, as ever he did.

She had managed one. She could manage two, she told herself, but when the notes of the first bar of music played she realised it was the *Volse.*

Devlin had known full well what the dance was. He smiled a knowing smile as he slid his hand around her waist.

She gritted her teeth and bore his touch.

'Why are you doing this, Devlin?'

'I thought we had put the past behind us,' he replied softly, his breath brushing against her ear.

'Given what happened, how can we ever do that?' She turned her face away from his and edged her body to maintain as big a distance as possible between them.

The music began in earnest.

It was bad enough that she had to dance with him, the man who had corrupted her brother and turned him into something else, but that it was this dance over all others, this dance that allowed him to hold her, that kept them close and almost intimate…

They danced. And whether it was the dance itself, or his proximity, or the way those dark arrogant eyes mocked her, she did not know. What she did know was that it stripped away all the defences she had built around herself. It made her feel powerless. It brought back that terrible night two years ago, fresh and raw as if it had been only last week. The night her brother had gone out with Devlin and his friends and lost everything. The night her family's lives had changed for ever. So many emotions, so long buried, that now here on this dance floor before all of the *ton* threatened to resurface. It shocked her. It frightened her. It made panic squirm in the pit of her stomach.

There was a lump in her throat the size of a boulder that no amount of swallowing would shift. There was a tightness in her chest that made it hard to breathe and a nausea that churned in her stomach. For a terrible moment she thought she might actually start weeping, which was ridiculous given she had not wept through it all. She did not understand what was happening. She did not know how much longer she could keep herself together. Only that every second seemed an eternity, balanced on that brink.

She forced herself to breathe deep and slow. Tried to calm herself. Knew that they were being watched. Knew that she had to get through this without embarrassing herself.

Across the dance floor she saw Ned standing by the arch of the doorway with the Earl of Misbourne, watching. His face was stoic, stone, revealing nothing of emotion.

Her eyes met his. *Ned.* He was the last man she should turn to for help, but in that tiny moment she did.

The dance progressed her and Devlin further away across the dance floor.

She felt Devlin's hand tighten around her waist. The panic threatened to rise up.

'Lord Devlin.' Ned's voice sounded close by, polite enough, yet with an unmistakable cold strength beneath it. 'May I?'

Chapter Nine

Ned did not wait for an answer.

While Devlin stood gaping and speechless in shock, Emma found herself smoothly wrested from his grasp and swept away by Ned.

She could not speak for a moment. Only felt the support of Ned's hand upon her waist, warm and strong. Only smelled the reassuring familiar scent of him.

The steps of the dance, fast and lively, put an ever-increasing distance between them and Devlin.

'What are you doing, Ned?' she asked when she could speak.

She did not look to the periphery of the dance floor, to where the dowager and the *ton* would surely be staring, just kept her eyes focused on his.

'I think they call it cutting in.'

'You cannot do that.'

'I just did.'

'There will be a scandal.'

'I'm trade. Such faux pas are to be expected.'

The last of her panic faded.

She took a breath to steady herself. 'You have just made an enemy of Devlin.'

'Devlin was not so enamoured of me beforehand.'

'He is a powerful man, Ned. A man used to getting what he wants. You should be careful of him.'

Ned gave an ironic smile.

'Why are you smiling? I am being serious.'

'Anyone might think you had a care for my welfare.'

She glanced away. Over at the side of the floor they had quite the audience. Already she could see the spread of the scandalised whispers and dreaded to think of the state Lady Lamerton and the ladies would be in.

Now that the panic had subsided she felt ashamed of her weakness, ashamed even more that she had turned to him. 'You really should not have intervened, Ned.'

'Shall I return you to him?'

Her eyes met his once more.

Their gazes held.

He would do it, too, she knew. If she said the word. And she should say the word, she knew that, but she could not.

'No.' She was very conscious of how close he was, of the feel of his hand upon her waist and the sensations that arose from it.

'What is between you and Devlin, Emma?'

'The past,' she said. Dangerous ground, too sensitive to tread near.

He did not smile at that.

Their eyes lingered on one another. Such a strange mixed-up strain of emotion between them.

She looked away and breathed until she had regained her composure, then steered the conversation to a safer subject. 'I saw you with Misbourne. Are you doing business with him?'

'In a manner of speaking.'

'Which means?'

'Managing the most important deal of my life.'

'Is that all?' She smiled.

And so did he.

The music slowed and came to a halt.

'Thank you, Ned,' she said quietly.

'For what?'

Her gaze held his.

His face was strong, serious, unsmiling as if they were strangers, his eyes steady and almost cool. Almost. But they had the same depth as those of the man who had spilled a drink upon a black-haired villain in the Red Lion.

She knew what he had just done.

And he knew she knew.

The knowledge sat awkwardly between them.

Neither of them said a word more.

He led her back to Lady Lamerton in silence, bowed and returned to stand by his steward.

She did not look at Devlin.

'Come, my dear, I have something of a head-ache. Let us return home.' And with that Lady Lamerton swept her companion from the Found-ling Hospital hall out into her waiting carriage and the grilling that awaited there.

Three hours after Emma left the Foundling Hos-pital dance, Ned stood within the study of his mansion in Cavendish Square. The fine engraved crystal glass containing gin sat untouched on the mahogany desk behind him. He stood before the grand bow window, staring out into the night.

The summer night was warm so the hearth was bare and black. A wall sconce on either side of the mantelpiece each contained two flickering can-dles. Their light was warm and amber in the dim-ness of the room, rendering the darkening blue night through the window black and sombre by comparison. A single silver candlestick sat on the desk behind him. He could see the reflection of its tiny flame in the paned glass, framed by the dark curtains that Ned never touched. The sweet expensive scent of burnt beeswax hung heavy in the air.

'You knew what they were doing as soon as they started dancing with her,' Rob accused.

Of course he knew. Devlin had nothing of subtlety about him. 'Making Emma Northcote the belle of the ball.'

'This ain't some sort of a jest, Ned!' Rob's anxiety made his speech revert to their Whitechapel days. 'They were making it clear they don't want you anywhere near her. They must have thought your dancing with her the other night was some kind of threat.'

'They can think what they like.'

'Aren't you forgetting something?'

'I forget nothing.'

'They're dangerous, Ned.'

'I know what they are.'

'They could destroy you and everything you've worked for.'

'You think I'd let them do that?'

'I think after tonight you might have just started

a war.' Rob raked a hand through his hair. 'What the hell were you thinking of, taking her from Devlin mid-dance? You might as well have taken off a glove and slapped him in the face, called him out and been done with it!' Rob shook his head. 'Why?'

He closed his eyes and saw again Emma in Devlin's arms and the way she had looked at Ned in that moment. He had understood what she was feeling, understood, too, her appeal and knew very well he should have turned away and ignored it.

'What the hell were you thinking of?'

'There is something between Emma Northcote and Devlin. She needed rescuing.'

'And you had to be the one to do it?'

'Yes,' he said simply.

'Are you deliberately trying to goad Devlin? Because if so you're doing a damn good job of it.'

Ned turned from the window to look at Rob. 'The woman I was seeing. My mystery woman as you called her. It was Emma Northcote.'

Rob stood very still, unnaturally so, as if he had suspended even his breathing for that moment.

The silence hissed loud. He heard Rob swallow even louder.

'Is this some sort of jest?'

'I wish it were.'

Rob stared at him slack-jawed, unable to comprehend the magnitude of what Ned was telling him.

The clock on the mantel punctuated the silence.

'Hell.' Rob raked a hand through his hair. 'Hell!' he said again, louder. He rubbed his fingers against his forehead as if by doing so he could wipe what Ned had just told him from his mind.

'Of all the women out there, you have to go and start messing with *Emma Northcote*…?' Rob stared at him in disbelief.

'I didn't know who she was when I met her.'

'How can that be?'

'It's complicated.'

Rob lifted his glass and emptied its contents down his throat. There was a silence before he said, 'Well, I suppose that explains things.' He looked pale even in the candlelight. His eyes shifted to Ned's. 'Are you still seeing her?'

Ned gave him a stony look.

Rob held up his hands. 'I was only asking.'

Ned refilled his friend's glass. His own remained untouched.

'What are you going to do about Devlin?'

No pause before Ned answered, 'Ignore him, as

I always do.' He looked out on to the barely visible rustle that was the sway of trees in the night.

'And Emma Northcote?'

He looked through the trees, across to the other side of the Square, to where the lights illuminated the rectangles of windows. 'It's over with Emma Northcote.' His voice was uncompromising. 'There's nothing between us any more.' But in his mind he heard again their conversation upon that dance floor and felt that same draw to her, that same attraction. And although he would not act upon it, he knew that it was very far from over between him and Emma Northcote.

'The audacity of the man,' Lady Lamerton was still talking of the previous night's Foundling Hospital ball at luncheon the next day. 'Does he not know that a gentleman does not cut in on another gentleman's dance?'

Ned knew all right, despite all that he said. And she knew that he had done it to help her. She knew what the *ton* would be saying about him and felt a level of guilt.

'Any other man would be castigated. Would have curled his toes in embarrassment when it was pointed out to him what he had done. Not Mr Edward Stratham. He gets away with it, because he does not seem to care if he is castigated or not. And probably the fact that he is such a handsome rogue goes a long way to helping.' Lady Lamerton sipped at her tea. 'Lady Routledge has quite a soft spot for him, you know.'

'I did not,' said Emma.

'But handsome rogue or not, he has danced twice with you, Emma, cutting in to secure you for one of them. A man who does not dance. It is quite the latest *on dit*.' She gestured to the mountain of letters that lay on the tea table. 'Everyone wishes to know if there is something between the two of you.'

'How could there be anything between us? I barely know the man.'

The dowager took another sip of tea, and gave Emma a shrewd look. 'Stratham is no fool. He has money. What he needs is power, influence and social acceptance.'

'That marrying into a title would bring.'

The dowager gave a smile. 'Precisely.'

Emma smiled and lifted the teapot. 'More tea?'

The dowager nodded. 'That would be delightful, my dear.' She gave a small satisfied sigh. 'And then, of course, there is Devlin and his friends.'

To Emma's credit she did not spill the tea. She finished pouring it smooth and steady, added a few drops of cream and three lumps of sugar and sat the cup and saucer before Lady Lamerton.

'I am so glad that you have managed to put the past behind you.' The same words Devlin had used.

Emma smiled. 'One has to move on with one's life.'

'One certainly does.'

She had moved on with her life after what Devlin and his friends had done to Kit. But could she so easily move on from Ned? When she had to see him every day? When she would have to watch him court and marry a title?

'I wonder if Devlin and Stratham will be there tonight. After last night, it will be very interesting to see.'

Emma glanced away. Interesting was not the word she would have chosen. 'I wonder,' she said. They both affected her, albeit in very different ways. And she had to pretend that neither did. She sipped her tea and hoped neither of them would be present that night. That was the only way it was going to get any easier.

That evening Ned and Rob sat with Misbourne and his son, Linwood, watching the first half of

Romeo and Juliet in the Botanical Gardens down near the river.

Ned was there, not because he was interested in Shakespeare or because he wanted a night in the Botanical Gardens, but because Misbourne had asked him. The day's business had been concluded in the study of Misbourne's Leicester Square home. The deal agreed in principle on handshakes and glasses of brandy, instructions given for the contracts and plans to be drawn up by their associated men of business. And when it was done, Misbourne had suggested coming here to this Shakespeare in the Gardens.

Misbourne was on board, but Ned needed the earl committed to the alliance so, until then, he would do nothing to jeopardise their arrangement.

Across the way on the other side of the grassy stage, he could see Emma and Lady Lamerton.

The dowager had given him a little nod of acknowledgement at the start of the evening, and he replied with a bow of his head. Emma did not. Following on from their dances he knew that speculation was rife about his interest in her and Devlin's, too. Her name was upon every gossiping tongue in the *ton* and he felt a degree of regret over that.

She was wearing a dark dress and matching pelisse, the colour of which he couldn't discern in the dying light of the dusk. The light of the flambeaux around the stage and the lanterns that lit the garden's paths lent a faint orange shimmer to its silk. Her hair was pinned up in a cascade of dark curls that stirred in the breeze. She might not have acknowledged him, but her eyes met his before she returned her attention to the players upon the stage.

It was halfway through the second act when Ned's footman came with the whispered message. His eyes moved to Emma once more and held for a second too long; such a tiny moment to make such a momentous decision.

He spoke quietly for Rob's ears only. 'It's important that you keep Misbourne sweet until I get back. Don't leave him.'

Rob gave a nod.

'If you will excuse me for a few moments, sir,' Ned said to the earl.

Misbourne gave a nod. Watched him with those black eyes of his before murmuring something to Linwood and returning his focus to the stage.

Ned made his way down the lantern-lit path towards the glasshouses.

* * *

Emma watched the footman deliver the message to Ned. Watched Ned slip away with so little disruption that she doubted too many others had noticed him leave and wondered what was so important to have him abandon Misbourne midplay. The fact that Rob Finchley remained suggested that Ned would return. She knew whatever business he had with the earl was important. The most important deal of his life, he had called it.

She turned her eyes back to the stage, to *Romeo and Juliet*, but the play could not hold her attention. She was too aware of Ned's absence. The act came to an end. The players' manager appeared to announce the interval and that footmen would be circulating with a selection of drinks. And still Ned had not returned.

There was an apprehensive feeling in her bones, a gnawing sense that all was not well.

Rob Finchley looked like he was worried, too, and that he was struggling to pacify Misbourne. The earl and his son's expressions were cool and remote. They were men that few others would risk insulting, having something rather dark and silent and sinister about them.

'I wonder where Stratham has got to,' Lady

Lamerton whispered in her ear. Other people were beginning to notice, too.

Unease made the skin on the nape of Emma's neck goosepimple.

When Lady Lamerton's friends wandered over to speak to the dowager, Emma exchanged civilities with them, then sank into the background and watched Misbourne.

The earl was saying something to his son. He looked irritated and as if he were on the verge of leaving.

The most important deal of my life. Ned would not have just walked out on it. Emma knew that something was wrong. She glanced at Lady Lamerton and her friends in full gossip, then slipped away into the shadows towards the glass-houses.

The first glasshouse had been set up with screens for use as a withdrawing room for the ladies. It was while on her way towards the second that she saw the dark still shape lying between the tall hedging that led into the maze. Her stomach dropped in dread and an iciness stole through her blood because, even in the darkness, she recognised that the shape was the body of a man; a man that the moonlight showed with white shirt and cravat...and fair hair.

Chapter Ten

Emma ran the distance and fell to her knees at his side.

His eyes were closed, his bottom lip grazed as if from a fist. She touched her hand to his neck, felt the beat of his heart beneath her fingers and knew he still lived.

'Ned!' she whispered his name urgently. 'Ned!' Delivered light butterfly slaps to his cheeks. Kissed his mouth to shock some response from him.

He gave a low moan, opened his eyes, looked directly into hers for a heartbeat and then another, sharing her breath, as the confusion cleared.

'Thank God,' she breathed.

He sat up, clutching a hand to his side. 'How long have I been away?'

'About twenty minutes or so.'

'Is Misbourne still there?'

When she nodded he got to his feet, with a wince. 'I need to get back to him.' But she glanced down to see his tailcoat open and the seep of a sinister dark stain over his pale waistcoat.

'You are bleeding!' Her heart twisted in her chest. 'I will fetch help.'

'No!' He caught hold of her hand. His eyes held hers, resolute and determined.

She gave a nod, understanding what he needed.

'I'll make a pad to staunch the worst of the bleeding, if you could rip long strips from your petticoat to tie it in place.'

She did as he asked. There was nothing of false modesty in his seeing her legs. They both knew the absolute urgency of this.

He pulled up his shirt. In the moonlight the smear of blood glistened wet and dark on his pale hard-muscled belly. She could see the dark slash of a wound before he pressed his folded handkerchief to it.

'What happened?' She began to wind the strips of petticoat tight around his waist to secure the handkerchief in place as best she could.

'I received a message from you that you needed my help and asking to meet here.'

'I did not send any message.'

'I realised that when I saw the welcome party waiting for me.'

She swallowed and did not ask how many men it had taken to fell him, just concentrated on tying the strips off.

As he dropped his shirt into place she saw the long tear in the material where the knife had cut.

'It's worse than it looks. They were paid to beat me, not kill me.'

'Someone does not like you,' she said.

'Quite a few people,' he replied as she dusted down the shoulders and back of his tailcoat.

But there was one name that whispered between them.

'Devlin would not stoop so low…not over a dance.'

Ned just gave a grim smile. 'Go back now so that we are not seen to return together.' He did not need to tell her what that would do to her reputation. 'I'll finish up here and follow in a few minutes.'

She nodded. 'Good luck with Misbourne.' Reaching a hand to his face, she wiped a smear of blood from his cheek.

Their eyes held for a tiny second more before she dropped her hand and hurried back to the play.

* * *

Lady Lamerton was still talking to her circle as Emma stopped to speak to an old school friend not so far away from where Misbourne stood…as if that was what she had been doing all of the time.

The bell rang to sound the end of the interval.

Emma headed back to Lady Lamerton.

'Was that Phoebe Hunter I saw you talking to?'

'It was.'

'I thought you and she no longer spoke.'

'We did not. But if I am putting the past behind me with so many people, Phoebe should be the first of them. You know she is having renovations done at Blackloch and a new nursery built.'

'Indeed?' The dowager looked pleased with the news. The bell rang for the end of the interval and they resumed their seats once more.

The players strolled upon the stage, just as Ned slipped into his seat.

He looked just as he had done when he left—smartly and expensively dressed, his tailcoat fastened neatly in place. No one save him and Emma would ever have known what lay beneath.

Rob eyed the wound as Ned changed the dressing on his belly later that night. 'Luck of the devil, a little bit deeper and they'd have spilled your guts.'

'Not the devil,' Ned said and thought how the ivory token tucked in the pocket of his waistcoat had deflected the blade. 'Besides, they weren't trying to kill me.'

'Doesn't look that way to me.'

'The knives only came out in retaliation for the loss of their friends.'

Rob's eyes were steady on his. 'What did you do with the bodies?'

'They were gone when I came round. They must have taken them with them.'

'And you dressed the wound yourself?'

'I had help.'

Rob looked at him in question.

'Emma Northcote.'

'You are kidding.'

Ned met Rob's gaze and raised his eyebrow.

Rob closed his eyes and pinched the bridge of his nose. 'I'm not even going to ask.'

'Better that way,' Ned said.

'What the hell was she doing with you, Ned?'

'I thought you weren't going to ask.'

'You've still got feelings for her.'

Ned pulled his shirt back down into place, and

threw the brandy-soaked bloodied rags on to the fire.

There was a silence.

Ned was not a man who talked about feelings. He had quashed 'feelings' a long time ago. Feelings made one weak and open to hurt. Feelings hindered, not helped with survival. But what was between him and Emma Northcote, this thing that he felt… He said nothing and his silence was as loud as if he had shouted his agreement to Rob's statement.

Rob glanced away, uneasy and nervous. Bit at his thumbnail. 'If Devlin organised what happened in the Botanical Gardens because you cut in on a dance with her, just think what he would do if you go after her.'

'I'm not going after her. How could I, knowing who she is? Besides, this isn't about Devlin.'

'No? If he talks, then you kiss goodbye to Misbourne. You kiss goodbye to it all.'

'You know Devlin can't talk.'

'There's something else you should know.' Rob looked away again, his manner awkward, his hand rubbing the back of his neck. 'I was asking around about her, sniffing for some gossip on her and Devlin. You said there was something between them.'

'And is there?' Ned felt his focus sharpen.

Rob gave a nod. 'Seems she blames him and his pals for leading her brother astray. Little Kit Northcote running with the big bad boys.'

Ned shook his head and gave an ironic laugh.

'I thought so, too,' said Rob. 'Just thought you should know.'

'Thank you, Rob.'

'You managed to smooth it over with Misbourne?'

Ned gave a nod.

'What did you tell him?'

'He didn't ask and I didn't tell.'

'Probably saw the bruise on your forehead and the grazes on your knuckles and guessed how you got them.'

'It was too dark to see.'

'It won't be tomorrow.'

Ned lifted the lid of the silver platter on his desk to reveal a thick slab of raw steak.

Rob grinned. 'I see you've thought of tomorrow already. Nothing stops bruising better than a raw steak compress.'

But when Rob left a few minutes later it was not bruises or Misbourne that Ned was thinking of, but the woman who had helped him that night. Had she not come looking for him, Misbourne might have walked. But she *had* come and she had helped him, not baulking from the blood or the mess or what had to be done, although it had shaken her. It seemed he could still feel the tremble of her fingers against his face, wiping away blood he could not see, and the brush of her kiss that had brought him to his senses.

He poured himself another gin and drank it down.

You know Devlin can't talk.

Once that had been a certainty. Now, Ned was no longer so sure. Because, for all his assertions to Rob, after tonight he could no longer deny he still cared for Emma. He cared for her and if Devlin was to realise that fact then all bets were off.

It was not an eventuality Ned could afford to risk.

He took another swig of gin and stared into the flicker of the flames upon the hearth.

He had to stay well away from her. For both their sakes.

Emma could not sleep that night.

Her mind kept reliving the bloodied mess of Ned's injury and the awful shock of finding him lying there on the grass. She had thought him dead. Dead! And that stomach-dropping moment had been one of the worst in her life.

She looked down on to the quiet moonlit street, watching the trundle of the soil cart and the skulking shadow of a cat creeping behind it.

Every time she closed her eyes she saw that seeping stain so dark against the white glow of Ned's shirt, the torn linen and, beneath it, the glistening gash that gaped in the muscle of his belly. Such a thin black line to produce so much blood. His skin had been slick with it beneath her fingers. It seemed even now that she could still smell it in the air and taste its metallic tang on her tongue. Her stomach knotted at the memory. It felt like a hand had taken hold of her heart and squeezed, and would not stop squeezing.

That Devlin could have stooped so low... He was a rake, a selfish, arrogant wastrel. But despite all of that she had always thought him a gentleman. Ned himself had said he had enemies. A man from trade would always have enemies amongst the *ton*.

She shivered and pulled her shawl more tightly around her shoulders. But it was not the cold that made her shiver. She still loved him. It was not a good realisation. She closed her eyes, knowing that it was all wrong.

He was looking for the daughter of a title, everyone knew that. He might desire her, he had always desired her, but he would never marry her.

Ned was ambitious. He was an empire builder. He had his plans. And she had both her pride and her duty. A hint of scandal and her position with Lady Lamerton would be lost and with it her best hope of finding Kit. Her father was relying on her. And given what had happened between them in Whitechapel… *Fool me once and shame on you. Fool me twice and shame on me.* The old saying whispered through her head.

She loved him, but she was not a fool.

So she would wish him luck in his search for a bride and leave him to the marriage mart.

Ned was sitting alone on a wooden bench in Green Park, looking out over a view that could not have been more different than the one from another bench a few miles across the city in Whitechapel. He needed space to think outside the walls of the mansion in Cavendish Square. He needed to be alone to think. And given his schedule for meetings tonight he could not go to Whitechapel. If he were honest, it was not the only reason he was not going to Whitechapel. He had not been back since Emma had arrived in Mayfair.

The sky above was leaden, the air unnaturally still. There was barely a breath of movement. The atmosphere seemed to radiate a tension that made people uncomfortable and unsettled and all the while not knowing why. The portent of a storm to come. It kept them indoors, or hurrying along the streets to get there. It cleared the sweep of undulating green grass and its paths so that he had the place to himself, almost, save for the odd figure or two rushing away into the distance to escape that feeling and what was to come.

Ned's feeling of discomfort could not be so easily remedied. Not by returning to the house in Cavendish Square. Or by anything as simple as waiting for the storm to pass.

I'm not going after her. How could I, knowing who she is? His own words seemed to ring in his ears, taunting him.

He couldn't get Emma out of his head. Maybe because of who she was. Maybe because she was the one woman in all the world he should not want and could not have. Maybe both of those reasons or neither of them, he did not know. What he did know, what he could no longer pretend to himself otherwise, was that he wanted her as Emma Northcote every inch as much as he had wanted her as Emma de Lisle. She had not changed, between Whitechapel and Mayfair. She was the same woman. He understood why she had lied and it did not alter the facts. That he wanted her. That he had feelings for her. And the realisation complicated everything.

It brought risks he had never contemplated. To his plan, to all he had spent a lifetime working towards. To himself and the very crux of who he was and what drove him.

Ned knew what he was and had always been comfortable with it. He saw things with a clear dispassion. But this thing with Emma Northcote was different. It pushed him to a place he had not been before, a place he did not want to be. It made him question things he did not want to question. It made him question what sort of man he was.

He moved the fingers of his right hand in that old comfortable reassuring rhythm, tumbling the token backwards and forwards, backwards and forwards.

Because being who he was, if he cared for her, how could he be with her?

Unlike all the other problems he had faced in his life, blind-ended problems, problems the size of a mountain, this was a dilemma to which there could be no solution other than walking away.

He had responsibilities. He had his destiny and

his duty. And regardless that he did not play by the rules of the world, he had his own moral code, his own sense of honour.

Every time he thought it through, all the arguments, all the logic told him to stay away from her. The decision was already made.

But it did not stop him thinking about her.

Emma's letter to her father had been posted. She had taken it to the Post Office herself so that no one else would see the Whitechapel direction written upon it, along with two of Lady Lamerton's letters, under the guise of a need for fresh air. The guise in itself was no lie. The air was not fresh, but still and ripe with uncomfortable promise. But since the Botanical Gardens incident she had not felt herself and she needed some time away from the dowager. She needed time alone, to walk, to clear her mind and to straighten her thinking.

Emma knew just how hard it was to live in a different world from the one you had been born to and raised within. One's roots coloured everything. To sever them and walk the other path was not easy. She thought of how much she had had to learn to survive in Whitechapel. Ned must have done, and indeed still be doing, the same here. He always seemed so confident, yet she knew that every small thing would be alien to him.

The sky was darkening, changing through shades of grey to a deep, menacing charcoal.

A storm was coming. She could feel the ominous stillness of the air. Smell the scent of promised rain, sense the slight winding of tension deep within. Knew she was still too far away from Grosvenor Place to reach Lady Lamerton's home before it hit. She cast a worried glance at the green silk of her skirt. Once a rain-ruined dress would have meant nothing more to Emma than an excuse to visit the mantua maker. Now it was different. She had walked the other path, where women had one dress to last a lifetime.

She gave a grim smile at that thought and took the short cut through Green Park.

Halfway through she saw the gentleman sitting on the wooden bench.

The image reminded her of another man sitting on a different bench, in a different place, at what seemed a lifetime ago. But within a few steps her heart began to thud harder and something trickled into her blood, making it rush, for she knew that figure with its dark-blond head and she knew that trip and magical roll of the token over his fingers.

It was like the replaying of a dream in her head, except it was real and happening before her eyes.

Her heart skipped a beat. Her feet faltered and ground to a halt.

He glanced up, met her gaze, as if he had been sitting there waiting for her. The token ceased its rhythmic tumble.

Time stretched between them. A tiny moment encapsulating something too big to contemplate.

Ned got to his feet. Stood there, his eyes never leaving hers.

Emma's heart was thudding fast and hard enough to escape her chest. Swallows were diving and swooping inside her stomach. She took a breath. Resumed her walking. But she did not look away any more than he did.

She stopped before she reached him.

'Emma.' Her name was low and husky upon his lips.

'Ned.'

The ensuing silence stretched tense. She could feel the strain of so much between them.

'How are you?' he asked softly.

'Well enough, thank you,' she said slowly. 'And your wound?' She glanced down to his tailcoat and what she knew lay beneath.

'Healing well, thanks to you.' His eyes scanned

hers. She saw the movement of his Adam's apple. 'You shouldn't have had to see any of that.'

'I have seen worse,' she lied. 'You forget that I worked in the Red Lion.'

'I forget nothing, Emma.' The undercurrent strengthened. Nights in darkened alleyways, passion and kisses, that last sunlit morning at the stone bench, promises and insinuations... All of it was there, whispering between them. 'You risked your safety and your reputation to help me, Emma.'

'Then we are even, Ned.'

'We will never be even.'

She did not understand his words, just saw the dark intensity in his eyes and the way he was looking at her, that made her heart race all the faster and ache for him.

She swallowed. 'I should be getting back. Lady Lamerton will be waiting for me.'

He said nothing. Just gave a tiny hint of a nod as if he agreed with her.

She gave a curtsy.

He gave a bow.

She walked on, leaving him standing there.

Only a few paces before she stopped. Touched her fingers to her forehead. Closed her eyes to stop the tears that threatened. Knew she might not get another chance to ask him, not in all of her life to come.

She turned and met his gaze.

He had not moved. He seemed tenser than normal and there were shadows in his eyes.

'May I ask you something, Ned?'

He gave a nod.

'Why did you come back to Whitechapel all those times?'

'It is my home. Where does a man go to relax but his home?'

'Cavendish Square is your home.'

'Cavendish Square is where I live.' *Not his home.*

'Can you find no relaxation here?'

'Here I must play the part of a gentleman and we both know I am nothing of that.'

'You seem to play it with ease enough.'

He smiled at that. 'I thank you for the compliment. But it took many tutors and much practice to achieve.'

She smiled, too, a sad smile. 'And the change of clothes was so that you would not draw unwanted attention.'

'Turning up at the Red Lion dressed in Weston's best...' He raised his rogue eyebrow.

She traced the scar through it with her eyes and

thought of her own trip to Whitechapel. 'I can imagine.' She paused before asking, 'Have you been back recently…to the Red Lion?'

The hint of a smile vanished. 'I have been too busy.' His eyes held hers with an intensity that lent other suggestions to the reason he had not returned to the chop-house.

The tension ratcheted between them, humming with the strain. The very air seemed to crackle.

Great heavy rain droplets began to fall, hitting her cheeks and rolling like tears. Big and slow. Hitting the olive-green silk to darken it with spots, each one so big and juicy that it seeped right through the thin muslin of her spencer.

She glanced up to find the charcoal sky dimmed almost dark as night.

'I have to go.' But her words were dwarfed by an enormous crack of thunder that peeled and rolled across the heavens. The rain began to pelt with a fury that matched the roar of the emotion between them, as the storm was unleashed.

'Too late, Emma,' he said and they seemed the most ominous words in the world. Ned peeled off his tailcoat as he spoke, wrapped it around her shoulders and, taking her hand in his, they ran through the weight of the drumming rain to the nearby oak trees.

He pulled her under the cover of the low leaf-laden branches to the shelter beneath. They stood facing one another, their hands still entwined. So close that she could see the glitter of raindrops on his waistcoat and the sodden linen of his shirt, moulded transparent to the hard contours of his chest. So close that she could feel the brush of his chest against her own, the rise and fall of his breathing. So close that she could smell the scent of rain-soaked material and beneath it the scent of him, clean, familiar, tantalising.

She tilted her face up to look at him.

His hair was sodden, turned dark with the rain and slicked back against his head. And his eyes, the most amazing eyes in the world, were like a window to his soul.

The trees and driving rain were like a curtain around them, locking out all of the real world, creating a moment they would never have again.

'The last time I saw you in Whitechapel... That day on the old stone bench...when you said that when you returned we needed to talk...' The rain ran in rivulets down her face.

He stroked the drops away from her cheeks with gentle fingers. His eyes studying hers.

'Yes,' he said, answering the question she had not asked. 'I would have told you of Mayfair. I would have told you it all.' And he really would have done because he had thought her the same as him. Hard-working, smart and ambitious enough to climb from her working-class roots. A woman who would have shared his vision, who would have understood. A woman who could straddle both worlds.

'Ned…' she whispered.

She was the same woman. The same woman beneath that name and there was such a cruel irony in that.

Emma let her gaze wander from his eyes to his lips and he knew that she wanted him as much as he wanted her. He was made for loving her. She was made for loving him.

And in the heavens above was the crash of thunder as if something of the world was being torn apart. Lightning flickered, illuminating her face in its stark white light. Illuminating everything she was, everything he wanted.

'God forgive me,' he whispered with shaky breath and lowered his face to hers.

He kissed her with tenderness. He kissed her with passion. Savouring this moment that was everything they could not have.

She slid her arms around him, anchoring them together. They lost themselves in passion and emotion, and need. Lost themselves with a fury that matched that of the storm all around.

Her heart beat with his. The thunder reverberated through them, the crashing and splitting of the skies only reinforcing what was happening between them. Fate and destiny proving that they would not be denied.

He kissed her until the furore of what flowed between them calmed enough to let them breathe again. They stood there entwined, chest to chest, lip to lip, the brush of his eyelashes against hers. Two lovers, beneath the old oak trees in a busy and fashionable park in London in the middle of the day, whose reunion the heavens had conspired to hide. The thunder was quieter now, the storm moving away. The lightning no longer flashed. In the silence there was only the drum of rain, drawn like a grey screen around them.

He held her in his arms, savouring these last few moments together. He kissed her one final time. And never again.

The sky was lightening to a pale dove-grey, its dark cloak moving to the north. The rumble of carts and carriages sounded from the nearby streets as normal life resumed.

Soon the rain would cease and they would once more become visible to the world.

He closed his eyes and dug down deep, knowing what he had to say to her.

'Emma...' His voice was low and husky.

But she shook her head. 'I know,' she said. 'You need to marry a title.'

'Yes.' But it was a lie. He did not need to marry a title. He just could not marry her. 'You will make a good match, Emma.' With any man other than him.

'I will,' she said. She had her pride. Her head was high. All her defences slotted back into place. She moved out of his arms, seemingly cool and calm and removed, but he was not fooled.

'I think it would probably be wise if we stayed away from one another, Ned.'

'I think you're right. It would be for the best.'

They looked at one another for a moment longer.

For the first time in his life he was doing the right thing but, ironically, nothing had felt more wrong.

Better she think him a selfish scoundrel than learn what he really was, yet it did not make this any easier.

The rain eased around them. The curtain began to draw back.

'We should not be seen leaving here together,' she said, practical and capable as ever, no matter what she felt. And he knew she felt. He could sense it in her. He could feel it in the way his chest ached. He was doing the right thing, he told himself again and gave a nod. But he could not avert his gaze and he did not walk away.

'Goodbye, Ned.'

'Goodbye, Emma.'

It was Emma who walked away, ducking under the low-hanging branches to make her way with such dignity back to the path. He stood there and watched her until she disappeared from sight.

Even then he waited before taking a breath and following that same path.

There was a glimmer of sunlight in the sky, but it did nothing to warm the cold in Ned's bones.

He thought of Emma and of what could not be.

And he, just like Emma before him, did not notice the tall dark figure that stood watching from the shelter of a distant doorway.

Chapter Eleven

Emma's eyes were fixed upon the page of the book in her hand, but she was not reading it. Fatigue blanketed her shoulders and head, the result of a night spent with little sleep and much regret. She knew she should not have kissed Ned. It did not matter what she felt in her heart, it was what she knew in her head that counted. He was seeking a titled and powerful alliance. She had known that before she kissed him. But when she looked into his eyes, she saw a mirror of her own feelings. She saw desire and connection and care. She saw respect and admiration and tenderness. And she saw love. Or maybe she only saw what she wanted to see.

He had no serious or respectable interest in her. He had told her plainly to her face. She could not trust him. Worse than that, she could not trust herself. It was just lust on his half, just physical desire, she told herself. But she knew in her heart that was not true, that physical desire was just one part of it.

Whatever it was that existed between them, this love and desire and passion, it would ruin her. It would cast her from society for a second time. It would destroy her only chance of finding her brother and make a mockery of the vow she had sworn to her mother. It would dash all of her father's hopes. And it would destroy her own pride and self-worth.

Emma had to stay very far away from Ned Stratham.

Far enough to watch him court a title. Far enough to watch him marry another woman and feel nothing.

And she would do it. No matter what she felt in her heart. She had to do it, for her family and for herself. She had to do it, because it was the right thing to do.

'You look tired today, Emma.' The dowager interrupted her train of thoughts.

She glanced up to find her employer no longer engrossed in her romance novel, but watching her. 'Do I?' She returned her eyes to the book in her hand, placing her bookmark within its pages. 'I am quite well.'

'And yet you do not seem your usual self.'

'Perhaps I am a little tired after all,' she admitted.

'You need not worry so over your papa. I am sure he is all the more at ease for knowing you are here.'

'You are right.' More so than Lady Lamerton could ever realise. But it was not her father she was thinking of. With his new job she had less cause to worry over him. The new job made her think of Ned again.

She was saved by the knocker sounding at the front door. Lady Lamerton exchanged a look with Emma. It was her look of intrigue and curiosity. 'I wonder who that might be. I was not aware that visitors were expected.'

'They are not,' said Emma.

The butler came in and announced that the Earl of Stanborough had come to call upon Lady Lamerton.

'Show him into the drawing room and have some tea sent in, Wilcott.'

'Very good, my lady.'

'Come along, Emma. Let us see what has brought Alfred calling upon me this fine afternoon. He was a dear old friend of mine. Such a pity he married beneath him. But I suppose the

March girl was dangling the heiress card and one might argue that one's papa owning a bank is not really trade. But I never believed it,' she snorted and gave a little wicked laugh.

Emma smiled. Lady Lamerton might be a terrible elitist, but she was rather endearing with it.

But the smile faded when she entered the drawing room and saw there were two gentlemen standing there waiting.

'Wilcott did not mention that you had brought your son, Devlin, with you.' Lady Lamerton smiled and flicked a gaze at the tall, handsome man who was a younger, dark-haired version of the one standing before her.

'I trust it does not inconvenience you…or Miss Northcote?' Lord Stanborough added, casting a concerned look in Emma's direction. 'But we go direct to a meeting at White's after this.'

'It is not the slightest inconvenience.' Lady Lamerton smiled again. 'Either for myself or for my companion. Is that not so, Miss Northcote?' Lady Lamerton looked at Emma.

'No inconvenience at all, Lord Stanborough.' What else could Emma say?

'I am most relieved to hear it, Miss Northcote,' Viscount Devlin said and bowed.

'Lord Devlin,' she said and sank into a polite curtsy.

'Now, Alfred, I take it you are here to discuss our little charity event?'

'Indeed, I am.'

'Excellent. I have already drafted a list of possible donors and guests.'

'Capital, capital.' Lord Stanborough followed Lady Lamerton to take the armchair opposite hers.

Emma was very aware that only left the sofa on which she and Devlin would be obliged to sit together. She walked over to stand by the window, looking out at the sunshine and blue sky.

'Such a pleasant day,' she said.

'Indeed.' Devlin came to stand beside her.

'What sort of numbers are we running to?' she heard Lord Stanborough ask Lady Lamerton in the background.

There was a shuffling of paper. The earl and Lady Lamerton leaned in closer and fell to conferring on the details in earnest.

Devlin smiled that so-charming smile of his, but there was something in the way his eyes held hers that stroked a sliver of unease down her spine, or maybe it was just the memory of their dance or the thought that he might have been behind the attack on Ned.

He looked at her. 'How have you been, Miss Northcote?'

'I have been well, thank you, Lord Devlin.' Unease stroked again. She knew with Devlin that his presence here was no chance event.

There was a small silence.

She lowered her voice, for his ears only. 'Why are you here, Devlin?'

'To enquire as to your welfare.'

She raised a cynical eyebrow.

He smiled again.

'And observe that Mr Stratham seems to have made quite the impression upon you.'

She glanced away. 'I am sure I do not know what you mean, or what business it is of yours.'

'Since we are speaking so plainly...I saw you together in Green Park yesterday...beneath the trees.'

There was a silence. In the background were the voices of Lady Lamerton and Lord Stanborough, convivial and chatty. But Emma's focus was all on Devlin and that sharp look in his eyes and the thud of her heart in her chest. She held her head up and eyed him with a calm confidence she did not feel.

'What of it?'

'I am not sure that your employer would have quite such a *laissez-faire* attitude.'

She stared at him with incredulity. 'You are here to blackmail me.'

'Blackmail is such an unpleasant term. Think of it more as a warning.'

She swallowed, glanced over to see if Lady Lamerton was listening, but the dowager was smiling and nodding over something that Devlin's father was saying. Her eyes moved back to Devlin's. His gaze was fixed and cool.

'And what is it that you want for your silence, Devlin?' She thought of the way he had sat beside her at dinner, the way he had danced with her and the probability that he had been behind the attack on Ned—because Ned had cut in on their dance. And there was a cold dread in the pit of her stomach.

A moment passed before he spoke.

'I want you to stay away from Stratham, Emma,' he said so softly that she thought at first she had misheard.

They were not the words she had expected to hear. She stared at him.

The silence hissed between them.

'Why?'

'Because he is not the man for you,' said Devlin.

'He is not the philanderer you portrayed him.'

'Maybe not, but he is not of our world, Emma. Not one of us.'

'I cannot believe your arrogance.'

'Oh, believe it,' he said quietly.

She still could not quite believe this conversation they were having.

'What is it to you what I do with Edward Stratham?'

'I have a care for you, Emma.'

The words hung awkwardly between them.

'Devlin…' she began.

'And what gentleman could stand by and watch a gently bred lady be devoured by a rat from the gutter?' he interrupted.

'Do not speak of him like that!'

'You may not like it, but it is the truth.'

She shook her head. Glanced away.

'I know I do not have to point out how well Lady Lamerton would take the news were she to discover what her latest companion has been up to.'

'You really would ruin me?' She looked into his eyes. This man who had already led her brother to his ruin. This man who professed to have a care for her but, in truth, had nothing of a care for anyone save himself.

'I will do what I have to, Emma.' The words

were uttered in a soft tone, yet beneath them she could hear both the steel and the promise. Then, 'Come, Miss Northcote,' in a voice loud enough to be heard by the dowager and his father. 'Let us rejoin the party.'

She had no choice but to do as he suggested, perching at one end of the sofa when she got there.

'May I?' Devlin asked, his face a mask of polite innocence.

She gave a nod of her head.

Devlin flicked out his coat-tails and sat down by her side.

'Now look at the two of you getting along so well,' said Lady Lamerton, glancing up at them.

'Aren't we just,' Devlin said and slid a gaze to Emma.

Emma said nothing.

'You and Devlin seemed to be having quite the conversation yesterday.' Lady Lamerton spoke without glancing up from her embroidery. 'What were the two of you whispering about?'

The smooth flow of the pen within Emma's hand paused upon the paper. 'The fine weather of late,' she lied.

'The most appropriate excuse.'

The words made Emma's heart stutter. She

lifted the nib of the pen, but too late—the ink had already blobbed, spoiling the letter she was writing on Lady Lamerton's behalf. She took a breath before she looked up at the dowager.

'Whatever do you mean?' She asked the question lightly, forcing a quizzical smile to her face.

Lady Lamerton set her embroidery aside. 'Why, just that Devlin seems wont to seek out your company these days. He is at almost every event we attend.'

'A mere coincidence. The Little Season has barely started. There are few enough events.' But now that the dowager pointed it out she realised it was true. Devlin seemed to be there in the background too often watching her.

'Tush!' exclaimed the dowager and flared her nostrils. 'Devlin is enamoured of you, Emma.'

'You are mistaken.' But after yesterday she feared that Lady Lamerton was right.

'Why else is he everywhere you go and always appearing by your side? And accompanying his father on a visit here...' Lady Lamerton raised her eyebrows and gave a knowing smile.

Emma said nothing.

'And then there is Mr Stratham.'

Her heart stuttered and missed a beat. In her

chest was the scrape of rawness. 'I do not know what you mean.'

'I am sure that you do. Stratham does not dance, but he danced with you. And I am not blind, Emma. I see the way he looks at you.'

She glanced away.

'And no doubt, so has Devlin.' Lady Lamerton smiled. 'You do know that Devlin has never liked him.'

'I had not thought Devlin to be so arrogant or prejudiced in his beliefs to dislike a man because he is self-made.'

'You sound like one of those political radicals, Emma. You will be telling me next that you think all men equal and we must do away with the class system!'

Emma averted her eyes to hide the truth in them.

'Devlin would be a very good catch for any woman, least of all one in your position, Emma. And there is nothing like a bit of competition between men to bring them to their senses when it comes to marriage.'

She could not dispute that Devlin was considered a catch. He was a viscount and one day would inherit an earldom. He was rich and powerful. His family owned a bank. But he had corrupted her brother and he was blackmailing her.

She was not foolish enough to think that marriage required either affection or love. It was an arrangement between two families for their mutual good. But she could not like Devlin and the thought that he was most probably behind the attack on Ned made revulsion curl in her stomach.

I want you to stay away from Ned Stratham.

The irony was she had had no intention of going anywhere near Ned Stratham again. It just galled her that Devlin would think it was because of his insistence. And there was the added worry of what Devlin might do to Ned, given what he had witnessed in Green Park.

'I wonder if Devlin will be at Lady Misbourne's little event this evening.' Lady Lamerton slid a knowing look at Emma before lifting her tambour once more.

It was not a thought on which she wished to dwell. Emma put the spoiled letter aside and took a fresh sheet of writing paper from the drawer.

She forced the worry aside and, after dipping her pen in the inkwell, began the letter again.

The Earl of Misbourne raised a hand and a butler appeared by his elbow. 'Champagne all round,' he instructed, then returned his attention to Ned.

'Everything is signed and sealed. The project will go ahead, I give you my word.'

Ned and Misbourne shook hands.

It was done. Ned breathed a sigh of relief and satisfaction.

The butler filled four glasses and passed them round to Misbourne and Linwood, to Rob and Ned.

'To new ventures and continued success.' Ned made the toast.

And all four men toasted it, chinking their glasses in the process.

'You'll stay for a while,' Misbourne said to Ned. 'My wife is hosting a card evening. We have invited a few people round.'

'Thank you.' Ned took a sip of his champagne.

'Capital.' Misbourne clapped him on the shoulder. 'Serious gaming in the dining room. Lighter stuff in the drawing room. If you'll excuse me for a few moments…' He slipped away to speak to his son-in-law, Knight, who had just come through the front door.

Rob gestured to the dining room ahead. 'Feeling lucky?'

Ned drew him a look and instinctively touched his fingers to his tailcoat, feeling the shape of his lucky token that was secure within the waistcoat pocket beneath.

'Just as well.'

Ned glanced into the dining room.

'Devlin still in there?' Rob asked.

'They all are. We'll take a drink in the drawing room to placate Misbourne, then leave.' He did not want to run the risk of meeting Emma. Staying away from her meant precisely that.

Rob gave a nod of agreement.

But as soon as Ned walked into Misbourne's drawing room he realised his mistake.

A line of tables ran down the centre of the room, crammed with ladies and several gentlemen on either side, all intent on playing whist.

On one side of the centremost table Lady Misbourne was trying to avert a scene. A young blonde woman, with eyes that were as dark and intent as Linwood's, was being helped from the room by one of Misbourne's maids. On the other side sat Lady Lamerton and Emma.

'Ah, here comes Mr Stratham. He will step in and save us, I am sure.' Lady Misbourne glanced over to Ned and Rob's arrival.

Emma followed her gaze.

'Lady Misbourne's daughter, Lady Marianne

Knight, has come over in a swoon, leaving her poor mama without a partner. And we are in the middle of a crucial match,' explained Lady Lamerton.

Ned stiffened. He made no pretence of smile or charm. For the first time since she had known him she saw something of obvious discomfort in his eyes.

'My apologies, ladies, but I do not play.' He bowed and made to leave, either uncaring or unaware of the insult he was dealing their hostess. Already Emma could see the disapproval and sneers on several faces. Already she could hear the whispers of 'trade' and 'lack of breeding.' But Devlin's warning whispered in her mind. As, too, did her own pride.

She should leave him to it. Maybe she should even be glad of it. But it was not gladness at his mistake that she felt. It was something else altogether. Something that pumped through her blood and was there in her bones, something that wrung at her heart. She looked away, trying to ignore it. Told herself that what they thought of him, what they did to him, was nothing to her. That if his slight of Lady Misbourne made her husband change his mind on whatever business deal he had with Ned, it did not matter to her. She swallowed.

Gave a grim silent sigh and knew she could not sit there and let it happen.

She stood up. 'Mr Stratham is too polite. He does not wish to tread upon the sensibilities of us ladies by winning. But I assure you, sir, Lady Lamerton is a formidable player. And I am not so badly skilled myself.'

Her eyes held Ned's across the room, sending the message that this was not an invitation he could afford to refuse, willing him to put what was between them aside for his greater good. 'You must play, sir.' She said it lightly as if it were a joke, but her words were in deadly earnest. 'You would not wish our hostess to feel injured.' The subtlety of that last comment would not be lost on him and if he walked away now, he would insult both her and Lady Misbourne.

'When you put it like that, Miss Northcote...' His lips curved in the hint of a smile, but his eyes were cool and focused all on her. 'How can I refuse?'

He gallantly helped Lady Misbourne to her chair. Then, once all the ladies were seated, he sat down by their hostess's side.

She saw him glance over at his friend, Mr Finchley.

Ned smiled, but it was a smile that did not touch

his eyes. For all intents and purposes he was his usual impassive self, but beneath it Emma sensed something else, something that was as tense and still and focused as the calm before a storm. Something dark and tumultuous. It was so palpable that she wondered that any of the other women did not sense it.

'Rest assured, sir, we will treat you gently,' she said to lighten the situation. The remark made all the ladies smile. Ned smiled, too, and he seemed almost as relaxed and confident as his usual self. But when his eyes met hers, she could see that it was a sham and she knew that he felt the same terrible conflict that beat in her own heart.

'You do know how to play whist, do you not, Mr Stratham?' Lady Lamerton enquired.

'I do, for my sins.'

Lady Lamerton smiled. 'Then let play begin and see if Miss Northcote and I cannot best you and Lady Misbourne.'

The dowager dealt the cards, one at a time in rotation, until the pack was exhausted. 'Ah, hearts are trumps, I see,' she said as she dealt the last card face up on the table.

Ned picked up his cards, spread them to a small fan within his hands. Across the cards his eyes met Emma's. In that moment it was as if his guard was lowered and she caught a glimpse of his soul—bared for her to see. And what she saw was such a blazing tortured intensity of emotion that it took her breath away. Their eyes clung together, as if they were the only two people in the room, as if they were the only two people in the world. As if there was nothing and no one except him and her and the force of this thing that raged between them. It shook her.

It shook him, too. She could see it in his eyes as they lingered too long on hers before lowering to his cards.

They played on. Lady Lamerton was in her element as she and Emma soon took the lead.

And then Lady Lamerton exchanged a look with her, giving a subtle gesture across the room. Emma followed Lady Lamerton's gaze to see Devlin standing there.

Devlin's eyes rested on Ned and just for a moment the expression on his face was one of utter loathing. Then he masked it and slid his gaze to Emma's. The words of his warning seemed to whisper between them.

She glanced down at her cards. Kept her face composed. Betrayed nothing. But when she glanced at him again, he was walking directly towards Ned.

She felt her stomach dip and begin to churn. Her eyes met Ned's in warning.

Ned understood. A tiny glance over his left shoulder to see where Devlin stood.

The change in his face was so small as to have been imperceptible, but Emma saw it. That slight tension and the way his hand moved to touch against the watch pocket of his waistcoat, which only she knew contained not a watch, but the small battered token that was his good-luck charm.

He played on. Lost. Again.

'Such terribly bad luck you are having today, Mr Stratham,' lamented Lady Misbourne.

Ned glanced over his other shoulder where Fallingham and Bullford now stood. 'Worse than you can imagine,' he said with a smile.

'One might almost think, sir, that you are determined to have Miss Northcote and me win,' said Lady Lamerton with a twinkle in her eye as she scooped the growing pile of winnings closer.

'As if I would,' said Ned in a teasing tone.

Devlin walked round to Emma's side of the table, came to stand close to her, close enough to have a slightly threatening possessive feel about it. For a moment she feared he meant to reveal her and Ned before them all. But then she saw the way he looked at Ned across the table. A challenging look. A look that was so obvious in its contempt that she felt her blood run cold.

As Monteith, Fallingham and Bullford crowded around Ned, the rest of the table saw only three gentlemen intent on getting a closer look at the game, swept along in the excitement and camaraderie. But Emma saw something else. She saw that the threat and danger was aimed not at herself, but at Ned.

Ned showed nothing of intimidation. He seemed relaxed enough, but Emma knew he had not been so since he had walked into the room. She could sense his tension as if it were her own.

The game dragged on, the pressure building ever higher. Every time Ned lost, Lady Misbourne scooped a trick and so they survived a little longer.

Sensing something of the atmosphere, people gathered round to watch. But closest of all were Devlin, Fallingham, Bullford and Monteith, like ravens in their black tailcoats waiting for the kill.

'All done,' said Lady Lamerton as she won the last trick.

'I must beg your forgiveness, Lady Misbourne, for having been such a poor partner,' said Ned.

'Not at all, sir. Luck was not on our side tonight,

but our losses were not so bad,' Lady Misbourne replied.

Their audience began to disperse, wandering back to their own tables. But Devlin and his friends made no move. The atmosphere hummed with menace. The tension felt drawn to breaking point.

'Lady Lamerton…Miss Northcote.' Ned's eyes lingered on Emma's for a heartbeat, before he made his apologies and took his farewell of Lady Misbourne. 'If you will excuse me.' He bowed and walked out of the room.

She watched with a sick feeling in her stomach as Devlin and his friends followed him.

'We did well, Emma,' said Lady Lamerton.

'Indeed,' she managed. But there was a panic in her ready to unleash, and a dread seeping through her bones over what might happen in that hallway. 'If you would excuse me for a few moments.'

'Of course, my dear.' Lady Lamerton gave a nod.

Chapter Twelve

Ned and Devlin stood facing each other in the corridor. The look on Devlin's face was one of ice-cold fury. Standing on Ned's side was Rob Finchley. Monteith, Fallingham and Bullford were sided with Devlin.

'You can dress yourself in fine clothes, Stratham. You can feign some pretence of manners and politeness. You can attend every opera, ballet and ball that you wish. But it cannot change what you are beneath. You are no gentleman. Not all the money in the world will ever buy you that.' Devlin's voice was quiet enough, but Emma heard every word.

Ned smiled as if Devlin's rant amused him.

'Playing whist with Miss Northcote...' Devlin sneered.

'Do you wish a game? I fancy my luck would return were I to play you.'

'I would not sully myself to sit at the same table.'

'Afraid you would deal me the winning hand, Devlin?'

Devlin's nostrils flared. Emma saw the muscle tighten in his jaw, saw his eyes darken with fury, saw the barely concealed violence. The air crackled with it. Devlin's fists balled. He stepped closer to Ned. 'You have gone too far this time, Stratham. Way too far.'

Ned still seemed relaxed, but she had seen him fight and she recognised that look in his eyes and the subtle shift in his stance. She knew what was about to happen. She knew Ned would annihilate Devlin. There would be violence, and blood and a fight that would not follow gentlemen's rules, here in Misbourne's home, before his family, before all his guests. Ned would best Devlin, but there would be a cost to it more than he realised.

She stepped closer as if about to pass them, brushed against Devlin and tipped the contents of her glass of lemonade down the front of his tailcoat and breeches. 'I am so sorry, Lord Devlin. Forgive me. I am too clumsy.'

It was enough to quench the fuse that had been lit…for now.

Devlin reacted by stepping away from Ned, glancing down at his soaked clothing.

His eyes met hers. There was nothing of his usual charming or smooth self. In their place was a cold promise that frightened her. He knew exactly what she had done. 'You have made a very foolish choice, Emma,' he said softly.

She sensed the movement in Ned. Saw the tightening of the muscle in his jaw. Stepped between him and Devlin to prevent what he was about to do.

But the two men glowered at one another. Two combatants. The fight was not over. It would never be over, but only grow worse in this escalating war of which Emma was a part.

'If you will excuse me, Miss Northcote...Mr Stratham.' Devlin walked away with his friends.

She saw the flick of Ned's gaze towards the door through which Devlin had just left. Saw the hardness in his eyes.

The breath shook in her throat. She could feel a slight tremble running though her body.

'Emma...' His voice was low, husky, quiet enough for only her to hear. He was looking at her with such strained control that she could see the storm of emotion that simmered beneath. He was looking at her as if he were committing her image to memory. She felt the surreptitious brush of his fingers against hers and glanced at where

Rob Finchley stood watching, before meeting Ned's gaze once more.

She knew that they did not have much time. Knew after what she had just witnessed what he would do if she told him that Devlin had blackmailed her to stay away from him and now meant to reveal her to Lady Lamerton. She could not tell him even to warn him.

'Ned,' she whispered with urgency, 'this is not Whitechapel. You must fight by different means here or be ruined.'

Their eyes held locked. They were still standing too close.

'Emma,' she heard Lady Lamerton's voice from the doorway of the drawing room and stepped away from Ned.

'If you will excuse me, Mr Stratham,' she said formally.

'Your servant, Miss Northcote.' He bowed.

She made her way back along to Lady Lamerton.

The violence she feared had not materialised, but that did not allay the worry churning in her stomach. She had the overwhelming sense that something had just happened between Ned and Devlin and herself, something from which there could be no turning back for any of them.

The Rubicon had been crossed.

* * *

Ned stood alone by the window of his bedchamber that night, staring out at the lamplit street and seeing nothing of it.

He could not stop thinking of that card game.

The choice had been between insulting Misbourne's wife in a very public way in her own home or sitting down at that table with Emma Northcote. And after all these years…after all he had striven for, on the brink of success, he had almost walked away. Almost spoiled the deal that was in the bag. And he knew why. He closed his eyes at that.

Emma had been right to stop him from walking away and delivering the insult. It was Emma who had saved the deal.

But to sit down at that table across from her… He had not thought it would affect him so. He had not realised the magnitude of his dilemma until that very moment. Now he understood it too well. He understood exactly what it was he had done two years ago.

This wasn't just about him. There were hundreds relying on him. Those who were nameless, faceless, voiceless, forgotten. How could he turn his back on them? But sitting down at that card table had not guaranteed their safety. Ned knew people and he knew the look of a man who had been pushed too far. He knew, too, how this evening must have looked to Devlin: that Ned was taunting him with a red rag, that he was rubbing his face in it. Every man had his limit and Devlin had reached his.

If Devlin knew what Ned felt for Emma, there would be nothing to stop him. He would strike. He would destroy Ned and all of his work.

What he felt for Emma.

He stared out of the window, knowing now what it was he felt for her, knowing, too, the impossibility of it.

Destiny had seen to that.

He slipped the token from his pocket and rubbed the worn surface between his fingers.

A man might gain the world and lose himself in doing so. A man's luck always ran out eventually.

Ned thought that maybe his time had come.

The weather turned cool and gloomy the next day. Within the little parlour at the back of Lady Lamerton's town house a small fire burned on the hearth to chase the chill from the room and banish the gloom. It did not banish Emma's megrim. Her head felt so thick with fatigue from a night sleepless with worry that she could not think straight.

She was on edge at every letter Lady Lamerton opened. Her stomach clenched every time the butler came into the room.

You have made a very foolish choice, Emma. Devlin's words rang in her head.

She knew what was coming and she had only herself to blame. Nor could she get Ned's expression out of her head. When he had looked at her across that card table, and afterwards, when his fingers had touched hers. Maybe she should have told him of Devlin's threat, but she had known what would have happened if she had done that. And now it was too late.

'You are wool-gathering, Emma. Have you reached the list of forthcoming events for the Little Season yet?' Lady Lamerton's voice interrupted her thoughts.

'Forgive me.' Emma forced her eyes to return to *The Lady's Journal* that lay opened on her lap. She turned the page and started to read aloud again.

It was almost a relief when Wilcott interrupted with the news that Lord Devlin had called and was waiting in the drawing room to speak to Lady Lamerton unattended.

'Very interesting,' said Lady Lamerton with a twinkle in her eye as she looked at Emma.

Emma could not smile. She knew what the dowager thought and how wrong it was. She knew what was coming and her blood was ice-cold with dread. The same dread that was pounding in her chest and tying her stomach in a knot. She should say something, utter some small warning to the dowager, it was only fair, but her mouth was too dry and the words would not form upon her tongue. By the time she opened her mouth Lady Lamerton was halfway across the room, smiling, happy as she made her way to meet Devlin.

The door closed with a click behind her, leaving Emma sitting alone.

She closed over the pages of the journal with bloodless fingers. Sat it neatly on the table and got to her feet with legs that were stiff and cold.

She thought of her father. She thought of her brother, Kit, and all that Lamerton might have achieved. She thought of Lady Lamerton's disappointment.

Only a few minutes passed before the dowager returned to the parlour and closed the door behind her. The expression on her face was unreadable.

Emma stood still as a statue. The beat of her own heart was loud in her ears as she met her employer's gaze and waited for the axe to fall.

'Devlin wishes to speak to *you*, Emma. Alone.' Lady Lamerton smiled.

Emma stared at her, shocked by this unexpected turn of events, not understanding what Devlin was doing.

'Says he has something very important to speak to you of...'

She could hear in Lady Lamerton's tone her romantic expectation, for, in the dowager's mind, why else did a gentleman call on a respectable lady at home and ask to speak to her alone?

Why else indeed?

'Well, off you go, my dear. You do not want to keep him waiting.'

'I do not.' She went to discover just what Devlin had in store for her.

Devlin was standing beside the white marble of the drawing-room hearth, with a dark look within his eye.

'Miss Northcote,' he said and then more softly, 'close the door behind you.'

She hesitated.

'Unless you have a wish for Lady Lamerton to hear our conversation...'

She closed the door with a quiet click. Came to stand before Devlin, facing him across the fireside rug. 'Does toying with me give you pleasure, Devlin? Tell her and be done with it.'

There was a silence as their eyes held.

'If I tell her, it would be the ruin of you, Emma.'

'Is that not what you want?'

'Contrary to what you think, it is not.'

'Then what do you want, Devlin?'

He smiled a strange sort of smile and glanced away.

Emma felt an uneasiness. 'Devlin?' she prompted softly.

That dark unreadable gaze met hers. He smiled again. This time his usual handsome charming smile, but it did not quite reach his eyes. 'I want you, Emma.'

All she could hear in the resounding silence was the hard thud of her heart.

She stared at him, unable to believe what he had just said. 'Is this some sort of jest?'

'I have never been more serious.' His voice was silky smooth and cold as ice. 'Marry me, Emma.'

'You cannot be in earnest, Devlin.'

The silence hissed loudly.

He stepped closer and, lifting a strand of hair away from her face, tucked it behind her ear in a gesture that was too intimate. 'You think I have no care for you?'

She stepped back out of his reach, trying not to show the horror slipping through her veins.

'And if I refuse you…?'

He stared at her as if he had not considered that as an option. Devlin was titled and rich, handsome and powerful. There could not be many women who would turn him down. Especially a woman in Emma's position.

'I think you understand the choice well enough. Marry me, or I will have to reconsider my position on speaking to Lady Lamerton.'

'You said you had a care for me. You said you did not want to ruin me.'

'Needs must,' he murmured in a voice that, for all its quietness, cut through her to make her shiver.

'More blackmail,' she said.

She thought of her father. She thought of her brother. She thought of Ned.

How could she marry a man that would think nothing of blackmailing a woman, a man who had organised that awful attack on Ned? Who despised another man simply because he had been born poor and made his own way in the world?

And how could she not, given what was riding on it?

'Do you understand what I am offering you, Emma?'

He was offering her a reprieve.

He was offering her a lifetime at his side and in

his bed. She would be his to do with as he pleased. A man who had led her brother to a gaming den and sat there and let him lose her father's fortune.

She looked into his eyes, and knew she could not do it.

'I recognise the honour you do me, Devlin, but...'

'You are refusing me because of him?'

'Lady Lamerton said you have always disliked him, even before my return. Why? Simply because he is trade?' she demanded.

'Is he?' Devlin asked. 'What do you really know of Edward Stratham?'

'I know enough.'

'Do you, really? Do you know he is a Whitechapel tough, Emma, in the guise of a gentleman? A wolf in sheep's clothing and one that means to eat you up for breakfast?'

'There is nothing between me and Ned Stratham.' *Any more.* Those small important words went unspoken. 'I will not be seeing him again, I promise you.'

'Somehow I do not believe you.'

'Then you are mistaken in what you believe.'

'In the same way I was mistaken in what I saw in Green Park?'

His words echoed in the silence.

'Believe what you will. Shall I fetch Lady Lamerton that you might tell her?'

'You really will not yield.' Not a question, but a statement.

She shook her head.

His eyes scanned hers. 'You fancy yourself in love with him,' he said slowly with the air of a man making a discovery.

'Do not be absurd!' she snapped, but felt the traitorous blush heat her cheeks. 'It is merely that, unlike you, I am not so prejudiced to judge a man on where he was born and how he came by his money.'

He laughed at that, but it was a hard, sarcastic sound. 'Such pride and principles, Emma. You really have no idea.'

'You think Whitechapel a hovel and Edward Stratham beneath a gentleman because of it.'

'No, I think Whitechapel a cesspit and Stratham the vilest of its villains.'

They stared at one another.

'He is not what you think him, Emma.'

'Whatever he is, Devlin, he is a better man than you.'

The words seemed to echo in the room between them.

'I am sorry that it has come to this, Devlin.'

'So am I, Emma.' He looked at her for a moment longer. 'So am I.'

He bowed and walked away leaving her standing there.

'Well?' Lady Lamerton was standing in the doorway, with her eyebrows raised in expectation of the news.

'He asked me to marry him.' Emma felt dazed.

'I knew it!' Lady Lamerton crowed. 'Many congratu—'

'I refused him.'

'You did *what*?'

'I refused him,' she said and sat down in the chair.

'Are you run mad, Emma?'

'Perhaps,' she said. And maybe she really was. She had refused Devlin and stoked his ire. And for all her justifications and moral high ground, she knew they were all just excuses. She knew the real reason she was jeopardising her position and risking Lamerton's assistance in locating Kit. She felt numb from what she had just done.

'Devlin is heir to an earldom. He is one of the wealthiest men in London. His mother is from a banking dynasty. And you are—' Lady Lamerton stopped herself just in time and sat down, clasping a hand to her forehead.

'A penniless companion,' Emma continued for her. 'Whose family name has been marred by scandal.'

'You are a young lady who holds too much against him, is what I was going to say.'

'Both are true,' Emma admitted. 'But given the part that Devlin played in my family's history, he and I really would not suit.'

'I think, Emma Northcote, that is a decision you will regret. And if it has anything to do with Edward Stratham then you would do well to think again. I saw you talking to him at Lady Misbourne's card party. Using him to bring Devlin to offer was one thing. But this is something else. Rest assured Stratham will have his eye on bigger fish than you, Emma, I thought you understood that. I am not unaware that young women are attracted to men who are, how shall I put it—rugged, untamed and rather dangerous. A rogue can set a lady's heart a-flutter. I was once young myself, hard to believe though it is. But trust me when I tell you that whatever else you might imagine, what Stratham wants from you is not marriage.'

* * *

Ned stood by the empty grate of his study in the mansion house in Cavendish Square. Rob sat in one of the nearby wing chairs.

'You'll have heard the whisper that Devlin proposed marriage to her and she turned him down,' Rob said.

Ned gave a nod. 'I've heard.'

'Because of you?'

'She loathes Devlin. She blames him for what happened to her brother,' Ned said, not answering the question. He let the words lapse into silence. 'I'm going to tell her. The truth. Of who I am.'

'Why?' Rob stared at him as if he had had a brainstorm. 'Have you gone mad?'

'I love her, Rob.'

His friend stared at him. Had never heard him say such a thing about anyone ever. 'I did not realise.'

'Neither did I. Until I had to sit down at that card table opposite her.'

'Hell!' Rob whispered.

'Yes,' agreed Ned. 'It was. It is.'

'If you tell her, you're risking everything.'

'Misbourne is signed in. He won't pull out.'

'And the rest of it? Everything else?' Rob shook his head. 'You could lose it all.'

'Then so be it. I am done with the charade. I cannot marry another woman. Nor can I sit back and watch her marry another man. I love her!'

'But if you tell her…you will lose her.' Rob looked in pain.

'And if I don't tell her, how can I be with her?' Ned shook his head. 'How can I ask her to wed me?' He knew what his friend was saying was right, but he knew, too, he had to do this. 'She has a right to know the truth. To make her own informed choice whatever that choice may be. I will not hoodwink her. I will not lie to her. Let the cards fall where they will.'

Rob glanced away. 'At the end of the day, she's one of them, Ned.'

'She's not what you think her. She's one of us, too.'

Rob shook his head. 'Have you thought about this? About what it will mean?'

'I have thought about nothing else for days.' He looked at his friend. 'I'll tell her tonight. There's a dance at Colonel Morley's. Lady Lamerton's name is on the guest list.'

There was a small silence during which Rob digested the enormity of what was about to happen. His face was pale.

Ned took the piece of paper from the top drawer

of his desk and handed it to Rob. 'You've been a good friend to me, Rob. Whatever happens to-night…you'll be all right.'

'Thank you, Ned.' Rob slipped the cheque into his pocket.

Ned lifted the bottle of gin from where it sat ready on the drum table between them. Poured them both a drink. 'Dutch courage,' he said and sat down in the leather wing chair opposite Rob's.

Rob accepted the drink with thanks. He hesitated, then asked, 'You said that you love her. Does she love you?'

'I believe she thinks she does.'

'I'm sorry, Ned. I never imagined…'

'Neither did I.'

They lapsed into silence. Sipped their gin from the engraved cut-crystal glasses in the splendour of the mahogany-lined study.

Because they both knew that Emma Northcote would not love him once he told her the truth.

Emma heard the stifled whispers about her and Devlin the minute she walked into Mrs Morley's ballroom and knew that it had been a mistake to tell Lady Lamerton. She ignored the gossip and concentrated only on Lady Lamerton's conversation with Mrs Morley, Mrs Hilton and Lady

Routledge. But the too-frequent flicker of their eyes across the ballroom warned her. She glanced across the room and saw Ned and his steward talking to Mr Dale.

The footman passed Emma the note surreptitiously as he brought the tray of lemonades across to the party of ladies. Slid it into her hand beneath the cover of tray as he offered the drinks.

She opened her mouth to ask who had sent it, but the footman was already weaving his way through the crowd. With the sudden race of her heart she thought that she already knew the answer.

Emma slipped the note straight into her pocket before anyone could notice. Her eyes found Ned's across the room. She felt the power of all that bound them together squeeze her heart, felt it twist and tug against the chains in which they were trying to confine it, felt it roar for release.

Inside her pocket the letter seemed to quiver and vibrate. She knew whatever he needed to tell her must be important for him to risk sending a note.

Their eyes held a second longer across the ballroom. His expression was intense, serious, watchful. His brows lowered. She felt her stomach tighten with worry.

She turned away, bent her head to Lady Lamerton's ear and whispered her excuse.

Lady Lamerton did not stop listening to the story Lady Routledge was relating. Barely glanced in Emma's direction. Gave a nod of her head to Emma to show that she was giving her permission.

Emma glanced at Ned again. Then she made her way from the ballroom.

Out in the hallway she stopped behind a large display cabinet and retrieved the note. The paper quivered in her hand as she opened it and skimmed her eyes over the few dark strong words written there. Her eyes widened. Her heart gave a stutter.

The note was not from Ned, but she did not even question the instruction written within it. Emma slipped it into her pocket and, with a deep breath, stopped a passing footman and asked him the way to Colonel Morley's study.

Chapter Thirteen

'The development of the site has started just as you required,' Mr Dale was saying by Ned's side.

Ned watched the footman slip Emma the note. Watched her pocket it with equal stealth. Her eyes moved to his. Held, before she turned away and whispered something in Lady Lamerton's ear. Dale's voice was still talking.

'Good. Keep me informed of its progress. If you will excuse me, sir.' Ned's eyes followed Emma as she left the ballroom.

The curtains had been drawn within the study. A single branch of candles had been lit, its soft flickering glow the only point of illumination in the darkness.

He was standing by the fireplace, staring into

the blackened grate, a half-empty glass of brandy in his hand. Waiting.

'Devlin,' she said and closed the door softly behind her.

'A word, if you please.' Ned collared the footman behind the column in the corner of the ballroom, the same footman who had passed Emma the letter, and pressed a Bank of England five-pound note into the man's palm.

The footman pocketed the money. 'For that you can have any word you like, sir.'

'The name of the person who gave you the letter for Miss Northcote.'

'That would be Lord Devlin,' said the footman. 'Saw him heading for Colonel Morley's study.'

Ned pressed another banknote into the man's hand and set his untouched glass of champagne down on the footman's tray.

Ned's face was grim as he made his way from the ballroom.

Within the dimly lit study Devlin made no move. He did not so much as glance round.

Emma walked closer.

'You said you had news of Kit.'

But Devlin still stood where he was. Gave no reaction, as if he had not heard her. Not until she walked right up to him. She could see the way he was staring at that grate, with such a dark brooding look upon his face that made her dread that the news was the worst.

'Devlin?' she said softly.

He finished the rest of the brandy from the glass in a single gulp. Set the crystal down on the black-marble mantelpiece with a thump. And finally turned to face her.

'I lied,' he said.

She stared at him. 'I do not understand... Why would you send me that note saying—?' She stopped as the sinking realisation hit her.

'I see you do understand after all.' He did not smile. Just looked at her. 'That I wanted to get you here alone.'

'How despicable of you to use my brother's name to do so. Especially after your role in his downfall.'

Guilt flashed across his face. He looked away. And when he looked at her again there was angry cynicism in his eyes. 'No one put a pistol to his head and forced him to the gaming tables.'

'Maybe not. But he was a boy and you and the

others, men of the world that he looked up to, you led him astray.'

'Kit was no child, Emma. He was a foolish man, but a man nevertheless. A man who made his own choices. And one who has to face the consequences of his actions. As all men do, Emma.' There was guilt in his eyes, heartrending and obvious before he hid it once more. 'You cannot blame others in his stead.'

'I am not a fool. I know my brother was not blameless. He gambled the money, after all. But you and the others let him stake his last penny. You let him stake it all. You should have stopped him, Devlin. You were supposed to be his friends!'

'We were his friends.' He gave a cold mirthless smile. 'We still are.'

'Spare me the pretence.'

'As you insist.'

The silence pulsed between them. His eyes held hers with cool determination.

'If you will excuse me, Lord Devlin.'

'I am afraid I cannot allow you to leave.'

His words stroked a shiver of fear down her spine, but she regarded him with disdain to hide it. She calmly turned to walk away, but Devlin's hand caught her arm and held her firm.

'You should not have turned me down, Emma.'

She felt the dread slip into her blood like a single splash into a still, deep pool. She looked pointedly at where his hand held tight to her arm, then raised her eyes to meet his, feigning a calm confidence she did not feel.

'What are you doing, Devlin?'

'Whatever I have to.' His voice was soft in contrast to the hard determination in his eyes.

Fear drummed loud and insistent through her heart. She tried to pull free, but Devlin's grip was unbreakable. She ceased her struggle and conserved her energy. Faced him boldly. 'What do you mean to do, Devlin?'

'Save you from Stratham.'

She gave a cynical laugh and shook her head.

Devlin did not smile. His expression was cold, un-amused, frightening.

She glanced again at where his fingers were locked around her arm. Then looked into his eyes with derision. 'And *you* lambast *him* for not being a gentleman?'

'Sometimes the end justifies the means,' he said quietly and pulled her close. So close she could see the striations in those dark eyes of his and feel his breath warm against her cheek.

Her heart was thudding so fast she felt sick. She

tried to resist, but he was too strong. 'Do not do this, Devlin,' she said. 'Please.'

He swallowed, glanced away, then back again. 'Just a kiss, Emma. Nothing more, I swear. Do not be afraid.'

He slid an arm around her waist. As he shifted his grip, she managed to break free and began to run, but he grabbed her shoulder and wrenched her back to him.

'No! Do not!' She fought him, but he was too tall and powerful.

He pulled her into his arms once more, holding her there as he looked into her eyes. 'I am sorry, Emma,' he said before his mouth closed over hers.

She kicked against him, fought harder. But none of it made any difference. All she knew was his overwhelming strength and the smell of his cologne and the possession of her mouth by his and a raging fear and anger at what he was doing.

She was struggling so hard she did not hear the opening of the study door. But Devlin did. He released her so suddenly that she stumbled back against the fireplace wall. She stayed there, her spine pressed against the wallpaper. She was breathing hard, shaking with shock and panic and fight. Devlin stood where he was facing her, his eyes cool and focused upon hers. But she was not looking at Devlin, only at Ned standing there in the door frame. So silent and still and with a calmness that was a promise of something very different. He stepped across the threshold, closed the door with careful control. The quietest of clicks in the silence.

Only then did Devlin glance over his shoulder and the expression on his face changed, so that she saw it for the mask it was. Shock flitted in his eyes.

Ned's eyes held hers for a moment. She saw them drop to the neckline of her dress and only then did she realise that it had been ripped in the struggle. Something changed in Ned's eyes. Something so dark and dangerous slipped into them that it frightened even her. His gaze swivelled to Devlin. She had thought him powerful when he had fought Black-Hair in the Red Lion, and that night in the Botanical Gardens. But this was different. Everything of his stance. Everything of his being. The very air around him. All of it shimmered with a dark deadly promise. The quiet before the worst thunderstorm. The promise to death.

'Ned.' It came out as a whisper. Husky. Broken. Part relief, part plea. 'Stop. Wait. It is not...'

But her words died away as she realised that

Ned was not listening. He did not shift his gaze from Devlin. And she knew in that moment that Devlin's fate was sealed. That Ned was going to kill him.

Devlin must have known it, too. He faced Ned. Tense. Moving ever so slightly. Ready to meet what was coming. Ready to fight for his life.

She saw the subtle gearing of Ned's body, the ripple and movement of muscles, the slight shift in balance, the honed deadly focus.

'You've crossed a line from which there's no retreat, Devlin.' Ned's voice was low and quiet. 'You may do what you wish to me. But Emma...' He shook his head.

Devlin stood his ground, a barrier between Emma and Ned. 'I will not let you have her, Stratham.'

'Step away from her.' Almost a growl.

Devlin shook his head. 'I'll see you in hell first.'

There was a moment, just the tiniest moment of silence. And then everything exploded with a speed and violence and fury as Ned ran full tilt at Devlin. The collision seemed to reverberate through the room, but Ned kept on going, the force of the momentum carrying both men across the room to land with an almighty thud on the floor. Then fists were flying, punches landing hard, feet kicking, as the two men struggled and rolled and fought. A round mahogany table was thrown over, its crystal decanter and glasses crashing in a mess of broken glass upon the hearth. One minute Ned had the upper hand, the next it passed to Devlin.

'Stop it, both of you!' Emma cried, but it was as a whisper against the roar of a hurricane. She could not even begin to get close.

Both scrabbled to their feet. The white of their shirts, cravats and waistcoats was speckled red with blood. Devlin's lip was burst. Ned's cheek was cut and the sleeve of his jacket was torn.

Devlin moved in fast, landed a blow in Ned's stomach, then, as he doubled over, Devlin let loose a series of punches to his face.

Ned staggered back.

Devlin came after him, with his fists.

Ned smiled. Caught Devlin's fist as it came again. Crushed it.

Like some kind of arm-wrestling game, the men's eyes held and their bodies strained motionless. Then Ned twisted Devlin's arm and slammed him hard face first into the wall. Devlin began to crumple, but Ned grabbed him by the neck, hauled him upright, put a hand round his throat. And squeezed.

'Ned!' Emma ran to him. 'Stop! Think what it

will mean, for us both, if you kill him.' She laid her hand on Ned's arm and could feel how hard he was breathing. 'Please, Ned. Do not do this.'

He slid his eyes to Emma's and in them was such love and fierceness that it took her breath away. Their gaze held for a second longer, then he gave a nod and returned his focus to Devlin.

'If you ever touch her again, I *will* kill you. Regardless of anything else that is between us. Do you understand?'

Devlin's face was turning purple. He managed a gesture of agreement.

Ned released him and Devlin sagged, catching his breath.

'Oh, Ned,' she whispered and only then realised that she was crying.

'Emma.' Ned swept strong arms around her, moving her away from Devlin's reach.

He gathered her to him, held her. She could feel the hard beat of his heart, feel the strong pump of his blood, feel all that was between them; this warrior of a man who had saved her so many times; this man who would kill to protect her.

She tilted her face up to his, looked into his eyes, as his hand cradled the back of her head.

'I am done with pretences. Things cannot go on the way they are, Emma. We must speak in earnest.' He caressed a thumb against her face. 'But not here, not now. First things first. We need to get you tidied up and back to the ballroom before your absence is noticed.'

She nodded, knowing he was right.

But then the door opened and there was a woman's gasp and a man's guttural exclamation of shock. And she knew it was too late.

It was only when the study door opened to reveal Colonel and Mrs Morley, and Lady Lamerton, surrounded by Devlin's tight circle of friends, that Ned saw the expression on Devlin's face and understood what was *really* happening. What Devlin's intention had been. That Devlin had expected the little party's arrival, but not Ned's. He shot a hard glance across at where Devlin stood.

Emma was in Ned's arms, her face wet with tears, the shoulder of her dress ripped, her hair tumbling awry from its pins, her lips kiss-swollen. She looked like a woman who had been ravished. And even if she had not, it would not have mattered.

'Good God, Stratham!' exclaimed Colonel Morley. 'You have ruined her!'

'No,' Emma began to say. 'It was—'

Ned knew what he was going to have to do. His

arm tightened around her waist, his eyes met hers in warning. He kissed the word she would have uttered from her mouth, hard and lusty, then released her and moved to stand in front of her, facing the men and shielding her from their view.

'Guilty as charged,' he said. 'If Devlin had not interrupted us…' He glanced at Devlin.

The viscount's eyes were dark and filled with loathing. But there was nothing he could do. Nothing he could say.

'Emma?' Lady Lamerton stared at her.

Ned's eyes met Emma's again, willing her to understand and say what she must.

Emma looked at Lady Lamerton and gave a nod.

'Well, sir,' proclaimed Colonel Morley, puffing himself up. He began to walk to Ned, but stopped when he saw the look on Ned's face. Morley glanced around him for support. 'Miss Northcote is a gently bred lady. There can only be one honourable outcome to this thoroughly dishonourable affair.'

'There can,' agreed Ned. It was either him or Devlin. And there was no way he could give her up to Devlin; not when he felt about Emma as he did and most definitely not after what he had just witnessed. 'I will wed her.' His face was grim.

Morley gave a nod.

There was a silence. He saw the dark expression on Devlin's face and those of Monteith, Fallingham and Bullford. Colonel Morley looked in a state of righteous indignation. Lady Lamerton looked shaken.

And Emma—she maintained a quiet dignity and poise, but he could see the relief in her eyes that it was him and not Devlin.

And something twisted in his gut, because he knew she would not be relieved if she knew the truth.

Destiny mocked him with her cold irony.

And he stood there and said nothing, to protect the woman that he loved.

'I warned you, did I not?' Lady Lamerton was in high dudgeon and Emma could not blame her. She had lost one companion. Now she was about to lose another. And Emma knew that Lady Lamerton had been good to her. Had treated her with honesty and kindness and ignored the scandal surrounding her family.

'I am sorry,' Emma said. And truly she was. For Lady Lamerton. For Ned. For her father and Kit. For all of this mess that had erupted around her.

'I knew he was no good.'

Emma swallowed. Pressed her lips firm so that she would not say the words she wanted to, to defend Ned. That it was not Ned with whom she had fought, but Devlin.

Ned looked the villain when all he was guilty of was saving her.

'Although none of us realised the depths he was capable of plumbing.' Lady Lamerton swallowed and her distaste for the words she was about to say made her purse her lips. 'To force himself upon a woman…' She shook her head. 'But I suppose that bad blood will always out. He is no gentleman, but a rogue in truth.'

Emma closed her eyes at that.

'What were you doing alone with him in the study in the first place? You told me you were for the ladies' withdrawing room.'

'I received a note,' she said slowly, hating the fact she could not tell the truth of what had happened in that study. 'It said he had information on the whereabouts of my brother.'

Lady Lamerton's face tightened to a scowl. 'A dirty trick worthy of only the lowest villain.'

'It was indeed.' Except that low villain was a viscount and one of the *ton*'s inner circle of disreputable gentlemen, not Ned Stratham.

'Thank God that Devlin arrived! I dread to think the state you would be in had he not.'

Emma looked away, unable to bear hearing Devlin so praised and Ned so vilified.

'At least he realised he could not wriggle out of doing the honourable thing. No doubt he would have tried had not so many gentlemen been present.'

Emma could have smiled at the irony of that statement. If they only knew... If it had come to fighting, Colonel Morley, Devlin, Monteith and the rest of them would not have stood a chance. She thought of Ned's grip round Devlin's throat and knew that Ned would have killed him had she not intervened.

When she gave no response, Lady Lamerton misconstrued her silence. 'I know it is difficult, Emma, but you are going to have to marry him. You are completely ruined if you do not. And there is nothing I or anyone else can do to change that. I have asked Colonel Morley and Devlin *et al.* to remain silent on the matter.'

Emma wondered if they would. She knew how much Devlin hated Ned. But after what he had done... She shuddered at the awful memory.

'And I have told Mr Stratham in no uncertain

terms he is not welcome here. Damnable cheek of him to think he could call this morning.'

Emma thought of having had to sit with Lady Lamerton in the upstairs parlour and keep on writing the dowager's letter while Wilcott informed Ned that neither Lady Lamerton nor Miss Northcote were at home to him. 'What harm would there have been in admitting him?'

'What harm indeed?' Lady Lamerton snorted.

'We will be married come Friday.'

'Let us just hope that Mr Stratham has learned enough about being a gentleman to keep the appointment.'

Ned Stratham was the most honourable man Emma had ever known. It killed a part of her to have to sit quiet and let him be so unjustly maligned. 'He would not—' she began.

'Indeed?' Lady Lamerton raised her eyebrows and looked down her nose. 'I do believe that when it comes to Mr Stratham any dishonourable thing is possible.'

Ned waited until the door closed behind his man of business before he spoke.

'It is done. All of the business and the project with Misbourne will always be taken care of.'

Rob gave a nod. 'You did good for this city, Ned Stratham.'

'It wasn't my money.'

'It was. You took an acorn and grew it to an oak whose branches stretch far beyond the petty privileged drawing rooms of Mayfair and the already-filled pockets of those that run the gaming clubs. That is where it would have ended otherwise. You can't deny that.'

'Maybe not. But it doesn't alter the truth of where the money came from.' Ned looked at the gleam of the bare mahogany desktop before him.

There was a silence.

'I didn't think he had it in him to stoop so low.' Rob sneered as he said it.

'Desperation pushes a man to his limits.'

'He went too far.'

'Way too far.' He closed his eyes at the memory of Devlin forcing himself upon Emma. It was an image that would remain branded on his brain for ever. And one that made his teeth clench and his fingers curl to fists and a cold fury of protective anger pulse through his blood.

'The irony is that Devlin only had to wait an hour. One hour more and I would have had a chance to speak to her. One hour and she would have known the truth. Of who I am, of what I am.

He wouldn't have had to say one word to her, or lift so much as a finger against her.'

Rob swallowed. 'Are you going to tell her before Friday?'

'Were I to do so, do you think there would still be a wedding?' He raised an eyebrow. 'Will she willingly marry the man who destroyed her beloved brother? The man who won his fortune, and was responsible for her family's ruin?' Ned gave a tiny shake of his head. 'If I tell her now, she will not have me. And if she doesn't marry me she's ruined.'

The two men looked across the room at one another with serious eyes.

'God help you both,' said Rob.

'Amen to that, my friend,' said Ned. 'God help us both, indeed.'

Chapter Fourteen

The morning sunlight flooded into the carriage, sending silver shimmers through the silk of Emma's dove-grey dress. Outside she could hear the song of a blackbird over the rattle and roll of the carriage wheels and the clatter of horses' hooves. Inside, the silence was loud. Neither Lady Lamerton nor Mrs Tadcaster sitting opposite uttered a word. Not until the carriage came to a halt outside Ned Stratham's mansion house, in Cavendish Square.

Then Mrs Tadcaster dabbed at the tears in her eyes and said, 'Oh, Emma, I can only be glad your poor mama is not here to witness your disgrace.'

'I wish with all my heart that she were here. And as for disgrace, you blame the wrong person,' Emma said with a fierceness that made the woman look at her as if she had just been slapped.

'I wish you well, Emma,' Lady Lamerton said.

'Thank you.' Emma's eyes held the older woman's with affection. 'For everything.'

Lady Lamerton gave a nod of encouragement. 'Are you ready?'

Emma gave a single nod.

Lady Lamerton smiled sadly and only then signed to the footman through the window to open the carriage door.

There was a gentleman waiting in the hallway of the house. It was only when he glanced round that Emma recognised he was her father.

'Papa?' She hurried the rest of the distance to reach him.

He smiled a small half-smile.

'You look very well, Papa.' The gaunt hollows had gone from his cheeks and his complexion held a good healthy colour that had been missing for too many of the previous months. She glanced down at his fine expensive tailoring.

He pressed a little kiss to her cheek. 'You look beautiful, my dear.'

She felt a lump form in her throat. Felt the tears threaten in her eyes. 'I did not know if you would come.'

'To my own daughter's wedding?' He looked at her, his eyes soft and kind. 'Even if the circumstance is not that which I would have chosen.'

'They told you what happened?'

'Stratham told me. Owned all of the blame. I cannot pretend to like it, Emma.'

'It is not what you think. *He* is not what you think, Papa.' She softened her voice to a whisper that no other would hear. 'I love him.'

He gave a nod. Smiled again, a sad smile. He held out his arm to her and she placed her hand upon it. And together they walked to the open drawing-room door. They paused. Stood there and looked at the room within.

It was the wonderful scent that hit her first, sweet and beautiful as a summer day that now seemed so long ago. She smiled as her eyes moved over the bloom of violets that decorated the room and the white-and-pink ribbon garlands that festooned the chandeliers. Violets. The significance of his choice of flower was not lost on her. The lines of chairs were filled with guests. A black-robed priest stood with his back to the fireplace. Ned, with Rob Finchley as his best man, waited patiently before him.

Ned was smartly dressed in his midnight-blue Weston tailcoat, a pristine snow-white shirt, white cravat and white-worked waistcoat. His hair was clean and shining gold as it fluttered in the slight breeze from the drawing-room window. He was tall and broad-shouldered. A man strong enough to best Devlin and every rogue in Whitechapel. Strong enough, too, to bear the villainy that belonged to another.

He had saved her from Black-Hair in the Red Lion and from two drunken sailors in the dark midnight depths of a lonely Whitechapel alley. He had saved her from Devlin's lecherous attentions. Now he stood there, saving her from ruin. Giving up his chance to marry a title and gain the acceptance and connections he could never otherwise have. She hated to think he might be doing this against his will. Stood there, frozen for a moment. Knowing that once she stepped across that threshold her life was going to change for ever.

'Emma?' her father whispered.

And just at that moment, Ned glanced round, his gaze meeting hers, and holding, so strong and true and honest that it vanquished all her doubts. She felt a surge of love for him, this man who was the other side of herself. As if it were he and she together, as one against the world. It was as if she had been destined to be his from the very first moment she had seen him.

'Emma,' her father said softly. 'Ned Stratham may be many things of which I cannot approve.

But I do believe that he loves you and that he will care for and protect you more than any other.'

She looked into her father's kind old eyes and saw love and wisdom.

'I am proud of you, Emma. And your mama would be, too.'

Tears pricked in her eyes. The lump grew bigger in her throat. She smiled and squeezed his arm with affection.

'Thank you, Papa,' she whispered, and let him lead her into the drawing room, to the priest and Ned Stratham.

Ned stood with his eyes facing front, aware in every possible way of Emma standing by his side. Aware, too, that she would not be looking at him like that if she knew the truth of him. She would not be marrying him.

She was wearing the dove-grey silk dress that complemented the warmth of her smooth tawny skin and made her eyes look such a soft velvet-brown and her hair shine like a raven's wing. She was the most beautiful of women, inside and out. She was intelligent and filled with vitality and a capacity to survive and to find happiness. Despite all that she had endured she was not embittered. Her heart was the biggest he had ever known. And she had given it to him. A man who had known no love in all of his life. The man who was unwittingly responsible for all that had hurt her.

Ned sensed her nervousness, saw the uncertainty in those beautiful dark eyes that met his. Felt the chill of her fingers when her father gave her hand into his and thought he would have done anything to undo what had happened to her, to save her from every hurt, every hardship.

He smiled to reassure her. Closed his hand around hers to warm it. Gave it a little squeeze that said everything was going to be all right.

She smiled at that and he saw something of her tension ease.

Then the priest started talking, reading from the small, battered, black-leather prayer book in his hand.

Ned blocked out all emotion. Got through the lines of ceremony until it came to the bit he was worried over. He tensed. Clenched his jaw. Waited for the priest's words.

'If any man can show any just cause, why they may not be lawfully joined together, let him now speak, or else hereafter for ever hold his peace.'

The silence hissed loudly.

Ned waited for it to break. Felt every muscle in his body tense and straining, ready for the interruption. Waited for the crash of the front door opening, for the sound of Devlin's voice announcing why Emma should not be allowed to wed him. And all that would follow.

But nothing happened.

He felt a measure of both relief and guilt.

The ceremony progressed and he said the words *I, Edward Stratham, take thee, Emma Northcote, to be my wedded wife*, and the rest of it and slid the heavy gold band on to her finger.

'Those whom God hath joined together, let no man put asunder…I now pronounce that they be man and wife together.'

She was his. His wife before God and the law.

He took her in his arms and he kissed her, this woman that he loved.

And it was the best moment in all his life. And it was the worst moment, too. Because he had saved Emma from penury and from scandal. He had married the woman that he loved. And in so doing he had proved himself the most despicable of all men.

The wedding breakfast was lavish. No expense had been spared. Champagne and a banquet of the finest foods, exotic and presented as if for a queen. The dining room was decorated with more violets. The tiny blooms had been woven into a garland across the mantelpiece. Every wall sconce held a tiny violet spray, and in the centre of the long dark mahogany dining table was a line of small crystal vases each containing yet more violets, interspaced with pineapples. Emma wondered how anything so lavish and thoughtful could have been arranged at such short notice.

A string quartet in the corner of the room played Vivaldi in gentle tones during the meal. There was a large white sugar creation just like those beloved by the Prince Regent, a sculpture showing a palace with sugared violets cascaded down its walls—it was both beautiful and secretly meaningful to both her and Ned.

There was the finest pork, beefsteaks and pot-roasted chicken. There were eels in wine sauce, baked soles and buttered crabs. Dishes of potatoes in garlic and cream, French beans and mushrooms. There was whipped syllabub and orange-and-almond cheesecake. And a selection of rich cakes. And on the table amidst such lavish finery, sitting like a brass farthing in a pile of gold sovereigns, a dish of lamb chops and fried potatoes.

The guest list was small but significant enough to give the illusion that the marriage was not a forced and scandalous affair: the Earl and Countess of Misbourne, Viscount and Viscountess Linwood, Mr and Lady Marianne Knight, The Marquis and Marchioness of Razeby, Lady Rout-ledge, Mrs Hilton and a few other tabbies who were there as a favour to Lady Lamerton, as well as Lady Lamerton herself. Mrs Tadcaster and Mr Finchley. And her father, of course. But no one who had any connection to Devlin or any other of the men who had been her brother's friends. And Emma could only be glad of that.

It was a wedding arranged as if it truly was a love match, and in a way, for Emma at least, it was. She could almost pretend that nothing had occurred in Colonel Morley's library. Espe-cially when she felt the warm clasp of Ned's hand around hers. And even more so when his eyes met hers and she felt the power of what bound them together pull and tighten and strain.

That he wanted her as a man wants a woman, she did not doubt. Even in her innocence she could feel the thrum of desire that was between them. That he loved her, she believed that, too. The way he looked at her, the way he touched her, was as if he felt all for her that she felt for him. Being here with him felt like coming home. It felt right. Like this was always meant to be. Yet she was aware that he was marrying her to save her and afraid that had not the incident with Devlin happened Ned would never have offered for her.

At last the celebration came to an end and their guests gradually drifted away to leave only Emma and Ned.

They stood alone in the dining room, the warm golden light of the late afternoon casting rainbows through the crystals of the magnificent chandelier, burnishing the darkness of her hair with a blushing halo and turning the soft brown velvet of her eyes golden. Dust motes drifted to sparkle in the air between them, making the moment seem all the more magical.

She was his wife. His *wife*. Captured through false pretences. But right or wrong, he could not regret it. He loved her. He wanted her. He would give her the world.

He reached a hand to capture a stray curl and rub it between his fingers.

'You are beautiful.'

She smiled. 'I bet you say that to all the serving wenches.'

'No,' he said. 'Only to you, Emma Stratham.' No longer Northcote, but Stratham, and that meant much to him.

'I am very glad to hear it.' She smiled again.

And so did he.

'Thank you, Ned. For the violets and the sugar palace with its doves. For making today so special. For making them believe it is a love match.' She glanced away, but he saw her sudden discomfort. 'I know that you were forced to marry me and that—'

He touched his fingers to her chin and guided her face gently to look into his. 'Do you think me a man to be forced against my will?'

'I think you a man who cares about my honour.'

Their gazes held, warm and intimate and honest.

'Emma, I have wanted to marry you since Whitechapel. That morning by the old stone bench when I said we should talk when I returned...'

'You were going to propose marriage?' She closed her eyes but not before he saw the glitter of unshed tears in them.

'Emma,' he said softly, 'you hold my heart in your hands. You always have. You always will.' From the pocket inside his tailcoat he slipped the white velvet box and gave it to her.

She opened the box to see the gemstone violet necklace that lay inside.

'Oh, Ned!' She clasped a hand to her mouth. The petals were amethyst, the centres, diamond and the leaves, peridot and emerald.

'The sweetest of all flowers,' he said.

Her eyes met his. 'You remembered.'

He crooked his rogue eyebrow, making her smile while their eyes shared the memory of that day and all the love that had since blossomed.

'Thank you, Ned.'

He fastened the necklace around her neck, watching how the gem violet sparkled and glittered against her *décolletage*.

'I love you, Ned Stratham.'

Their mouths came together, kissing, showing with touch and taste and tongue the truth of their words. Her arms slid beneath his tailcoat to wrap around his waist. Their bodies cleaved together, ready for the union for which they had striven so long.

He scooped her up into his arms and carried her up to bed.

Ned plucked the pins from her hair, unravelled it, to let it hang long and loose down her back and over her shoulders.

'You have such beautiful hair.' He leaned in to inhale it.

Lifting a strand, he ran it between his fingers as if it were as precious as smooth polished jet. 'Like ebony silk.'

'As dark as yours is fair. We are the opposites in so many ways.'

He glanced away into the distance, a sombre look in his eyes. 'So many ways,' he echoed in a low voice.

'But opposites that were made to counterbalance each other. Together we are whole.'

His eyes returned to hers and held with such love that it made her want to weep. 'You speak the words that are in my heart,' he said softly and brushed the back of his fingers against her cheek.

He smiled and cradled her face in his hands, kissed her with such exquisite sweetness. He was her man, her husband, her love. She wanted him, wanted this union that would seal their marriage and bind them together for ever.

He slid his hands round to the back of her bodice, unfastened the line of pearl buttons with unhurried fingers that tantalised every time they brushed against the skin beneath. The dress began to gape, slipping from her shoulders. She shrugged it off, letting the silk slide down over her legs to land at her feet. She reached to him, slid her fingers over his lapels, then opened his tailcoat, intent on easing it from his shoulders, but the fit was so perfect that she struggled.

He peeled off the tailcoat and threw it to land on a chair. His white-worked waistcoat followed.

She unfastened the knot of his cravat, unwound the length of pale silk and let it flutter to the floor, like a ribbon in the wind.

The open neck of his shirt exposed the bare skin beneath, making her blood rush all the faster. She stared at it, fascinated by the sight of him. Reached tentative fingers to pull his shirt free from where it was tucked into his breeches.

He shed the shirt, pulling it over his head and dropping it to the floor.

'Oh, my!' she whispered.

He smiled.

She reached for him, trailed her fingers light as feathers against his muscle-contoured chest, marvelling at the difference in their skin tones. Her fingers were golden olive against his paleness. She touched more boldly, exploring the unknown landscape of a man's body. She had thought him a warrior fully clothed, but half-naked, with his chest exposed like this, he was truly magnificent, all hard honed muscle, all long strong limbs, all power and strength. There was not an inch of softness in that granite sculpted frame.

The sight of him dried her mouth and sent her heart thudding in a frenzy. The feel of him made her shiver, made her thighs burn hot, sent urges and sensations and needs to throb through her body.

Her fingers trailed lower. Over the ribbed muscle that banded his stomach and abdomen. Over the thin line of scar that the tough's blade had left.

'It has healed well.'

'Thanks to you.'

The memory of that night whispered between them.

She felt the ripple and clench of muscle beneath her hand, felt how hot his skin burned beneath the chill of her fingers. She dipped a finger into his belly button and heard him catch his breath. Emma saw the blue fire burn all the hotter in Ned's eyes and realised how much she was affecting him. It was a heady feeling of power.

She laid her hand flat against his chest, covering his heart so that she could feel its beat, strong and steady as the man himself. Looked up into his eyes, the most amazing eyes in the world, that smouldered with a desire that was all for her.

He moved his hands slowly, stroked her shoulders before he untied her petticoats. The layers of linen fell away unnoticed. His gaze dropped to her lips and lower again to the swell of her breasts over the tight-boned stays, his focus so hot and hungry that she felt it as clearly as if he had touched her there. Her heart was thudding like a horse at full tilt, her blood rushing so fast to make her dizzy. Her breath was ragged with need and desperate anticipation as his eyes rose once more to hold hers.

Every second was a torture of waiting. Every second was an ecstasy of wanting.

She was desperate to feel the skim of his fingers against the exposed skin of her breasts, to feel his mouth hot and hard upon hers. But he did neither of those things. Instead, he turned her around and gently collected the lengths of her hair to bunch them over one shoulder while he unlaced her stays with firmer hands than any lady's maid had ever done. She felt them fall away, heard them tumble and land with a thud on the Turkey rug beneath their feet.

She trembled with anticipation. Wanted him to touch her. Needed him to take her. Maybe she was brave because she had her back to him, or maybe it was just her own boldness. Regardless of the reason, she slipped the straps of her shift from her shoulders and let its transparent fine silk slide down her body.

She stood there, naked save for her stockings and shoes. Stood there, waiting, until she felt the caress of his fingers against the bare skin of her back, felt their trail all the way from the top of her spine right down to its tip, sending shimmers to tingle in unexpected places. The breath escaped her in a soft gasp.

She felt his smile, felt the warmth of his breath against her shoulder blade, making her shiver, before his lips touched a kiss there.

Her breath came faster and harder.

His arm slid around her waist, pulling her closer. His palm splayed flat against her belly, anchoring her to him, her spine to his chest, her buttocks to the hard muscles of his thighs. His body was so different from her own in every way, yet it felt like they had been moulded to fit together.

She felt him caress her hair again, felt him kiss the nape of her neck, the touch of his lips to that one small place making her gasp louder.

'Oh, Ned,' she whispered as she closed her eyes and angled her neck to invite him to more.

He understood what she wanted, nuzzled kisses against her neck, her throat, did something wonderful with his tongue where her blood pulsed strongest and hardest.

His hands slid slowly up over her belly. 'You have the softest skin,' he said as he stroked higher to her stomach.

Her breathing quickened, the rise and fall of her chest only making her all the more aware of those strong manly fingers that rested so close. Of their slow teasing caress, that was making it hard to think. Of their promise to reach the destination she craved.

'Ned…' she whispered his name like a plea.

He nibbled kisses to her neck and finally moved his hands to capture both breasts.

She gasped a long low sound of pleasure and moved her arms behind, holding to him, her fingers gripping tight to the muscle of his lower back.

His weighed her breasts, stroked them, wove magical patterns upon them, but never let his fingers stray to their pebbled peaks.

She arched, driving her breasts all the harder into his hands, needing that touch, demanding it. And he finally obliged.

When he plucked her nipples for the first time her knees went weak, her fingers clung all the tighter to stop herself falling. She groaned aloud.

His strong arm snaked again around her hips, his hand covering her sex. And then those warm long strong fingers began to move slowly, enticingly.

She groaned again, opened her legs and felt him touch her there in that most secret of places. He did not stop. One hand between her thighs, the other going between her nipples. He pleasured her without mercy. Pleasured her until she was gasping, until she was writhing, until she was begging…

Only then did he stop and still his hand over her heart as she had done to him. 'Emma.' Her name was a whisper on his breath. 'My love.'

Her fingers moved to find his, clutched his hand to her heart all the tighter. 'My love,' she echoed.

She turned in his arms and looked up into his eyes.

He swept her up and, carrying her over to the bed, laid her down upon it. He stripped off her stockings and her shoes. Stripped off the rest of his clothing.

She stared at the sight of him fully naked, at the huge wonder that made him a man, and felt a *frisson* of fear. But then he covered her body with his own, somehow taking his own weight so that he did not crush her, and she forgot the fear.

He kissed her and all she knew was her love for him and that she wanted him with all that she was.

He moved between her legs and showed her the full wonder of the love that was between them. Together they reached a place she had not known existed. A place of exploding stars and magic and ecstasy and all of it because she loved him and he loved her. A union not just of bodies but of hearts and souls. A union that could never be undone.

And in their loving she knew that they were meant to be together. That they had always been meant to be together. Destined to love. This man who was her heart and her soul and the very breath in her lungs.

His body merged with hers. And together, at last, they were as one.

Those first heady days following the wedding were the closest Ned would ever get to heaven. He wanted it to be special for her. He wanted to show her just how much he loved her. They spent every moment together; spent many of them in bed, making love. A cocoon in which only the two of them existed and there was nothing and no one else. No past. No future. Only the now, only their love.

Everything about her brought him joy. Her smile, her laughter, the sound of her voice, the way they could talk for hours and never grow weary, the passion that burned between them. He treasured each moment. Savoured it and etched it carefully on his memory so that he would never forget. As if he ever could. But even then there was a part of him that knew the transience of those moments. They were a dream. The world would not for ever stay locked outside. Reality was already knocking at the door. He did not want to let it in. But in the end he had his responsibilities, which could not be ignored. Reality knocked and Ned answered.

Chapter Fifteen

It was late by the time Ned got home from the meeting with his man of business. Emma had not eaten, but waited for him so that they could dine together. She dismissed the footmen and butler. Lifting a covered plate from the heater in the middle of the table, she brought it over to him.

'I had cook make your favourite,' she said as she lifted the lid from the plate of lamb chops and fried potatoes. 'And…' She smiled and produced a bottle of porter, unstoppered it and poured it into a new silver tankard which she set before him.

The candlelight reflected on the symbol engraved upon it, a diamond shape enclosed within a circle. He traced the outline with his finger and felt his heart expand to fill the whole of his chest and the threat of tears in his eyes.

'The symbol from your lucky token,' she said softly.

He slipped the token from his pocket and laid it down next to the tankard. 'You remembered it exactly.' His voice was low and gravelled with the strain to control all that he felt for her.

'How could I forget, when it brought us together? Do you remember the night you dropped it in the Red Lion?'

'I remember.'

She placed her hand upon his and followed the trace of the pattern. 'What does it mean?'

'It is a gaming token, Emma.' He had never told anyone in his whole life. But he told her. 'And it is the only connection I have to my mother. She slipped it into my pocket when she left me at the Foundling Hospital. It was the only gift she ever gave me.'

Her hand closed around his, holding him, supporting him. 'I am sure your mother would not have given you up lightly.'

'She didn't. I was four years old when they took me. I still remember her, and that day.'

Emma's eyes glittered with tears, but what he saw in them was not pity but compassion.

'She gave you to the best life she could. And the Foundling Hospital raised you well, Ned.'

He gave a wry smile. 'They tried, but I was a troublesome child. I ran away, time and again.'

'Why? Where to?'

'To Whitechapel and its streets.'

'To seek your mother?'

'Whitechapel was my home, not some other un-known place on the other side of town miles away from everything I knew.'

'That is why you can relax there. Because it really is your home,' she said softly.

He gave a nod. 'And despite all, I miss it. And I never want to forget. It is dirty and gritty, but it is the real world in a way that this place can never be.'

'This beau monde of wealth and luxury. But you are right, when one has seen men and women and children fight for survival and savour the small-est things in life...' She shook her head. 'If there is nothing of substance beneath, the sparkle and glitter soon tarnishes.'

As ever, she put into words everything that he felt.

She glanced again at the token where it lay on the table. 'It must be the most precious thing in the world to you.'

'It was, Emma. But now I have something much more precious.' He raised their joined hands and kissed her fingers. 'I have you.'

'Oh, Ned,' she whispered as she leaned down

to him and pressed her mouth upon his. 'Do you know how much I love you?'

He closed his eyes. Felt his chest tighten with the strength of emotions that fought and vied within him, love and guilt and shame. She loved him, but he was not the man she thought. If she knew who he was... That he was not her saviour, but her nemesis—the man who had caused all of her troubles. That he had married her under false pretences. That by loving her, by continuing to allow her to blindly love him, all the while not knowing the truth of who he was, what he was, was making a mockery of all that was between them.

It felt like the shadows of guilt were gathering, to whisper from the corners of his mind, taunting him for the charlatan he was.

It felt like the dark secret was starting to devour him from the inside.

Every night Ned loved her. And it was wild and sweet, and afterwards when they lay together in the big four-poster bed in their bedchamber her heart thumped in unison with his. And everything had a brilliance and a wonder, enough to overcome all else, so that she could only marvel at this love that was between them and think that beside it everything else was as nothing. And he stroked her hair and he looked deep into her eyes, and told her that he loved her, again and again, as if it would be the last time he would ever have the chance. Only then did that look appear in the back of his eyes; that veiled worry he thought she could not see.

She cupped a hand against his cheek. Looked deep into his eyes and tried to reassure him. 'We have each other, Ned. Nothing else matters, does it?'

He smiled and kissed her again. Kissed her until she forgot the question she had asked.

It was only later, much later, that she realised he had given no answer.

Ned stood by the window of his study looking out over the Square—the magnificence of the mansions, the neatly kept gardens whose shrubs and trees and flowers cost more than families in Whitechapel had in a year to live. Luxury and splendour and riches beyond what he once would have been able to imagine. It should have made him happy. And once it had, before he had realised the cost that went with it. Now every time he looked at it, it reminded him of the truth. Not that he needed any reminding. The knowledge was like a burr in his side, needling him, never giving him peace.

He sipped the gin from the glass in his hand, the juniper-berry smell filling his nose, the heat hitting the back of his throat and travelling all the way down to his belly. But it did not ease the weight of the burden that sat upon him, nor deaden the pain of the knowledge.

Dishonour. Deception. The accusations whispered in his ears and would not be silenced. Not now. Not ever. He had to tell her. He knew that. She had a right to know the truth. She deserved to be treated as an equal and not patronised as a simpleton or a child. But how did a man tell the woman he loved that he was not the man she thought him? How did he tell her without hurting her beyond belief?

He would lay down his life to protect her. Take every hurt upon himself to save her. How could he then plunge a knife in her heart?

They were wedded. Bound together in law. For ever. She could not just walk away from him. Move on with her life. Meet someone else. Marry. All of those options were gone.

A part of him told him to keep quiet, to shoulder the burden himself. If she never knew, she would never be hurt. And the temptation was great. So great. She had been through so much, he could not bear to hurt her. And yet, if he did not tell her, that only made him all the more despicable.

He had to tell her. For honour. For integrity. Because everything she thought him was a lie.

He had to tell her. It always came back to that. He had to tell her, because he loved her and it was the right thing to do.

Ned had spent a lifetime doing the difficult thing. He had never shied away from doing what he had to. Right or wrong. No matter how hard, no matter what it cost him. Until now.

Now, standing here, with Emma asleep in their bed upstairs, he did not know if he could do this hardest of things.

Shafts of rich autumn sunlight spilled through the window of the private sitting room that adjoined Emma's bedchamber in the mansion house in Cavendish Square. It shone warm against her back where she sat at the little bureau, writing the letter to her father. The nib was a heavyweight silver and so smooth and precise that it glided across the thick white paper without so much as a snag or a scrape. The ink flowed fine and even without a blob. She dipped the pen into the inkwell again and signed her name. She glanced over at where Ned stood by the window, staring out with a hard, distant look in his eyes.

'You have something on your mind.' She did not blot her letter, just left it to dry. Walked over to him, concerned at his preoccupation that seemed to grow only worse as the weeks passed.

'I always have something on my mind.'

'You work too hard, Ned.'

'Not hard enough,' he said and picked up the battered little oval miniature painting that sat upon the side table, the gold leaf of the frame worn smooth. Her eyes moved to the beloved miniature.

'It is a portrait of my brother, Kit, painted not six months before he was taken by Devlin and Hunter and the rest of that rakish gang to lose my family's fortune.'

'You blame Devlin for what happened that night.'

'I blame all of them. They took him to that gaming hell. They let him gamble his everything.'

'Maybe they chose the lesser evil.'

'What more could he have lost? Tell me, for I do not know.'

Ned said nothing.

'They should have stopped him. True friends would have stopped him.'

'They were not the ones who took his money.'

'Even so,' she said, unconvinced by his words.

There was a small silence.

Ned returned the miniature to its place on the table, but his eyes lingered upon it. 'Do you ever think of the man that your brother played against?'

'Oh, I think of him,' she said with feeling. 'To win a fortune is one thing. To take the coat from a man's back, his home, his dignity, to take his all…I do not know how the villain can live with himself.'

'Maybe he can't.'

She gave a cynical laugh. 'Somehow I doubt that. I bet he could not believe his luck when he saw my brother sit down at his table. A rich young fool ripe for the fleecing.'

'Perhaps. But he could not have realised the far-reaching repercussions of his actions that night. He could not have seen the family behind the rich young fool. Or the wreckage caused to their lives. He could not have known the fool had a sister or how much she would suffer.'

'It does not excuse him,' she said.

'It does not,' he agreed. His gaze returned to the miniature. 'You do not look so very like him.'

'I have the likeness of my mother, God rest her soul, whereas Kit favours our father.'

'But there is something of a similarity in your eyes.'

She smiled at that. 'My mother always said he had mischievous eyes.'

'So do you,' he said, but he did not smile. Instead, his focus remained fixed on the portrait, the expression on his face closed and unreadable.

'Kit was a rascal of a child. Always dragging me into scrapes and adventures. Teasing me, when he grew older, in the way only a brother can do.'

'You are close to him.'

'I am,' she said. 'Although not so much in the months before he left. I could not seem to reach him then. No one could. He was…troubled over what had happened.' She glanced away at the memory of those difficult days.

'You love him very much.'

'He is my little brother. There has not been a day when I do not pray he is safe and that he will come home. I swore a vow to my mother as she lay on her death bed that I would find him. It is why I did not wait for you, Ned. Why I had to accept the position with Lady Lamerton. Her son works in Whitehall—he has connections—and is trying to trace Kit as a special favour to his mother. But as the time passes and there is still nothing… Sometimes, I fear that perhaps…it is in vain.'

She saw something tighten in Ned's jaw. 'Sometimes hope is all that keeps us going,' he said. His fingers still held Kit's portrait. His eyes stared at it with an expression that was brooding and dark. As if he were not seeing her brother's portrait, but something else all together. As if he were locked in some other world of worry and unhappiness and danger. 'My connections may be of a different class to Lamerton's, but I swear to you, Emma, I will do all that I can to find your brother.' But he did not look at her, only at the tiny painting still gripped in his hand.

She gave a nod, knowing that if any man could find Kit it was Ned. And yet, knowing, too, that things were not right with him.

She took the miniature from his fingers. Set it upon the table once more. And took his hand in hers.

Her thumb caressed his. She looked up into his face. 'What is wrong, Ned?'

He did not look at her for a moment. His gaze still lingered on the miniature. There were shadows beneath his eyes, a tight tension within his jaw.

'Ned?' she prompted softly.

His eyes met hers at last and what she saw in them was a glimpse of something tortured, something at which what she had seen in Misbourne's hallway after the card game had only hinted.

He shook his head. Looked away again.

'You are not yourself.'

'I'm not. I'm someone else all together.'

The words disturbed her, reminding her of the taunt Devlin had thrown at her— *What do you really know of Edward Stratham?* Unease whistled like a cold draught through her.

'You are frightening me, Ned.'

'I would not have you frightened for all the world.' He looked at her then. Raised their joined hands to his lips, pressed a slow kiss to her knuckles. 'You're right. Forgive me, Emma. I have too much on my mind these days.' He smiled a smile that did not quite touch his eyes.

'Ned Stratham, what am I going to do with you?' she said softly and pressed a tender kiss to his rogue's eyebrow.

He took her in his arms and held her. Where her cheek lay against his chest she could hear the beat of his heart and feel the warm protection of his arms around her.

'That is the question I ask myself, Emma,' he murmured against her hair. But there was nothing of jest or tease in his words. He pressed a tender kiss to the top of her head and he held her, just held her as if he were afraid to let her go.

Each night he loved her. Loved her as tenderly as if it were for the first time and as passionately as if it were the last. He took her with gentleness and reverence. He took her with urgency and fire. Driving into her, hard and fast as if this act purged away all of the worry she saw in his eyes. She wanted him. She needed him. And she knew, too, that he needed her.

They strove together, lost in the union of their souls and hearts and bodies. And in those blissful hours in the darkness there was nothing save each other and the power of their love.

They moved together, matching each other's rhythms, knowing each other's needs. They moved together until she was crying out his name, until she was gasping her pleasure and exploding in a thousand sunbursts of wonder. Again. And again.

And afterwards when she lay in his arms, he cradled her against him, and stroked her hair and kissed her forehead, but the worry was back in his eyes. He held her until she slept, but often she woke in the night to find the bed beside her empty and Ned standing by the window staring out at the black night sky.

There was something he was not telling her. Something that was badly wrong. She just did not know what it was or how to reach him. And she began to wonder if maybe there had been something more in the battle between Ned and Devlin than just class.

Chapter Sixteen

Ned sat at the great mahogany desk in his study. The house was still and quiet, sleeping as the rest of London did beneath the dark cover of night. But Ned could not sleep. Not tonight, or last night or the nights before that. He doubted he'd ever be able to sleep again.

He had lit no candles. The hearth was empty and black. The moon lit the room in silver shadows, gleaming against the dark polished wood of his desk enough to show the single sheet of paper that lay upon it. But Ned did not need the light to read the words that were written upon the paper. He knew each one by heart. They were etched upon his soul, words that could never be unwritten.

He heard the faint creak of the floorboard, saw the flicker of light beneath his door a second before the study door opened and Emma appeared.

She was wearing her nightgown. One hand clutched a shawl around her that was slipping from her shoulders. The other held her candlestick and the half-burned beeswax candle that flickered within it. Her hair hung long and mussed from their earlier lovemaking, dark and beautiful as ebony. She had not taken the time to find her slippers, but stood there, her bare feet a pale golden olive against the dark polish of the floorboards. There was a look of worry on her face that made his heart ache all the more with love for her.

He lifted the sheet of paper from the desk, folded it closed within his hand. Rose to his feet and moved to meet her.

'Could not sleep again?' she asked.

He shook his head.

She glanced at the paper within his hand, then back at his face. Walked to stand before him.

'Something is wrong.' She sat the candlestick down on the desk.

'Yes.' He did not deny it.

'Will you not tell me, Ned? I might be able to help.'

'You might.'

'I'm worried about you.'

The silence hissed loud and strained.

'Tell me, Ned,' she said. 'You know you have to tell me.'

'Yes,' he whispered. 'I have to tell you.'

He looked into her eyes, eyes that were dark and warm and tender, and filled with love. And he savoured that moment, all of her love and all of what she was, all of the wonder of what was between them. Love. Something he had never known throughout a lifetime. Something so glorious and powerful and strong he never could have imagined. He loved her with all that he was, and because he loved her he knew that he would do the thing he had feared and dreaded more than any other thing in his life. More than hunger and starvation. More than beatings and the icy fingers of night that stole lives from slumbering forms in doorways and alleyways. The hardest thing in the world. And the easiest.

'I love you, Emma.'

'I know you do. And I love you, too.'

He smiled at that. Took the words and the sound of her voice and the gentleness in her eyes and stored those most precious of treasures in his mind for the dark days ahead.

'I love you,' he said again. 'Always remember that. It is the truth, no matter what else you might think.'

'I would never think anything else.'

But she would. His eyes held hers, clinging to these last precious moments. He reached a hand to her face, stroked his fingers against the softness of her cheek. And she nestled her cheek against his fingers and placed her own hand upon his and held it there.

He leaned forward, breathed in the scent of her hair, placed one final kiss upon her lips.

'I am sorry, Emma. I would give everything to undo what you have suffered…everything to change what I did.'

'Ned,' she said softly, the little worry line etching between her brows. 'Tell me what it is that you have done.'

He took a breath, gave the slightest of nods.

The seconds stretched, but he felt almost relief in knowing that the time was now, that the tortuous waiting was over.

The paper was clutched tight between his fingers. He opened it out, smoothed the creases from it and offered it to her. And in so doing he pierced his heart with a dagger made of words that had destroyed a family's world.

She took the paper and held it closer to the candlelight to read the words penned upon it.

'I do not understand,' she said. 'This is Kit's

vow, for our home and my father's fortune, for everything that he owned…' She shook her head, frowned. 'I do not understand, Ned,' she said again. He saw the moment that she did, the cold horror of realisation that crept across her face.

She raised her eyes to his.

'Yes,' he said in answer to the question he saw in them, the question that could not form upon her lips. 'I am the man your brother gambled against and lost. I am the man who took your family's fortune.'

She stared at him as if she could not believe it. But she did believe it. He could see it in the horror and pain and shock in her eyes. He could see it by the way the paper in her hand began to tremble.

'You?' she whispered.

'Me,' he confirmed.

'You are the man who ruined my brother… The man who destroyed my family.'

He said nothing.

'No.' She shook her head as if to deny the truth. 'No,' she whispered the word again. Scrunched her face as if in pain.

'Yes, Emma,' he said. 'I would give anything to deny it and say it was not me, but I cannot.'

'Oh, God!' she gasped and clutched a hand around her stomach. 'Oh, God, please, no!'

He reached a hand to steady her, but she pulled back from his touch as if scalded, seeing the monster he was for the first time. 'Do not touch me!' she whispered fiercely.

He held his palms up. Stepped back to give her space.

Her breath was ragged. She pulled her shawl around her. Leaned back heavy against the desk. Stared at the floor, but he knew she was seeing nothing of what was around her only the horror within her mind. 'This cannot be happening.'

Ned had said the same thing to himself a thousand times.

'How could you do it?' she asked.

He said nothing. Just swallowed.

'You knew all along who I was.'

'Not all along. Not at the start.'

'You are lying! Everything between us has been a lie!'

'I have never lied to you. I never will.'

'I do not believe you!'

He said nothing.

'You knew who I was. You tricked me. You made me love you.'

He stood there and accepted the wrath he deserved.

'How could you do it, Ned?' she asked again.

This time louder, more of a cry. This time the question was not of what he had done to her, but what he had done to her brother. 'Tell me what happened that night.'

He glanced away. But she grabbed hold of his coat lapels with white-knuckled fists and stared up into his face. 'Tell me,' she said. 'I have a right to know.'

He nodded. She had every right to know.

His voice was low and empty as he relayed a very brief sketchy outline. 'A group of rich young aristocrats had taken to coming over to Whitechapel, to Old Moll's gaming den in Half Moon Alley. They liked the play there. It amused them to come amongst us and see how the other half lived. To dice with living on the edge. Devlin, Hunter, Bullford, Fallingham and your brother. They were drinking deep and playing deeper.

'I did not set out to fleece him, Emma. He...' Ned thought back to that night. To Kit Northcote. And the truth of what had happened. He looked into Emma's eyes, eyes that had something of that foolish young arrogant man who was her brother. The brother whom she loved. The brother whom she had cherished. And he thought he would do anything to save her, to take her pain upon himself. 'He was neither skilled nor lucky with cards,' he finished.

'He was young and foolish!'

'Yes.'

'He was out of his depth in such a place.'

'Way out.' She had no idea.

'And yet you took everything from him.'

'I took all he had staked upon the table.'

'You did not have to do that.'

'Yes, I did, Emma,' he said quietly.

But she did not understand. And she never would if he could help it. She shook her head.

'Because you wanted to be a gentleman?'

He said nothing.

'Because five thousand pounds were not enough that you must have even more?'

Silence.

Her fingers loosened their grip upon his lapels. She pushed him away. Hard. With disdain. 'You bastard!'

He made no defence. Because he was a bastard in every sense of the word.

She moved away, perched on the edge of the winged chair before the dark empty hearth, the small distance like miles between them. A gulf that would never be breached.

* * *

The silence seemed to echo and hiss in the room around her. She wanted to strike out at him, to hit him, to yell and scream and cry and weep. But Emma did none of those things.

She sat in that armchair and her mind was reeling. Part of her unable to believe what Ned was telling her, part knowing that it was the truth she should always have guessed. So many thoughts tumbled through her mind, terrible possibilities making themselves known, although beside the magnitude of what he had just told her she did not know why they should be so very terrible at all. She felt as if he had taken a knife and cut her heart from her chest.

'You should have told me,' she said.

'I tried.'

'Not hard enough.'

'No.'

She placed her knuckles against her lips, pressed hard to control the words, to control everything that was whirring with such fury and shock within her.

'Or maybe I was just part of your plan.'

'With you there was no plan.'

'No?' She felt flayed and betrayed, raw and weeping. She could not think straight, could only feel a gaping hurt and a roaring anger and endless uncertainty.

'What were you really doing in Whitechapel, Ned? Those nights you came to the Red Lion to eat when you lived here, in a mansion in Mayfair, with the finest of chefs to cook for you?'

'I've already told you the answer to that question.'

'And if I do not believe you?'

He said nothing, just held her gaze, strong and silent, but she saw the tension that clenched in his jaw.

'Your steward, Rob Finchley, does he know the truth? Of who you are? Of who I am?'

'He was in the crowd at Old Moll's that night.'

'How you must have laughed together at my naïvety.'

'We did not laugh.'

'He did not accompany you on your trips to Whitechapel.'

'No.'

'And you just happened to find me the Red Lion?'

'I just happened to find you, Emma.'

'Why there?'

'Because it was far enough away from my old haunts that I would not be known.'

'You expect me to believe that your being in the same chop-house, in which I worked, was just coincidence?'

'I don't expect anything.'

There was an ache in her chest, a churning in her stomach, a bitterness in her throat. All of her fears rose up, vile and goading her to the worst of imaginings.

'You took everything my family owned. Why not me? Was I just the final prize to be added to your winnings? That you could have everything from my brother: his money, his home, his position in society. That you could have even me, my heart, my body, my life? The ultimate revenge against a people you hated. Because we were rich and you were not. Because you wanted to taunt him. Because—'

A lightning of emotion flickered in his eyes. He moved then. Fast. Closed the distance between them in a breath. Grabbed her by the top of her arms. Pulled her up from the chair and stared down into her face.

'Never!' he said and the whispered word shook with the force of controlled emotion. 'I did not know who you were, not until Lady Lamerton introduced us. And, yes, I should have walked away from you then, once I knew, and God knows

I tried. Hate me all you will, Emma. Despise me. Loathe me. But never ever think that I would use you so poorly. I may have nothing of honour. I may not be a gentleman. I may have been a thief and a beggar and a rogue in my life. But never doubt that one thing.' He held her eyes with a fierceness that belied the quietness of his voice.

She could feel the press of his fingers around her arms.

She could hear the tremor in his breath and feel the extent of the control he was exerting over himself.

There was a pain and rawness in his expression that shocked her almost as much as his revelation had done. And an utter sincerity.

Their gazes held, locked in a torture. The seconds stretched in agony. Until he suddenly released her. Backed away. Sat down in the winged chair opposite and stared at the empty hearth.

She was shaking so much that she dropped down into the chair beneath her.

Only the clock punctuated the silence between them.

She did not know what to say.

She did not know what to do.

Her whole world felt like it had exploded around her. Love, hope, trust, a future—all gone in one fell swoop. She did not know who he was. She did not even know who *she* was any more. And the thought that thrummed through her head constantly, insistently, was that it had been Ned there that night in the gaming hell with Kit. The enormity of it obliterated all else.

'You promised to find him, when all along it was you who drove him away,' she said almost to herself.

She got to her feet.

He glanced up at her, the look in his eyes touching the rent in her soul.

She bled. The pain was piercing. It engulfed everything, everything, so that she could not think, only feel and what she felt was agony. An agony that was tearing her apart. An agony she could not bear. She needed to be alone.

'I cannot be with you, Ned Stratham.' Not right now. She could not look at him. Could not speak another word to him. Only shook her head and turned and walked away.

Ned sat in the study for the rest of the night. This was a beating like none he had ever taken. A wound that would never heal. But he did not allow himself the luxury of self-pity.

He locked his emotions away. Thought through

the steps of what must be done. The only things he could do. Nothing would make this right. But then he had always known that. He could bear her hatred, but her hurt—that was a lot harder. But Ned would bear it. He had borne much in his life. Things that would have made men like Devlin and Kit Northcote quail. He would bear it and know he had done all that he could. And that knowledge at least was something.

Ned did not drown his sorrows in gin. He did not stare aimlessly down on to the darkened street. He went to the desk and he found the papers that he needed. Then he sat there in that expensive leather-winged armchair, in a room that was bigger than any house he had lived in. He waited for the night to pass, and the dawn to come.

When daylight finally came he washed and dressed himself in fresh clothes. And with the papers safely stowed in his pocket he slipped out of the front door.

Emma stood at the edge of the window of her bedchamber and watched Ned's figure disappear along the road.

She was still wearing the nightdress and shawl. Her feet were bare and tinged blue from the cold.

Her head was pounding from a night filled with a storm of misery and disbelief and nothing of sleep. Her eyes were swollen and heavy from weeping. But she did not weep now. She was empty. Numb.

She stood there even after he was long gone.

She stood there because she did not know what else to do.

What *did* a woman do when she discovered that the man she loved was not who she thought him? That everything upon which their life and love was based was a lie?

I have never lied to you. I never will.

Maybe not in words. But he had deceived her just the same. And she did not know where they went from here. Because she did not know what it was she felt for him any more. Because she was his wife and he her husband and nothing could change that.

He was her husband.

He was her lover.

And he was the man who had taken her family's money.

She thought of her father having to give up their family home in Berkeley Street and move to a string of increasingly cheaper accommodations. And of the slow ignoble decline to obscurity.

She thought of Kit's running away, of what that

had done to her mother, of first Spitalfields and the consumption that had taken her mother's life. And then Whitechapel, and the dockyards and the Red Lion.

'Kit.' She whispered his name in the quietness of the room, as if he would hear her. *Kit*. In her mind she saw his face, the laughing eyes that were so like her father's, the grin that he wore when he teased her.

No one put a pistol to his head and forced him to the gaming tables. Devlin's words sounded again in her memory. She tried to close her mind to that truth, just as she had always done, but this time there was something in the way and the door would not shut completely.

She closed her eyes and it was not her brother's face she saw, but that of another man. A face that was not refined or beautiful. A face that was rugged, with its own harsh handsomeness. It made the hole in her chest, where her heart had been, ache. But it could not change who he was and what he had done. It only ridiculed it all the more, even if what had brought them together really had been just a cruel trick played by fate. Did she even believe that?

The memory of the pain in Ned's eyes, the force of emotion pulsing through him when he had denied her accusation. A man on the edge. She believed him. But it did not change anything. He had kept the truth from her. And, in a way, that deception hurt more than what it was he had been hiding.

She thought of packing the little travelling bag with which she had arrived here. Of returning to her father.

She thought of turning up at the Red Lion and asking for her old job back. Of earning enough to rent a room with another girl.

But in the end she knew she could do neither of those things.

So Emma went through the motions and she washed and she dressed, and she waited for Ned to come home.

It was six o'clock in the evening when Ned returned to the Cavendish Square mansion.

The sky was grey outside, the light already beginning to fade even at this early hour. Rain pattered softly against the bow window, trickling down the panes of glass like tears. She sat on the Queen Anne armchair by the fire in the drawing room, pretending that she was reading a book, pretending that she had not been pacing and anxious.

'Emma.' He came to stand by the fireplace. She could see the sparkle of raindrops where they sat upon the shoulders and sleeves of his coat, not yet absorbed by the wool. His hair was damp, swept back as if he had raked his fingers through it.

The silence was strained.

'Where have you been all day?' He looked tired. There were shadows beneath his eyes. And she already knew that he had stayed the long night in his study.

'To see my man of business. And a few other people, too.'

There was the slow tick of the grandfather clock in the corner of the drawing room and the clatter of horses' hooves passing from the road outside. It felt everything that her relationship with Ned had never been—awkward, uncomfortable. The accusations she had thrown at him last night still hung between them, jagged and sharp, still cutting.

'I don't expect you to forgive me, Emma.' His eyes held hers for a moment and her heart began to pound and the pain was back, making a lump in her throat.

'I am not sure that I ever can.' She had to be honest with him.

The silence hissed.

He nodded, then looked away. Took some papers from his pocket, legal papers by the looks of them.

He sat them down on the table by her side. 'Everything is yours. To do with as you see fit. My only request is that you keep the businesses running. My man of business, Mr Kerr, will call upon you in the morning to explain the details. As far as everything else, if there are any problems, if you are ever lost, go to Rob Finchley in South Street. He will help you.'

'You are leaving?' Her heart contracted small and tight with shock and too many other confused emotions.

'I didn't think you wanted me to stay.'

The silence roared

Stay! her mind whispered, but her tongue held the word captive and would not let it escape. Her fingers were gripping so hard to the book between them that her knuckles shone white. Pride was all she had left. Pride and the pretence that he had not flayed her raw, that his leaving was not hurting her all the more.

That moment was the longest of her life. Stretched precarious. Painful. Cutting to the bone.

'Goodbye, Emma.'

Do not go! The plea pounded through her head.

Whispered through her blood. But she sat there and said nothing, and let him walk away.

The drawing-room door shut softly behind him. She heard the quiet murmur of voices, then the open and close of the front door.

He could not be gone. So quickly. In the space of a few heartbeats.

She ran to the window, saw the familiar figure walking away down the street. Alone. No carriage. No travelling bag. Nothing save the clothes he was wearing. The darkness of his tailcoat disappearing into the grey gloom of the evening.

He could not really be gone, she thought again. Just like that. With nothing. He had to be coming back, for his clothes, for his possessions. Didn't he? But there was a terrible empty feeling in her chest because she knew, absolutely knew, that Ned was not coming back.

The book slipped from her fingers to thud on the Turkey rug below.

She did not stoop to pick it up. She did not even know its title or a single word that was written within its blue-bound covers. The rain lashed harder against the windows like fists beating to gain entry.

And a little part of Emma's soul shrivelled and died.

Chapter Seventeen

Emma received Mr Kerr in the drawing room at ten o'clock the next morning.

He was a small tidy man, with short grey hair neat around a balding pate. His age was middling, but his eyes were sharp and honest. Everything about him exuded competence and efficiency.

His gaze moved to the documents that still lay untouched on the table where Ned had left them.

She met his eyes, held them. 'What are you here to tell me, sir?'

'Mr Stratham had this house and the other property, and all of his assets, moved into a trust. He then gave the trust into the management of Mr William Northcote, with the stipulation that it be all for the "separate use" of his daughter, Mrs Emma Stratham. It effectively means that legally you own it all.'

'But he is my husband, and as such, everything that I own is his.'

'Not in the case of the trust. It is one of the few devices that may be used to circumvent certain particulars of the marriage property laws.'

She looked at him as what he was saying sunk in. 'I own it all?'

'Down to the last farthing.'

She frowned. 'You mentioned another property.'

'A house in Berkeley Street. Number nineteen, as I recall.'

The house in which she had been born and grown up.

'Mr Stratham purchased it almost two months ago.' He slipped a pair of spectacles to his nose and peered down at his notes. 'On the thirteenth of September.'

A few weeks after she had come to work for the Dowager Lady Lamerton.

'I have taken the liberty of producing a summary of your financial situation, which I thought would be of assistance.' He passed her a single-page document. 'I think you will find everything to be in order, but if you have any questions or instructions please do not hesitate to contact me.' He removed his spectacles to the safety of his waistcoat pocket, put his papers away in his leather folder and rose to leave. 'I will bid you good day, Mrs Stratham.'

Emma's eyes moved over the sheet, scanning the figures written there. 'A moment, sir.'

He stopped and looked at her with polite enquiry.

'These figures…the sums in the bank accounts… They cannot be accurate.'

'I assure you, madam, they are entirely correct.'

'But…' Her father had been wealthy enough, worth five thousand a year. She totted up the balances of the bank accounts. 'One hundred thousand pounds?' she said weakly. It had to be an error. It made no sense.

'Your husband is a very shrewd businessman. There are not many men who could grow an investment twentyfold in the space of two years.'

She stared at him. 'How did he do it?'

'A nose for knowing what to invest in and when.'

'He spoke of "businesses."'

'A variety throughout the East End—a vinegar manufactory, a dye house, several timber yards, a cooperage, a large brewery and a distillery. He also owned several mills—for wool, cotton and silk. Investments in the East and West Indies, and in the Americas. Shipyards in Portsmouth. And then there were the London Docks with all the warehousing, storage and loading operations located there. As I said, a very shrewd gentleman.'

She sat very still.

'So it seems,' she said and thought back to the conversation that had passed between her and her father on the day of her wedding, specifically to that one subtle slip. She understood it now, although she had barely noticed it then, let alone understood what it meant—that her father knew that Ned Stratham was the man who owned the dockyard and provided employment to him and all those men in the warehouse.

'Are there any other questions with which I may help you, Mrs Stratham?'

'No, thank you.' She let the butler show him out before untying and opening the uppermost legal document. It was the trust deed that Mr Kerr had spoken of.

Her eyes scanned over the list of all it encompassed. All the monies and properties and businesses. Bonds and shares and investments. Everything that Ned had owned. Wealth that must best almost every other man in England. And then her eye saw the date on the document.

The house was silent. Empty. Not another sound within it save the sob that caught in her throat.

Ned had signed the document on the morning of their wedding.

The days passed and Ned did not return. Everything went on in the house just as before, everything running like clockwork. Well oiled and efficient without her. The servants never asked when their master would be returning. If they knew he was not, they made no mention.

After a week of hiding behind closed doors she left Cavendish Square and went to visit the house in Berkeley Street.

The family to whom her father had sold the lease had changed much, but some things were still the same. As she walked from room to room there were echoes of memories from far-off days: her mother smiling and entertaining in the drawing room; Christmas Day with twenty gathered round a banquet in the dining room; Kit pulling her ponytail and laughing as he chased her down the stairs; cold winter evenings in the parlour with her father telling them stories as they all sat round a roaring log fire, drinking warmed milk with honey. And the feeling was bittersweet because all those times, all that happiness, and what had Ned been doing in those same years?

Children are not children for long round here.

A boy alone in a harsh world. With no warm cosy house. No proper home at all. A foundling. A runaway. No banquets at Christmas. No love.

The thought scraped at her insides. She closed her eyes, tried to suppress it, but it remained there silent and stubborn.

Poverty. Struggle. Hardship. What would a man not do to escape that life?

The house was empty now. A past gone never to be reclaimed. Inside Emma was keening. But it was not that long-lost life of plenty that she grieved. It was the loss of something much more precious. And it did not matter if she closed her eyes because she still saw him standing there with those intense blue eyes. And it did not matter if she blocked her ears because she still heard the gentleness of his voice.

She hugged her arms around herself, clutched her skin tight, but she still ached for his caress. A man stronger and fiercer than any she had known. A man who she did not doubt could kill another. And yet towards her she had never known a more gentle man.

She left Berkeley Street and knew she would not return. The past was just that. Gone, as much as Ned.

Emma sought out Rob Finchley in his house across town in South Street the next day.

He received her in his drawing room.

'Mrs Stratham.' For all the polite tone of his voice she could see his reserve and judgement when he looked at her. He knew Ned had left and why.

'Is something wrong, ma'am?' Worry flashed a frown in his eyes, there, then masked.

She did not waste time in niceties. There was little point in that for either of them. 'Where is he, Mr Finchley?'

'If you are referring to Mr Stratham's whereabouts, the answer is I don't know.'

'You came with him from Whitechapel. You are his friend. You must know where he has gone.'

'He would not tell me.'

She held his gaze, not sure whether he was telling her the truth. 'And if you did know…would you tell me?'

'I'm afraid I wouldn't, ma'am,' he said.

They looked at one another.

'I just want to know that he is all right. That he is…safe.'

'Ned is a survivor. He was on the streets alone at four years old. His home was a corner in a derelict manufactory. He's survived things you couldn't even begin to imagine.'

She said nothing. Because she knew it was the truth. And nothing she could say could make it better, only worse.

'Ned is hardly blameless in all of this,' she said to justify herself against the accusation she sensed in him. 'He did take the money.'

'He took the money all right, the money your wastrel brother would have drunk and whored and gamed elsewhere…'

'My brother—' she began in Kit's defence, but Rob Finchley kept on talking.

'The money that you would have frittered on fancy frocks and balls and fripperies. Yes, he took it, and he did something good with it. He created jobs for those that had none. He set up soup kitchens for the hungry, and is building a children's home for those that live on the streets of Whitechapel. You may think what you will of him, but Ned Stratham is a better man than any I've ever known.'

'A home for children?'

'His project with Misbourne. An annexe of the Foundling Hospital. Ned's idea, Ned's money and means. But no matter how worthy the cause, he still needed a title to sway the prejudice of the powers that be. Misbourne is chief amongst the Hospital's governors.'

'I did not know,' she said softly. So many things she had not known about him.

'Happen you didn't. But you should know how hard he tried to do right by you.'

She thought of all the times that Ned had saved her.

'He would have married a title. Achieved the influence and acceptance he needed to drive his charities forward, to grow his businesses and provide more employment for the poor. And then you appeared…and everything changed.' Rob Finchley stopped. Reined himself in. 'Forgive me, ma'am, if I've spoken out of turn. But it's a matter close to my heart.'

And a matter close to her own. She felt cold and alone. She felt the battle of conflicting emotions—of hurt and anger, of love and longing. *An annexe of the Foundling Hospital.* He was a villain; a rogue whose every action only proved all the more why she loved him. There was an ache in her heart that grew only worse, but Emma showed nothing of it. She gave a dignified nod and, with her head held high, walked away.

Emma rose early the next day, despite another night in which she had managed snatches of sleep and nothing more. Entered Ned's study for the first time since he had left. Just needed to have a sense of being near him.

The autumn sunlight was cool and pale through the window. The trees that lined the Square were ablaze with fiery leaves rustling in the breeze, a last show of colour before they withered and fell.

She stopped where she was. Felt her heart turn over. For there on the great desk lay a letter. One small pale shape upon that stretch of dark polished wood, just like Kit's IOU that had lain there on that terrible night.

She knew before she walked closer, before she stood before it and read the single name, written in a hand that was cramped and uncomfortable with writing, that it was for her. And she knew, too, who it was from.

Her heart was pounding hard and heavy. Her stomach clenched and twisted. She bit her lip to stop its tremble. Reaching out, she lifted the letter. Something slid and moved within its folds.

On the back it was sealed with a blob of red

wax, the letter S imprinted within the waxen circle. She broke the wax and carefully opened out the letter. Inside, the paper was blank. Not one word written there. Instead, in its centre was a small ivory disc, dented and scraped, its edges unevenly clipped. The shape of the diamond carved within it was worn smooth by his touch through the years, its red stain now faded to the faintest blush. The only thing Ned's mother had ever given him. Ned's lucky token.

She took it in her hand and held it as if it were the most precious thing in the world. And the tears welled in her eyes and overflowed to spill down her cheeks because she knew then that he really had given her his everything. All that he owned. All that he was.

Rob knew he was coming and yet he jumped as Ned stepped out of the shadow of the wall beside him. The narrowness of the mews behind the house in Cavendish Square was quiet at this time at night.

Ned glanced towards the house with its lights that glowed behind blind closed windows, then asked the question. 'How is she?'

'She's like a ghost.'

Ned closed his eyes at that. 'The pain and anger will fade eventually.'

'Will it?' asked Rob.

'For her, I hope.'

'And for you?'

Ned said nothing to that. He had no anger. Only pain, and that was unremitting. He held it to him and would never let it go because it was entwined with her memory.

'You haven't told her anything, have you?'

'Just as you instructed.' Rob glanced away to the side. 'She asked me where you had gone.'

Ned's eyes met those of his friend. 'And what did you say?'

'The truth—that I don't know.'

There was a little silence.

'Where are you staying, Ned? If you need some money—' Rob began to pull some banknotes from his pocket, but Ned stopped him with a touch to the shoulder.

'No.'

He could see the worry in Rob's eyes. Knew it was time to go. 'Thank you for doing this for me, Rob. For looking out for her in these early days until I know she's going to be all right.'

Rob gave a nod. 'It's the least I can do.'

They looked at each other for a moment longer,

before Ned gave a final gruff nod. 'Take care of yourself, Rob.'

'You, too, Ned. You, too.' Rob stood and watched while the figure of his friend walked away to be swallowed up by the night.

She went to Whitechapel the next day. Walked there to the dockyard.

'Emma?' Her father took one look at her face, gestured the other two men in the office to leave and closed the door quietly behind them before turning to face her. 'You look tired, my dear.'

'I am well enough.' She brushed away the observation, forced a smile to her face. 'I am here to ask you to come home with me to Mayfair. You do not need to work, Papa.'

But he shook his head. 'I may not need to work, Emma, but I want to. I like it here. I am useful. I have purpose. I am good at what I do and what I do makes a difference, to the men that work here, and more. My home and life is here now. Life moves on, Emma. There is nothing for me in Mayfair. Not any more.'

'There is me,' she said.

He touched the back of his fingers to her cheek. 'You are my daughter wherever we are. Nothing will ever change that.'

'Do you have no wish to resume your life as a gentleman?'

'What makes a man a gentleman is not his birth or right, not his money or wealth or abode. It is the way he lives his life. And I live my life as a gentleman, Emma, whether it be in Mayfair or Whitechapel.'

A vision of Ned swam in her mind. Not dressed in the finery of Weston's tailoring, but in the shabby old leather jacket and trousers. Standing up for her honour that night with Black-Hair in the Red Lion. Protecting her from drunken sailors in the alleyway. His expression grim and measured. His voice quiet. And his face when he had opened the door of Colonel Morley's library and saved her from Devlin. She forced the thoughts away. Tried to swallow down the sudden lump in her throat. But when she looked into her father's wise old eyes, he seemed to see too much.

She glanced away. Folded her fingers together in the semblance of a composure she did not feel inside. Tried to find the right words.

Her father did not rush her. Just waited. Let the silence act like a cushion around her.

'The man who is my husband…' *My husband*—the words sounded strained upon her lips. She swallowed again. 'He owns this dockyard. But then you already know that, do you not? I should have realised when you referred to him as *Ned* Stratham on the day of the wedding. How could you not know, working here?'

'Ned Stratham does not own this dockyard, Emma. I do.'

She stared at him in shock.

'The business is mine. The money. The responsibility that all I employ here earn a decent wage in decent conditions. Ned transferred it to me, just before the wedding, when he came to speak to me.'

There was a resounding silence while she took in the magnitude of what he was telling her.

'Is he here, today…?' She tried to make the question sound casual and unimportant.

'He has not been here all week.' But he misunderstood her reason for asking. 'You may rest assured our conversation will not be interrupted by Ned or any other.'

Her stomach squeezed tight.

There was a silence. She knew she had to tell him, all, not just a part.

'It was not Ned that tried to…compromise me… in Colonel Morley's library. It was Devlin.'

'Devlin?' Her father frowned.

She nodded. 'Ned stopped him, then swapped

their roles. He took the blame and made Devlin the hero.'

'He did not tell me that part of it.'

'There is something else I need to tell you, Papa. About Ned.'

He did not ask what. Waited with his usual restful patience that helped ease the hard heavy beat of her heart.

'You had better sit down.'

But he did not move. Just stood there, with an almost peaceful expression.

She touched her knuckles to her mouth. Then let her hand fall away. Took a breath and looked up into her father's face. 'Ned...' She swallowed. Took another breath. Tried again. 'Ned Stratham is the man Kit gambled against that night, Papa.'

Her father's face registered nothing of shock. Only calm acceptance.

'You already know?'

He nodded. 'Ned told me who he was when he came to ask for your hand.'

'And you let him wed me?' She stared at him aghast.

'Would you rather have faced ruin and condemnation?'

'Why did you not tell me?'

'Because you would not have married him had I done so.'

'And you wanted me to marry the man that ruined us?' She could not believe what she was hearing.

'No, Emma,' he said gently. 'I did not want that.'

'But that is what you got. What we both got.'

'Is it?' he asked, his eyes raking hers. 'If we are honest with ourselves, hard though it is to admit, my dearest girl, we both know that is not true.' He touched a light kiss to her cheek. 'You should go home to your husband, Emma.'

She could not tell him that Ned had gone. She just took her leave of him and began the long walk home.

Home. To the mansion in Cavendish Square. But her mind was a myriad of confusion and her cheeks were damp from silent tears when she got there.

She kept his bedchamber exactly as he had left it. Stopped the maid changing the linen on the bed. Where Ned's head had lain upon the pillow still held the faint scent of him. In the long dark hours of the night she held it to her. And her body throbbed for him. And her heart ached for him. And her soul felt small and empty without him.

There were so many thoughts going round in her head. So many emotions conflicting and confused. Love and anger. Blame and injustice. Guilt and regret. Grief and loss. They clamoured relentlessly through her body, stoked her mind in constant motion. One thought more than all the others.

There could be nothing of sleep. She rose. Pulled a shawl around her nightdress. Crossed the darkened room. She opened the curtains and stood there at the window, looking out into the darkness of the night.

The street lamps had extinguished. There was no moon. Only a scattering of tiny stars, silver-bright sparkling pinheads on the black velvet of the sky.

Her father's words whispered again through her head: *If we are honest with ourselves, hard though it is to admit, my dearest girl, we both know that is not true.*

She understood. She had always understood. All of the rest of it had been excuses and misplaced blame. She had lied to herself because it was easier than facing the truth.

Ned Stratham was not the man who had ruined her family. It was Kit who had done that. She allowed the thought freedom for the first time. It hurt. But the hurt was less than she had expected. It was pale in comparison to the rest of what she was feeling.

Ned might have taken the money, but coming from where he did, how could she honestly blame him? Had she walked in his shoes, would she have turned away so readily from such temptation?

And her heart ached all the more for the man who was her husband.

At five o'clock the next morning Emma sat at Ned's desk. She was still wearing yesterday's dress and her head throbbed with fatigue.

The house seemed dead. The street outside had not yet woken. Silence hissed in her ears. She glanced down at where her hands lay upon the desk, and the token within them. Rubbed her fingers upon it, wondered if it really would bestow luck.

'Bring him back to me,' she whispered. 'Please, God, bring him back to me.' Because he might be the man who had faced Kit across a card table in a smoky gaming den, he might be the man who had won her family's money, but none of that changed the fact that she loved Ned Stratham. And none of it changed the fact that in her bones she felt he was a good man.

She tried tipping the token along her knuckles as Ned always did, but it fell off and rolled to land upon the desk's surface time and again. So she left it where it lay. Stroked a finger against it. An old gaming token. What had his mother lost that she would give up her child? She thought of Kit and the night he had left for the gaming hell with Devlin and Hunter. She thought of Kit facing Ned across a table in Old Moll's Den. She lifted the token and flicked it to spin upon the smooth dark polish of the desk.

She did not hear its soft whir, only the whisper of the words Devlin had spoken, *No one put a pistol to his head and forced him to the gaming tables.*

Devlin had been there that night. Devlin must have known exactly what had happened. The thought only struck her then. So obvious that she wondered that she had not realised it before.

If Devlin was there that night, then he must always have known who Ned was. It explained Devlin's contempt, the tension that had always crackled between him and Ned—indeed, between Ned and the rest of her brother's friends who had been with him on that fateful night. It explained, too, why Devlin had tried so hard to keep her away from Ned.

What it did not explain was why Devlin did not just tell her that fact? He must have known that telling her that one truth would have worked far better than any warnings or threats or innuendoes.

If Devlin wished to save her from Ned, what better way than that? And yet Devlin had not.

Something uneasy stroked down her spine. That sense that there was something she was missing. A feeling that something was not right. That there was more to the story than Ned had told her. The token stopped spinning and landed flat on the desk before her with a soft clink.

The air rippled with mystery. She frowned and stared down at the token as if it held the answer. It did not, of course, but she knew who did and she knew, too, where to find him. She smiled a grim determined smile and, scooping the token up from the desk, placed it safe inside her pocket. Then she rang for the carriage and went to fetch the long dark winter cloak that Ned had bought for her.

Chapter Eighteen

The footman who opened the door of the St James's town house had a face that did not betray the least shock to find a woman standing on the doorstep at six o'clock in the morning, almost as if it were not so unusual an occurrence.

'If you would be so good as to call back later, madam. His lordship has not yet risen.'

'Then you had better wake him and tell him that Mrs Stratham is here to speak with him.'

Only once she was inside did she push back the hood of the cloak and look around her.

It was a distinctly masculine drawing room. Dark red walls. A black-onyx fireplace rather than the usual white. And above it a painting of an exotic-looking woman in a shockingly intimate pose. Emma studied it in horrified fascination.

* * *

He appeared some fifteen minutes later, smartly dressed in a shirt and cravat so white that they gleamed in the soft autumn daylight. But his dark hair was ruffled and his chin and cheeks were blue shadowed with beard stubble.

'Devlin.' She tried not to think of the last time they had been alone together.

'Emma.' His voice was gravelled in a way that hinted at his excesses of the night before. 'Or rather I should say Mrs Stratham.' He smiled in that easy way of his. 'Coffee, or perhaps you take chocolate in the morning. Kit always did.'

'No, thank you. I am not here for refreshment.'

'No, I rather suspected as much.' He walked over and poured himself a brandy. Glanced up and saw her watching him with disapproval. 'Hair of the dog. I over-imbibed last night,' he said by way of explanation, and took a swig. 'Does your husband know you are here?'

'He does not.'

'I see.'

She should have been afraid. Given what he had done to her, being here with him alone was a foolhardy position in which to place herself. But she felt nothing of fear because, with Ned's confession, she finally understood.

There was a small silence in which he topped up his glass again and moved to stand before the fireplace. He looked at her. Waited for what she had to say. Almost as if he knew.

'In Colonel Morley's library that night…' she began. Stopped. Glanced away in embarrassment.

'My sincere apologies over our little…misunderstanding.' He looked as uncomfortable as she felt at the mention of what had happened between them that night.

'It was hardly that.'

He dipped his head, raised an eyebrow, half-agreement, half-disagreement, and took another sip of brandy.

'You said I should have married you.'

'And so you should have.' There was nothing of jest or humour in his face now, only a deadly earnest. 'But it is too late now. You should go home, Emma. Married woman or not, I do not need to tell you what it would do to your reputation were you to be seen here.' He looked remote, cool, emotionally detached. A world away from the man that night in the library.

But she just stood there. 'You really were trying to save me, just as you said.'

'You know,' he said so softly that it was almost a whisper. 'Who he is. That is why you are here.'

She nodded. 'He told me.'

Devlin closed his eyes momentarily. And when he opened them he glanced away. 'I did try to save you from him.'

'I know.' She understood everything that Devlin had done had been to save her from Ned. 'That is why you proposed marriage.'

'Yes.'

'Why you tried to compromise me when I refused—to force me to the altar.'

'Monteith and the others were supposed to interrupt us kissing. I am sorry for forcing you, but I would have done anything to stop him getting his filthy hands on you.'

'Anything,' she said. 'And yet all you had to do was tell me who he was. That he was the man who won against Kit that night. Why did you not just tell me, Devlin? That one small fact?'

'Because of the oath, of course.' He finished the brandy from his glass. Moved to the decanter and poured himself another. 'Had I told you, Stratham would have made Kit's cheating public and none of us could allow that.'

The world seemed to fall away from beneath her feet. Her stomach plummeted to meet her shoes. There was a cold seeping dread of realisation through her blood. She stared at Devlin as the full horror of his words hit home. 'Kit cheated?' The voice that asked the question did not sound like her own.

'Ah,' said Devlin softly. 'Stratham did not tell you that bit.'

'No,' she said. 'He told me nothing of any cheating. But you are going to tell me what happened that night, Devlin. You are going to tell me it all.'

And he did. How they had taken to frequenting Old Moll's Den in the East End. How Stratham had toyed with them, and baited them, winning from them, night after night.

'Sitting there, tumbling that token of his over his fingers without cease. Taunting us.' Devlin's face was hard at the memory. 'We would have called it quits, but Kit would not have it. He was convinced he could beat Stratham. I laughed at him. Ridiculed him. *Like you did the last time?* I said to him. I did not realise what it would push Kit to do.' Devlin closed his eyes, but not before she had seen the guilt and pain in them. 'He persuaded us to go back to Old Moll's. *One more time*, he said. *Knew he could win*, he said. So we went. And we played again against Stratham and his friends. And low and behold, Kit did it, just as he said he would. He won. Then Stratham and his toughs accused Kit of cheating. We thought at first it was just bad form on their half, just a ruse to get out of paying.'

There was a grim tortured look on Devlin's face, and a faraway look in his eyes, as if he had gone back two years and was there once more in the smoky haze of Old Moll's Den.

'*Pull up your sleeves*, Stratham commanded. Kit refused, of course, as every one of us would have done. We were all incensed on his behalf. All of our honours slurred. All ready to fight.

'*Pull up your sleeves or I will do it for you*, said Stratham again. And Kit did.'

Devlin met her eyes. 'There were cards hidden there. He had cheated.'

There was a deafening silence in the room.

She swallowed down the bitterness in her throat.

'Have you any idea what happens to men that cheat at cards in Whitechapel, Emma?'

'I think I might hazard a guess.' But she knew. She knew in detail and it sent a chill through her bones.

He looked away, his expression hard, reliving the memory of that night. 'He would have been found washed up on the banks of the Thames.'

And that would have been a mercy after what else they would have done to him.

'They were going to lynch him. But Stratham

said he would settle for all or quits. Everything that Kit had staked on that table. One turn of the cards. Just Kit and Stratham.

'They would not trust Kit to deal. We would not trust Stratham. So Stratham had me deal the cards.' Devlin held her gaze hard. 'I dealt your brother that final hand, Emma. Not anyone else. I dealt and he lost.'

Lost the money, but kept his life and all of his limbs, she thought.

'Stratham struck a deal. We were to say nothing of who he was and how he had come by his wealth. In exchange he would keep quiet on Kit's cheating. But he never lost an opportunity to remind us. He was a card shark who played us. Then, and now. Every time I look at him I remember.' There was both loathing and guilt in his eyes as he spoke the bitter words. Then he met her gaze. 'But better to lose every penny, Emma, than bear the other disgrace.'

Of being a cheat. Within a society which deemed gambling debts ones of honour, there was no greater disgrace. She nodded, knowing that if it ever got out that her brother had cheated at cards there would no way back for any of them.

'I am sorry, Emma, for Kit, for the marriage to Stratham and for the rest of it.'

She gave another nod. 'I blamed you for corrupting my brother, but the truth was Kit needed no corrupting. You tried to protect him…and me.' And she had blamed Ned for taking the money, when what he had done was something much more.

'But not well enough,' said Devlin quietly. 'I did not stop Stratham when it came to you.'

'And I am glad of it,' she said. 'He is not what you think him, Devlin. He is a man of integrity and honour.'

Devlin said nothing, but she could see in his eyes that he did not believe her.

'I love him, Devlin. I love him with all my heart.'

Silence echoed her admission.

'I cannot pretend to agree with your measure of Stratham, but I am glad of your happiness,' Devlin finally said.

They looked at one another for a moment.

'You should go to him.'

'Yes,' she said. 'I should. I will.'

'I wish you all the best,' he said and bowed.

Emma pulled up the deep hood of her cloak and, with her identity hidden from any early morning prying eyes, she slipped away from the St James's town house.

* * *

She did not go home, but went instead to another man's house in a respectable street not so very far away.

'Mrs Stratham.' Rob Finchley received her as uneasily as the last time.

'Mr Finchley. Ned said I was to come to you, if I had a problem.'

'How may I be of help?' He gestured to the red-covered sofas in the neat and tidy drawing room.

But Emma shook her head and stayed where she was.

'You can tell me where Ned is.'

'I've already told you, Mrs Stratham, I don't know where he is.'

Silence.

'You were there that night in Old Moll's Den.'

'I was there.' His expression was cool, his jaw stiff and tight.

'Ned did not tell me that my brother was a cheat.'

His eyes moved to hers. 'Who told you?'

'Devlin let it slip. He thought Ned had already told me.'

'Ned would never have told you.'

'I know.' And she knew, too, why. 'I love him,

Mr Finchley. I want him to come home. So you see why I need to find him.'

An uncomfortable expression crossed Rob Finchley's face. He looked away.

'Please, sir. I am begging you. Please tell me where he is.'

Rob Finchley swallowed. She heard him blow out a breath. He raked a hand through his hair before finally meeting her gaze once more; and when it did she saw compassion in his eyes.

'I really don't know the answer to your question, Mrs Stratham.'

'But he must have left a means for you to contact him.'

Rob Finchley shook his head.

She stared at him, feeling her hope shrink and diminish with what she saw in his face.

'Loving you, knowing who you were…it tore him apart.'

Just as she was tearing apart. She had spoken such cruel words to him. She had let him walk away when he had looked at her for one single word to stay.

'I have to find him, Mr Finchley.'

'I wish you luck, truly I do, ma'am. But if Ned doesn't want to be found, I don't think that you will find him.'

* * *

Panic was rising in Emma, and cold dread. Back in Ned's study in Cavendish Square she pulled open every drawer, rummaging through them, emptying the neat piles of legal papers that Mr Kerr had left on to the surface of the desk. There was nothing else there. She opened cupboards and checked the shelves of the library with their blue leather-bound books.

She searched his bedchamber and dressing room, went through the pockets of every tailcoat in his wardrobe. But there was nothing.

She worked her way through his clothes' chest, through each pair of breeches and every waistcoat folded neatly within, and found not a single clue as to where he might have gone.

She pressed the waistcoat to her nose, inhaling the scent of him. She would not let herself weep, just pressed on with an utter determination to find him.

She moved to the wardrobe. Inside hung the shabby leather jacket and trousers he had worn in Whitechapel. Once they had been brown, now they had faded to a soft silvered birch. She traced her fingers against the jacket, remembering the very first time she had seen him, remembering the first moment those blue, blue eyes had looked into hers and tilted the axis of her world, and made beautiful butterflies flutter in her stomach.

Just as with everything else, the pockets were empty. But these clothes were not like all the others. Because they whispered to her another place she might seek him.

'Emma.' Nancy glanced up from behind the bar of the Red Lion Chop-House. 'Didn't expect to see you back here, girl.' The older woman's eyes darted over Emma's fine clothes, over her face, taking it all in in an instant.

The hour was still relatively early. Three die-hard regulars sat at a table, eyeing Emma with curiosity. Other than them the place was empty.

There was the sound of the cleaver chopping against the wooden block and Tom's cheery whistling coming from the kitchen. A new girl was mopping a spill from the floor without enthusiasm.

Paulette wandered over from where she was scraping wax from a table in the corner. 'All right, Em? Look at you! Ain't you the fancy lady!'

Emma gave both Paulette and Nancy a hug.

'I'm looking for Ned Stratham.'

'All right.' Nancy raised her brows. 'You and him still walking out?'

'In a manner of speaking.'

'Is it serious?' asked Paulette.

'Very,' said Emma. 'I need to find him. Urgently.' She saw Nancy and Paulette exchange a look.

'Like that, is it?' Nancy set the cloth she had been wiping the ale taps with down on the counter.

'Has he been in?' Emma asked.

'We've had neither sight nor sound of Ned Stratham in months,' Nancy replied.

'Since I told him you'd gone for a lady's maid, he ain't been back,' said Paulette.

Emma closed her eyes and took a breath. She knew both women were staring at her. 'If he does come in...if you see him at all, will you tell him I am looking for him? Will you ask him to come to me?'

'Does he know where to find you?' asked Nancy.

'He knows.' She paused and then added, 'Will you tell him that I love him?'

They looked at her with eyes agog and nodded.

Emma did not go to bed that night. She sat in Ned's chair in his study. The drawers all still hung open from her earlier frantic search, the legal papers still lay scattered across the desk. She made no effort to tidy them.

All the accusations she had thrown at Ned. All

that she had believed of him. When all along her heart had known the truth of him, if only she had listened to it.

Ned had gone because of her and he was not coming back. And she would have to live with that knowledge for the rest of her life.

She had blamed Devlin and Hunter.

She had blamed Ned.

She had blamed Kit.

But when she stripped everything away and looked at the bones of what lay beneath, there was only one person she could blame and that was herself.

She had as good as sent him away; the man whom she loved, the man who had saved her brother's life and protected her honour. The man who loved her and had given her every last thing that he could.

The knowledge cut deep in her soul. She knew she never would forgive herself.

Her gaze moved over the documents that covered the desk's surface, documents that made her one of the wealthiest women in the country. She had every material thing. All that her family had lost and far more. And it was all as dust. Because the only thing that mattered was who one loved.

She loved Ned and she had as good as sent him

away. He could be anywhere, anywhere in the world. And she did not know how to find him. Rob Finchley's words echoed through her mind. *If Ned doesn't want to be found, I don't think you will find him.*

On the desk lay the deeds from the house in Berkeley Street that he had bought back for her, the details of manufactories that he had built to give men in the East End work, the returns from the London Dockyards where he had given her father back his dignity. And the plans for the children's home in Whitechapel—*the most important deal of his life*. All the money he had made and all the good he had done with it.

She closed her eyes, but the tears still leaked down her cheeks. She rummaged in her pocket for her handkerchief and as she pulled it out Ned's lucky token came with it and fell on to the mess of papers on the desk.

She picked the little battered token up, rubbing it between her fingers as she had seen him do so many times. But it would not bring him back, no matter how much she wished.

Emma let it fall from her fingers back down on to the papers.

Her eyes lingered on where it lay, then shifted to the paper beneath—the plans for the children's home. She looked a little closer. Moved the token aside and opened out the folded paper to reveal the plan in full.

It was a technical drawing, detailed and carefully executed by a draftsman. It showed what the building would look like when finished. It showed the layout of the rooms and corridors and their scaled dimensions. It showed the playgrounds and the gardens—and the note for the planting to contain violets. It showed, too, the precise location in Whitechapel where it was to be built.

I grew up here. It reminds me of my childhood. The words he had spoken on a summer morning echoed in her mind. Now she understood what he had told her in a way she had not at the time.

A hand squeezed around Emma's heart. The tears flowed all the more down her cheeks as the tiny spark of hope kindled in the dark despair of her soul. She did not fan it. Dared not allow herself to hope too much. But the beat of her heart was strong and in her bones was a knowledge that she was afraid to admit. That she knew where he was. That she should always have known. For where else did a man go other than the only place he felt his home?

He had told her with his own lips and she knew

now, in truth, that Ned Stratham was a man who had never lied to her.

She lifted the gaming token and pressed a kiss to it. Then she slipped it in her pocket and went to ready herself.

The morning bell sounded from the distant view. From his stone bench Ned watched the men moving about like ants in the dockyard below. The sky was a clear blue, the sun warming something of the autumn chill from the air. Overhead the leaves hung like red-and-gold pennants fluttering in the breeze.

He heard the carriage before he saw it. There were not many fine town coaches in this part of London. He recognised it before it came to a halt at the end of the road. Knew that she had come before the footman opened the door and she climbed down.

Emma stood there for a moment and looked at him. Just as she had done on that summer's morning. She even wore the same sprig muslin and shawl she had worn then, the same faded straw bonnet trimmed with the matching ribbon. The sight of her squeezed tight at his heart. Made him think that she was a vision and this was a dream.

He got to his feet. Stood there. Everything else around him faded to nothing. There was only Emma.

She walked towards him, never taking her eyes from his, and he could not look away even had he wanted to.

She walked and everything seemed to slow and quiet so that all he could hear was the beat of his own heart.

She walked right up to him. Stood there two feet before him. Her soft brown eyes striped golden in the dappled light of the sun.

'You found me,' he said.

Her mouth did not smile, but her eyes…her eyes held things he dared not hope for. 'I would have searched a lifetime to find you, Ned Stratham.'

He swallowed.

She moved to the bench, sat down next to where he had sat.

He resumed his seat by her side.

'The old vinegar manufactory.' She looked across the road to the tumbling derelict walls. 'It was where you lived as a boy, when you ran away from the Foundling Hospital to come back here to Whitechapel, was it not?'

'It was,' he admitted.

'And it is the site of the children's home you are funding and organising.'

'There are too many homeless children in Whitechapel.'

'There are.'

They sat in silence for a little while, looking out over the scene.

A gentle breeze blew, rustling the leaves above their heads. From the dockyard came the sounds of hammering and the creaking of cranes and the sound of men at work.

'You should have told me about Kit, Ned. That he cheated that night.'

'You love your brother. I did not want to hurt you. I would have given anything that you were any other woman than Kit Northcote's sister.'

'I would not.'

He looked at her. 'I took his money. I bankrupted his family. I sent you to a life of poverty and hardship, while I pretended to be a gentleman.'

'You saved his life. We both know what happens to men who cheat at the card tables in Whitechapel.'

He did not deny it.

'And as for pretending to be a gentleman... My father told me that what makes a man a gentleman is not his birth or right, not his money or wealth or abode, but the way he lives his life. And you, Ned Stratham, are more of a gentleman than any other man I know.'

He looked into her eyes. Felt her hand move to cover his where it lay upon the stone bench between them. He took her hand, entwined their fingers together.

'I regret my cruel words to you, Ned. I never meant for you to go, but my foolish pride would not let me tell you. I came here to ask your forgiveness.'

He stared at her in amazement. 'I am the one who should be down on my knees begging before you.'

'My brother made the decision to go to Old Moll's. He made the decision to cheat. My family suffered because of the decisions he made that night, not yours. And we would have chosen the same path a hundred times over to save Kit's life.'

He could feel the pulse of her blood where their hands held, feel the warmth of this woman whom he loved so much.

'I love you, Ned. Please come home.'

He reached a hand to cradle the softness of her cheek. 'I love you, Emma Stratham.' He slid his hand beneath her bonnet to the nape of her neck and his mouth moved to hers and he kissed her, sitting there on the quiet stone bench beneath the flaming spread of the old beech trees.

He kissed her with all the love that was in his heart. And then he scooped her up into his arms and he carried her down the road to the waiting carriage.

Later, when day had faded to night and the moon glowed like a giant opal in the sky, Emma and Ned made love with a tenderness and understanding beyond anything else. And afterwards as the moon bathed them in its soft silver light Emma lay in the warm protection of her husband's arms, her face resting upon his chest, listening to the strong steady beat of his heart.

He stroked her hair and kissed the top of her head.

'How did you know where to find me today?' he asked.

She reached her arm across to the bedside cabinet, felt with her fingers until they closed upon the small battered token. As he watched she looked up into his eyes and pressed it to her lips. 'Just a lucky guess,' she said and tossed the token to spin in the air above them.

Ned reached up and caught it.

'With maybe a little help from destiny,' she added.

They laughed together.

And then they kissed, and showed each other how very much they loved one another all over again.

* * * * *

MILLS & BOON®

Why shop at millsandboon.co.uk?

Each year, thousands of romance readers find their perfect read at millsandboon.co.uk. That's because we're passionate about bringing you the very best romantic fiction. Here are some of the advantages of shopping at www.millsandboon.co.uk:

* **Get new books first**—you'll be able to buy your favourite books one month before they hit the shops

* **Get exclusive discounts**—you'll also be able to buy our specially created monthly collections, with up to 50% off the RRP

* **Find your favourite authors**—latest news, interviews and new releases for all your favourite authors and series on our website, plus ideas for what to try next

* **Join in**—once you've bought your favourite books, don't forget to register with us to rate, review and join in the discussions

Visit **www.millsandboon.co.uk**
for all this and more today!